The MIZPAH Ring

Dorothy Stewart

 Zaccmedia

Published by Zaccmedia
www.zaccmedia.com
info@zaccmedia.com

Published November 2015

ISBN: 978-1-909824-99-7

British Library Cataloguing-in-Publication Data
A catalogue record for this book is available from the British Library.

ACKNOWLEDGEMENTS

In the early1990s I became fascinated by the Klondike Gold Rush and am grateful to Taunton Public Library for finding me two wonderful books: Edwin Tappan Adney's *The Klondike Stampede of 1897-1898,* originally published in 1899 by Harper & Brothers, New York. (The version I used was republished in 1968 in a limited edition by Galleon Press, Fairfield, Washington.) And Pierre Benton's *Klondike: The last great goldrush, 1896-1899.* I used the fourth edition, published in 1977 by McClelland & Stewart Ltd.

I am grateful to Anne King and Andrea Rogalski for invaluable information about childbirth and what can go wrong; to Doreen Leith for impressions of Buenos Aires; to the Wick Society for permission to use photographs from The Johnston Collection; to Revd. David Gibson for the American Automobile Association atlas of the USA and Canada 1989; and to my sister, Anna Rogalski, for family stories, the 1901 Census Returns for Wick Parish, research wanders around Wick, long Friday evening phone calls and general unstinting support and encouragement. All errors are mine alone.

For those interested in language, a few non-English words occur in the book:

teuchter (possibly Gaelic) a (usually derogatory) term used by non-*teuchters* for folks from the Highlands

cheechako (Chinook) ignorant newcomer to Alaska or the Yukon

mackinaw (derived from Lake Mackinac, from Menomini or Ojibwe) coat made of heavy water-repellent fabric in plaid

sleekit (Scots) sly

porteños (Spanish) inhabitants of a port city, commonly applied to Buenos Aires

CHAPTER 1

Wick, Scotland, 1897

'Don't be ridiculous! I wouldn't marry you if you were the last man on earth.'

Belle Reid tossed her head, sending the red-gold curls dancing. In one swift, derisive move, she whirled, her long skirts swishing, back into the house and slammed the door shut in the young man's face.

Geordie Sinclair's dark eyes narrowed with fury. This time she had gone too far. He had tolerated her coquettish ways – flirting with each of the young men who flocked around her, favouring one this day, another the next. But he was not a puppy to be toyed with and then discarded. He was a man, and one day he was going to be a great man. A rich man. And he knew Belle was the wife for him. She was a kindred spirit – someone with an appetite for the good things in life, and the willingness to reach out and take them.

But her dismissal cut bitter and deep. One day she would regret her heartless rejection of all he had to offer her. One day, he promised himself, he would get even with her.

A noise from the stables that bounded one side of the large yard behind the Reid family home reminded Geordie that he was not alone. That little scene with Belle was sure to have been seen and heard by the men working there, and would no doubt be reported back to her mother and father.

Geordie cast his eyes along the row of stables, now empty of the big horses that pulled the carts that were the foundation of the family's prosperous business. The byre on the other side of the yard was empty too. The cows that supplied the adjoining dairy plenteously with milk were out grazing in the fields on the edge of town, a stone's throw away. Everything in the yard was as neat and spick as a new pin. A far cry from the broken-down cottage where his mother had brought up her family.

'Have you nowhere better to go?' a voice challenged him from the stables and one of the men emerged, pitchfork warningly in hand.

'I'm going. Nothing to keep me here.'

Geordie put a sneer in his voice and a defiant swagger in his step. As he reached the big gate out into Murchison Street, he aimed a deft kick at a bucket standing to one side, toppling it so a stream of dirty water poured across the newly cleaned yard.

'Oh dear!' he mocked and dodged smartly out of the gate, followed by the curses of the stableman.

He ambled idly down through Pulteneytown and into the main streets of Wick, still smarting from Belle's rebuff. Strangely he felt aware as never before of the disapproving glances that greeted his appearance. Small-town people and small-town attitudes, he told himself. None of it was new, but today it stung afresh. One day, he told himself, it would be different. One day they would treat him properly – not simply as one more by-blow on the wrong side of the blanket, one more wastrel from a disreputable family, but as himself, made good.

Geordie stifled a mocking laugh. He had no intention of ever becoming *good*. He knew in his heart it just was not in his make-up and he saw no reason why it should be so. There was no advantage in being *good*.

He smiled cynically as he saw a respectable married gentleman of the town cross the road to avoid him, in his embarrassed haste having to dodge between a couple of laden carts. The man had not been so unfriendly the other day when Geordie had opened the door to him to come visiting his sister. And the coins he had given Geordie to pay for his pleasure had not been forgotten.

At the corner of Bridge Street and High Street, a group of loiterers greeted him with noisy acclaim, drawing more sour glances from the worthies that passed by.

'How are you, lads?' Geordie acknowledged the whistles and ignored the disapproval. The lads had been useful on a few jobs in the past and they knew he would cut them in on any opportunities that were going. Not on the right side of the law, of course, but that did not matter to any of them. There were always easy pickings for clever men.

Geordie's steps slowed as he considered Belle's rejection once again. Maybe down in her greedy little heart there was a trace of the Puritan, a desire for respectability, and in this, his home town, there was no way he would ever be seen as respectable. Not with his background. But one day, he told himself, he would be rich and that wealth would buy the respect he coveted. Money solved all problems, covered all inequalities.

Then he would return to the so-high-in-the-instep Reid household – this time to the front door – and just when they were pleading with him to take that over-indulged hussy off their hands, he would spit in their faces and walk away. That would take the scorn off her face! See if it wouldn't.

All he needed was money, serious money. He frowned. All his schemes to date, while successful, had been low earners. He needed something more. Something bigger, but what?

~

'Gold! Gold! Gold! Gold!' screamed the newspaper headlines.

'Give me that!' Geordie demanded.

The young fellow that lounged against the wall beside him raised his eyes in surprise. 'But you said I was to read the newspaper,' he protested. 'So nobody would be suspicious...'

'Yes, yes,' Geordie said irritably. They were waiting for the home owners to leave so they could let themselves into the house and see what sellable items they could remove. 'It will look just as natural if I'm the one reading the paper.'

Reluctantly the boy handed over the newspaper.

'So what'll I do?' he whined, but Geordie just flapped at him to be silent as he took in all the details of the report. A steamer had docked in San Francisco laden with half a million dollars' worth of gold recently found in the Klondike. Another had landed more men newly rich with Klondike gold in Seattle. It was reported that sixty-eight miners had unloaded a million dollars' worth and the town had gone mad with gold fever.

Geordie devoured the information. One ounce of Klondike gold was worth more than two weeks' wages and some of the miners spoke of finding ten or more ounces of gold in one pan of river gravel. The gold was washed down from the seams in the hills into the river valleys and all a man had to do was wash away the gravel and pocket the gold.

4

The home owners walked past Geordie and his accomplice but Geordie did not see them. The boy tugged his arm but he waved him away. His attention was totally taken with the prospect forming in his mind. *Gold.* All that gold just there for the taking, and easy taking by the sound of it. Geordie saw himself idly rinsing a large pan of gravel in a sparkling stream in the Canadian mountains and picking out nuggets of gleaming gold.

Yes, it sounded just the thing for a man like him. Easy pickings.

The boy plucked at his arm again.

'Yes,' he said irritably. 'What is it?'

'They've gone out,' the boy said, waving at the now empty house.

'Yes, well, we'd better get on with it before they come back,' Geordie said as he led the way round the back of the house. There might not be much in the way of easy disposable stuff, but every little helped. He smiled. Every little would now go towards his fund for getting to the Klondike and making his fortune.

He smashed the kitchen window cheerfully.

'Go on,' he told the boy. 'In you go.'

CHAPTER 2

Geordie's lip curled in scorn as he watched the young man walking purposefully down the road alongside the harbour. Dressed in his best, the lad's eyes were averted as if he planned to hurry past him but Geordie was having none of that. He stepped out purposefully into his path.

'And where might you be going?' Geordie challenged him. 'As if I need to ask! Off to the afternoon rendezvous with the lovely Belle?' He laughed. 'You're wasting your time with that hussy!'

Young Hughie Mackay blushed to the roots of his guinea-gold hair. He was a regular member of the group of young men who danced attendance on Belle Reid. Sunny Sunday afternoons always found them gathered around her on the grassy clifftop at the South Head.

'She's not interested in the likes of us,' Geordie told the boy, rancour from Belle's rejection thick in his voice. 'She'll find herself a rich man from out of town.'

Hughie frowned. He raised his eyes to Geordie. 'I don't think so,' he protested. 'She's not like that!'

Geordie sneered. 'You need to grow up,' he said. 'You've got a lot to learn about women.' He watched the seventeen-year-old's discomfort with amusement. Another hapless youth who fancied himself in love with Belle!

'You'd better be going.' He stepped back out of Hughie's way. 'Won't want to be late – in case one of the other boys gets the best place next to Miss Belle.'

Hughie flushed as Geordie's barb hit its mark. There was always a jostle for who could get closest. It was only natural, Hughie told himself. She was so pretty. Of course all the young men in town would want to be near her.

Hughie sighed. He had been in love with Belle for so long and had hopes that perhaps she was looking on him favourably. But perhaps the others thought so too, even Geordie who had once been a familiar face amongst the group.

'Aren't you coming?' he asked.

Geordie laughed. 'I wouldn't waste my time. No, I've got better things to do.'

Hughie's face spoke so clearly of his disbelief that Geordie, riled, announced, 'I'm on the way to making my fortune!'

'Oh yes?' Hughie responded, expecting he was being mocked, but Geordie replied with solid conviction, 'Oh yes. And soon! Just you wait and see.' And in the face of Hughie's amazement, Geordie proceeded to boast. 'I'm going to get myself to Canada. To the Klondike. To the gold rush. And I'm going to make my fortune in gold! You'll have seen it in the papers?'

Hughie nodded. He too had read the reports and wondered at the huge finds. Now he listened as Geordie described his plans.

'It will be easy!' Geordie was declaring but Hughie was distracted by the sight of another of Belle's admirers making his way down the road towards their meeting-place. He quickly excused himself and hurried away.

As he feared, by the time he clambered up the cliff to the grassy top where Belle was holding court, there were several other fellows there. But Belle looked up as he arrived and, smiling, patted the ground next to her.

'Come and sit down,' she said, smiling sweetly as she extended the singular favour to him.

He gazed into her eyes in adoration and blurted out, 'I got held up... by Geordie.'

At once the smile vanished as her lids shut down over the beautiful blue eyes.

Hughie licked suddenly dry lips. To suffer Belle's disfavour was like the sun vanishing from the sky. He hurried to make amends.

'Geordie says he's going to the Klondike. To the gold rush. To make his fortune.'

The other lads began to clamour for more information but Hughie was aware only of Belle's sudden piercing gaze.

'Is he now?' she murmured.

Grateful for the reprieve, Hughie rushed to answer. 'Yes, he says he's going as soon as he can get the money together for his fare and the things he'll need.'

'And come back a rich man?' one of the lads guffawed.

'That's what he says.'

The other lads burst into laughter. They had heard Geordie's schemes before. But Belle was distracted and it was not long before her usual courtiers drifted away. Only Hughie remained.

'There really is gold to be found out there?' Belle asked him suddenly.

'Oh yes,' Hughie answered. 'There are huge quantities so they say and easy to get at. It washes down into the rivers and you just have to scoop up the shingle and sieve it and there it is – great lumps of the stuff! It's been in all the papers.'

'And Geordie's going?'

Hughie nodded.

'A great adventure,' Belle commented thoughtfully. 'I admire that in a man. Setting off to make something of himself. He'll come back a rich man and he'll have the pick of all the girls in town!' She looked up at Hughie from beneath her eyelids. 'Why, even my father would be willing to let such a rich man come calling!'

Belle's words worried Hughie. The youngest son of a poor crofting family, scratching a living from a stony hill down the coast, he knew he would never be a rich man.

'Belle?' He reached tentatively for her hand and was surprised and delighted that she let him take it.

'Yes, my dear?'

'Belle, you know I'll never be a rich man…' he began. 'Is that any impediment…?'

'My father,' she said, shaking her head sadly. 'He wants only the best for me. A lad with no prospects… compared with a man with Klondike gold…' She left the words hanging.

Hughie swallowed hard, his eyes fixed on his beloved. It seemed that love could not compete with money when it came to Belle's father.

She reached up and patted his cheek. 'But think about it,' she coaxed. 'You could be a man with Klondike gold too.'

'What?' he stammered. 'How?'

She smiled. 'You said Geordie's not ready to go yet. That he hasn't got enough money for the fare or the things he'll need. So you could get there ahead of him.'

Hughie stared at her, perplexed by her words.

'Your mother…' Belle began. 'I think you said she had some savings laid up for you?'

Hughie nodded. 'But it's for when I leave home, get married, to give me a start…'

'Well, maybe it would give you the start in life that you need now,' Belle said. 'Your ticket to the Klondike, ahead of Geordie…' Her eyes were fixed on Hughie as he pondered her words.

'That's a thought…' he began.

She smiled again. 'And then it would be you returning with Klondike gold and going to see my father and…' Belle turned her eyes down demurely.

Sudden wonder flooded Hughie's heart.

'You would have me?' Hughie blurted, his eyes ablaze. 'If I came back from the Klondike rich with gold, you would marry me?'

Belle brought the full beam of her smiling gaze upon him. 'Yes, of course,' she said.

'Oh Belle!' Hughie breathed.

She leaned over and placed a tiny kiss on his lips.

'Oh Belle!' Hughie reached for her but she moved away.

'You'll need to speak to your mother…'

'Yes, of course. I'll speak to her when I get home today.'

Belle smiled. 'We could be secretly engaged till you come back,' she suggested.

'Secretly engaged?' Hughie asked, a delicious panorama of promise opening before his dazzled eyes.

Belle nodded, and when Hughie reached for her again, she did not draw back.

'Oh Belle,' Hughie said. 'You've made me the happiest man alive.'

11

CHAPTER 3

'You've got to help me!' Belle cried, throwing her hairbrush down on the dressing table and bursting into angry tears of frustration.

Hannah was already dressed and on the point of going downstairs but her younger sister's words stopped her and she turned back into the bedroom they shared. There was never any point trying to ignore Belle in one of her moods. She would simply work herself up into such a state that the whole household would be disrupted. And Hannah, as usual, blamed.

Hannah sighed and picked up the brush.

'Get on with it!' Belle commanded, tears forgotten. She tugged out all of the pins she had inserted so the cloud of red-gold hair fell around her shoulders to await Hannah's ministrations. 'I mustn't be late!'

Carefully, Hannah started brushing out Belle's hair, thick and lustrous and so unlike her own soft, ordinary brown hair.

'I really don't see why you're so bothered,' she said. 'There will be a whole crowd at the station to wave Hughie and Geordie off.' She pondered aloud as she worked on Belle's hair. 'I know they're friends of yours... but I thought you'd fallen out with Geordie?'

Belle waved that away. 'That was a long time ago. I only pointed out to him what anyone with any sense would have known.'

Hannah, her mouth full of pins, grunted.

'Well, of course he was sweet on me but nobody would expect anything to come of it. Well, I mean,' Belle said derisively, '*me*... and the likes of him!'

Hannah carefully placed pins in Belle's upswept hair but, as she thought about Geordie Sinclair, she had to agree that Belle was right. Geordie's family was one of the least respectable in town and his reputation for sharp practice – if not downright dishonesty – had done him no favours. No one would expect the beautiful Belle, favourite daughter of one of the most prosperous businessmen in town, to look favourably on him.

But Geordie was not renowned for having a forgiving nature.

'He's got over it,' Belle assured Hannah airily. 'Nothing to worry about.'

Hannah considered. 'But what if he comes back from the Klondike a rich man? Would you look at him differently then?'

Belle arched wide innocent eyes in the mirror. 'If he comes back a rich man...?' she echoed, then she smiled a small secret catlike smile.

'Belle,' Hannah said warningly. 'What have you been up to?'

'Me?' Belle batted her eyelashes at her older sister. 'I really don't know what you mean.'

'Have you said something to Geordie...' Hannah began but Belle simply laughed.

'Don't be silly,' she said. 'I'm not interested in Geordie.' But the secretive smile came again.

So if this was not about Geordie Sinclair, Belle's interest had to be in the other young man leaving today for the Klondike – Hughie

Mackay. Hannah brushed her sister's hair and pondered. Hughie was a nice-looking young man, but maybe a bit too young and easily led to be any good for a minx like Belle.

'I must admit I was surprised when I heard that Hughie Mackay was going to the Klondike,' Hannah commented. 'It seems out of character for him. He's more of a stay-at-home lad, I'd have thought.'

To Hannah's surprise, Belle smirked, decidedly pleased with herself. And at once Hannah knew.

'Did you put Hughie up to going to Canada?' she demanded. 'Was it your idea?'

Belle's eyes narrowed as she viewed her sister in the mirror. Finally she shrugged.

'And if it was?'

'He's just a bairn,' Hannah said bluntly. 'He'll never manage without his mother to look after him.'

Belle's silvery laugh rang out. 'Well, that's why he's going with Geordie. He'll have Geordie to look after him,' she said with surprising satisfaction.

Hannah paused and stared at her sister.

'Was that your doing?' she asked. 'I heard that Geordie was furious when he found out Hughie was set on going to the Klondike too.'

Belle's pretty lips made a moue. 'He came round,' she said airily. 'Geordie soon saw sense. They'll do better as a team.'

'No good will come of it,' Hannah said shortly. 'That boy is an innocent and Geordie Sinclair...'

'That's the point,' Belle said irritably. 'Geordie had everything worked out – how to get there, what was needed. All that was lacking was a bit of money. Hughie, now – his mother had a bit of money she was willing to give him but she didn't want him to go on his own.

Once I realised her money was enough for the two of them…' She threw up her hands. 'Well, it just made sense.'

'I don't know,' Hannah began slowly.

Belle shrugged. 'It will all work out.' She raised an eyebrow as she examined the progress on her hair. 'You need to get a move on,' she told Hannah. 'I have to be there to see them off.'

'But you don't care about Geordie,' Hannah stated.

'Of course not!' Belle said. She swung round from the dressing table and fixed Hannah with a fierce stare. 'You must promise not to tell or I won't tell you anything!'

Hannah blinked. 'Well, yes, of course I promise, but what is there to tell?' she asked. 'And you'd better sit still or I won't ever get this finished.'

Belle turned back round to face the mirror. 'I have given my word to Hughie Mackay that when he comes back from the Klondike a rich man, I will marry him,' she announced grandly. 'We are betrothed.'

'What?' Hannah exclaimed, dropping the last of the pins. 'You can't be! You can't just decide… Father would never allow it!' She ducked down to pick up the pins, her head reeling.

But Belle merely smirked again. 'Well, I have, and we are. But it's a secret.' She preened. 'Hughie's wanted to marry me for ages now. But I couldn't consider it, not when he didn't have any prospects.'

Hannah rose from her knees, heart heavy at the worldliness of Belle's words. Where did love come into it, she wondered. The man *she* wanted to marry she loved with all her heart. Firmly, Hannah set the thought aside and concentrated on her sister. She had to concede that Belle was merely speaking the truth. Their father would never have considered Hughie, the youngest son of a poor crofting family, a worthy suitor for his daughter. And that daughter would never settle for a poor man.

'So when Geordie told Hughie about going to the Klondike and making his fortune…' Belle laughed. 'Well, I realised that was the solution. I'd get Hughie to go to the Klondike and make *his* fortune. And then when Hughie comes back a rich man with all that gold, Father will welcome him with open arms.' She sat back, openly admiring herself in the mirror. 'And so will I! Hughie will come back and claim me as his bride,' she said dramatically. She glared at Hannah. 'And that's why I have to be there looking my best to wave him goodbye. So I'm the last person he sees as he leaves Wick, to remember while he's gone…'

Romantic nonsense, Hannah thought, pushing in the last pin. First Hughie had to get to the Klondike, a journey of thousands upon thousands of miles, then he had to strike gold…

Even then, she was not sure their father would welcome him back as a husband for Belle. And Belle – well, Belle was not exactly famous for her steadfastness. She was like a butterfly that darted from flower to flower, and since she was never short of admirers, her family had got well used to not knowing from one day to the next which young man was in favour and which not.

'I hope he knows what he's doing,' Hannah muttered.

'He loves me,' Belle said with smug satisfaction.

'Yes, well,' Hannah said dryly. 'That's as maybe. You'd better get your hat on if you want to get to the railway station in time to wave him goodbye.'

CHAPTER 4

The cavernous railway station thrummed with noise. The big steam engine readied for the journey south kept up a deep rumbling roar, puffing out clouds of smoke and showers of sooty cinders. Doors banged as latecomers leapt on to the train and the guard slammed the doors shut behind them. Hurrying porters shouted warnings as they struggled with their heavily laden luggage trolleys through the knots of folk gathered to make their farewells. Passengers leaned out of carriage windows calling out to their friends on the platform and they shouted back, trying to make themselves heard above the din. Sudden great noisy puffs of steam spurted up on to the platform and rose to hang with the clouds of smoke in the iron latticework of the roof.

Hannah Reid put her gloved hands over her ears. She had never enjoyed the overwhelming din and smoky atmosphere of the station. There was one benefit though… She peeked up at the man beside her, then leapt back as a sudden blast of hot steam from between two carriages caught her ankles.

Rab Cormack laughed, not unkindly, and reached out a hand to steady her.

'Are you all right? You didn't get burned?' he asked.

Hannah nodded and fought to ignore the blush that rose in her cheeks as she felt his strong touch on her arm. But Rab's attention was only momentary as he instantly resumed his concentration on the touching scene further along the platform.

Hannah's eyes followed his gaze to where her sister Belle, dressed in her very best, was mopping at her eyes with a lace-edged handkerchief – eyes, Hannah noted wryly, that somehow did not get red and puffy like hers did when she cried. Belle always managed to look beautiful. And Hannah had to admit that she looked very beautiful indeed in her best blouse and skirt, her tight-fitting jacket showing off her tiny waist. By the looks of admiration Belle was receiving as she stood on the railway station platform, Hannah's efforts in helping Belle to get ready this morning appeared to have been well worth the effort.

Belle was teetering on her toes, in a dramatic pose of desperate longing, her gaze fixed on one of two young men leaning out of the window of the nearest carriage. The object of Belle's attention, Hughie Mackay, looked proud and happy. He was waving delightedly, clearly eager to be started on the long journey to Canada. Geordie Sinclair, a scowling figure at his side, glanced at Hughie glowing with excitement beside him and suppressed an irritated sigh.

A small shabbily dressed country woman was wringing her hands just a few steps away on the platform.

'Oh Hughie!' Her hands came up to her mouth to stifle the tears.

'Don't worry, Mother!' Hughie called. 'I'll be home in no time!'

Geordie Sinclair glanced cynically at the woman whose life savings were funding his trip. 'Don't you worry,' he told her. 'I'll take good care of him.'

But her eyes snapped angrily at him and in a swift movement she stretched up to the carriage window and thrust a battered Bible into Hughie's hand.

'You take this with you and read it every day, my son,' she admonished Hughie. 'And the good Lord will look after you.'

Hughie, blushing, bent down to tuck the Bible into the pack at his feet.

'There's a good boy. You do what your mother says,' Geordie murmured mockingly. A sudden spark of anger flared briefly in Hughie's eyes. Geordie laughed again.

A shout came from a friend in the crowd. 'Good luck, lads! Go and make your fortunes!' And a cheer echoed along the platform.

Hughie's face cleared at once, the moment's cloud gone. The future lay ahead, bright and shining, and there was the promise of his beloved Belle to come home to. He could cope with Geordie Sinclair's taunts for the short trip to the Klondike till they found gold and went their separate ways.

Whistles blew. The crowds on the platform stepped back to safety, still waving and calling out farewells and last-minute messages.

'I'll write!' Hughie called.

Belle waved her handkerchief, her other hand in a little fist against her mouth, holding back the sobs. She presented a very touching picture, Hannah had to admit.

And Rab? Hannah cast a quick glance up at him. One more of the beautiful Belle's admirers, he probably thought he would have more of a chance now that two of the competition were going to be out of the way.

The huge locomotive seemed to stir like a sleeping monster coming awake. With a great screeching of metal against metal, the big wheels began to turn. There came a loud shriek of the whistle and great puffings of smoke and the train gathered itself and slowly pulled out of the station.

For a few moments the folk on the platform remained waving till the train disappeared out of sight. Then they turned back, the empty track running out into the darkness of the early morning as bereft of life as a hillside cemetery after a funeral. People spoke quietly as they prepared to leave.

Rab Cormack went over to Belle and put a hand on her shoulder.

'I'll walk you home,' he offered with new confidence.

Belle gazed up at him through her eyelashes. 'Oh, that's very kind of you,' she said and placed her hand on his arm, giving one last dab at her eyes with her handkerchief. Rab brightened and patted her hand as he tucked it into the crook of his arm and guided her out of the railway station.

Hannah made to follow but Belle turned her head sharply. 'You don't need to come. Don't you have some errands to do for Mother?' Rab made to speak but Belle forestalled him, saying with a pretty laugh, 'She's so forgetful! It's just as well I'm here to remind her.' She turned back to Hannah, 'Now then, Hannah dearest, off you go and don't forget! You know I need to go home and rest.' And as they turned away, she looked back and winked wickedly at Hannah.

Hannah's mouth pursed in annoyance. But yes, it was true their mother had asked them to bring home a few things from the town, so Hannah simply nodded and headed away from them towards the shops. Patience, that's what she needed.

'I think I'm going to need plenty, Lord!' she prayed.

She sighed. It would have been nice if Rab had taken her hand and tucked it into the crook of his other arm so they could all walk together. A dreamy smile touched her lips as she conjured up the picture but it was soon dismissed. She knew it was her sister that Rab wanted to be with.

CHAPTER 5

Belle had been fidgeting all through family prayers and the generous breakfast that followed. Now as her father rose from the table, wiping his mouth fastidiously with a pristine white starched napkin and laying it beside his plate, she hurriedly rose and darted to his side.

'Darling Papa!' she cried and kissed his cheek. 'Shall I walk to the corner of the street with you again this morning?'

He smiled down at her eager smiling face and patted her hand.

'I'll be delighted to have your company, my dear,' he replied. 'I'm sure a little breath of air will do you good. Go get your hat and wrap.'

Without a backward glance, Belle rushed away to get them.

'The Lord has blessed me in my family,' Mr Reid intoned ponderously. 'My dear' – he glanced at his wife – 'I have a luncheon meeting with a new client today but I should be home in time for tea.'

Mrs Reid smiled fondly. 'Yes, my dear. There will be fresh scones waiting for you.'

'And you will see that your chores are all done,' he said austerely to Hannah. 'There can be no slacking, especially when your younger sister is so delicate. You must help her as much as you can and see that she does not overtire herself.'

Hannah swallowed down the hurt that rose at her father's words. Weren't her chores always done to satisfaction? And didn't she always do most of Belle's? Her mother caught her eye with a silent warning and Hannah bowed her head in submission. Just at that moment, Belle hurtled breathlessly into the room.

'I'm ready,' she cried gaily.

'But your father is not,' her mother chided gently.

Belle's lip trembled rebelliously but when her father turned to her, her face once more showed only a sunny expression.

'Ready?' he queried. 'Oh, the energy of youth!'

He laughed and followed his wife into the hall where she helped him on with his overcoat and handed him his hat and walking stick. Then he bent and kissed her on the cheek. 'Goodbye, my dear.'

Belle held her impatience in check as she watched this show of marital affection. For a moment she let herself dream of how it would be between her and Hughie when they were married. Why, he would hardly be willing to leave her side! No perfunctory husbandly kiss for her! He would adore her, worship the ground she walked on…

'Come, Belle.' Her father's words woke her from her dream and she remembered to smile at the interruption.

'Yes, Father,' she answered obediently and took his arm as they left the house. Quickly she scanned the street. Surely she had timed it correctly? The postman should be on his way.

As she engaged her father in light meaningless conversation, her eyes kept a sharp watch for the postman's bicycle. And at last, there he was, turning the corner from Vansittart Street into Wellington Street. Her heart began to race but she calmed herself. She was sure she could easily intercept him.

She kept her feet walking at a placid pace beside her father, keeping the conversation going pleasantly. She had no interest in the topics he discussed but she was adept at inserting little murmurs and comments at the right intervals. It was not difficult and he seemed suitably pleased in the company of his beautiful youngest daughter. She preened, then caught herself. The postman was coming nearer.

As he drew within speaking distance, Belle addressed him.

'Good morning, Mr Flett. I wonder, do you have any letters for us? I'll be happy to take them home with me.'

She waited, her eyes fixed on him as he sorted through the letters in his basket.

'Would you, Miss Reid? That would be kind,' the man said as he placed a bundle of letters in her outstretched hands. He dipped his head to her father then continued on his rounds.

'That was thoughtful, Belle,' her father said appreciatively. He bent to kiss her cheek. 'You're a good girl.'

She smiled and managed to sweep her eyes down under suitably modest brows, hiding her inward satisfaction.

'Well, we part here,' he said as they reached the corner. 'You take those letters home. I shall see you at tea time.'

'Yes, Papa,' she said and dimpled prettily.

With trembling self-control, she waited till he had gone out of sight before she allowed herself to look down at the letters in her hand. Swiftly she sorted through them. They were mainly for her mother, one for Hannah – and yes! Her heart soared in triumph. There was one for her.

Belle examined the postmark carefully. It was from Liverpool. She held it tightly. It had to be from Hughie. He had promised, as he was leaving, that he would write to her. And she had cleverly intercepted it! With the pleased smile of a cat fed the richest cream, Belle tucked the letter into her reticule and turned for home.

'What are you so pleased about?' Hannah enquired when Belle waltzed into the kitchen where she was putting away the breakfast dishes.

'Sour puss!' Belle mocked her. 'I'm just happy,' she said. 'But I must go upstairs and put my hat and wrap away. Oh, by the way, I met the postman on the way and brought the letters back. There's one for you.'

She was aware of Hannah's suspicious gaze following her as she made her way out of the kitchen. Let her wonder, Belle thought, amused. She wasn't getting a letter from her lover! She never would, old plain-faced Goody-Two-Shoes Hannah! She would never have a lover.

She put her things away hurriedly then threw herself on the bed to open her letter.

'*Dear Belle…*'

Belle's mouth turned down. It was not exactly the most romantic start to a letter. Could he not have put 'My darling Belle'? Still, maybe he was being careful in case the letter fell into her parents' hands. Yes, she decided, that would be it. It was not that he did not adore her. Hughie was simply being thoughtful to spare her any embarrassment. Yes, that would be it. She read on:

'*Dear Belle,*

We're here in Liverpool, waiting to get on the boat to Nova Scotia…'

'Belle?'

Belle jumped guiltily and clutched the letter to her chest. Her sister stood in the doorway.

'You didn't say you'd got a letter?' Hannah queried curiously.

Belle scowled at her.

'Who is it from?' Hannah asked as she came into the room. She waved hers at Belle. 'Mine is from Cousin Jane. She's had a lovely holiday.'

26

Belle sneered. Boring Cousin Jane. Boring holiday. She wanted Hannah to go away so she could read her letter. She turned away.

'Belle?' Hannah turned to look at her, waiting for the answer to her question.

Belle tried for an innocent bland gaze but her eyes sparked fire. Go away, she wanted to say. Go away!

Hannah took a step nearer and Belle clutched the letter closer to her chest. Hannah's brow furrowed. 'So who's your letter from? What's the matter? Why don't you want to let me see it?' She held out a hand for it but Belle squirmed back on the bed.

'It's mine,' she said. 'And I haven't read it yet, so you can just go away and read your own letter and leave me alone.'

'Just tell me who it's from,' Hannah said. 'That's all I want to know. Why are you hanging on to it as if I'd take it away from you! It's your letter. I just wanted...'

'Yes, I know,' Belle burst out. 'Well, I won't tell you...'

'Girls!' Their mother's voice cut into their argument. She stood in the doorway of their room, her disapproval clear on her face. 'This is not good. Sisters should live together in harmony.' She looked from one to the other. 'What were you arguing about?'

Hannah swallowed hard. 'Sorry, Mother. It wasn't really an argument...'

'I heard raised voices. I do not like to hear raised voices.'

'No, Mother.'

'It was Hannah,' Belle said. 'She was being horrid to me.'

'Hannah?'

Hannah sighed. 'I'm sorry, Mother,' she said again. 'I simply asked Belle...'

Belle gasped as she saw the ground open up under her feet. 'But I forgive her,' she said hurriedly in an attempt to sidetrack her mother. 'So we needn't talk about it.'

'It's good to forgive, my dear,' her mother said but her eyes were on Hannah. 'What were you asking Belle that caused such an argument?'

'I asked her who her letter was from.'

Mrs Reid's brows drew close and she turned to Belle. 'And that caused an argument?'

Belle's lips closed tight. Her mother's gaze fixed on the letter held close to Belle's chest. It was too late for her to try to hide it. Belle watched in dismay as her mother held her hand out for the letter.

'I think I had better see this letter. Belle?' It was not a request but a command and Belle found herself handing over the letter.

'I haven't read it,' she said defensively, glaring at Hannah. But her mother ignored her as she studied first the envelope and then the letter.

She raised her eyes to Belle in enquiry. 'From young Hughie Mackay?'

Hannah drew in a quick breath. So that was why Belle would not say who the letter was from. It also explained why she had been so willing of late to walk with her father in the early morning. It was all a ploy to intercept the postman!

Her mother's eyes lingered briefly on Hannah, then she turned back to Belle.

'And what would Hughie Mackay be doing writing to you?' she enquired gently.

'Why shouldn't he?' Belle bridled. 'He's a friend. Poor boy, I suppose he's got no one else to write to about his adventures now he's off to the Klondike!' She laughed a pretty, careless laugh. 'I shouldn't think his mother can even read!'

Her mother's eyes narrowed. 'I think we'll let your father see this and he can decide what is to be done.' She looked at her daughters.

'There will be no more arguing. And we will all hear what Hughie has to say about his adventures at tea time.'

She left the room, taking the letter with her.

'Now look what you've done!' Belle threw at her sister before flinging herself onto her pillows.

'Me?' Hannah said. 'I wasn't the one who got the letter and tried to hide it and…'

Belle turned round to face her, blotches of angry tears disfiguring her pretty face. 'Oh, I'm so tired of all of this!' she burst out. 'I wish Hughie would come back so we can be married and I can have my own house and run it the way *I* like so I don't have to do any of this any longer! I won't have to do any horrid chores and get my hands chapped and sore and we won't have any silly prayers and long boring reading out of the Bible in our house every morning! It's so…'

'Belle!' Hannah protested but her sister cut in angrily, 'Oh, it's all right for you, Miss Goody-Two-Shoes! You with your Bible on your bedside table so everybody sees it!'

Hannah flushed. She did keep her Bible on her bedside table – but that was because she liked to read from it every morning and evening. Belle's taunt hurt. Maybe it was a bit like the Pharisees flaunting their prayers in public? Oh dear. Maybe she should tuck it away, under her pillow?

Belle was well wound up by now. 'Well, all that Bible-reading won't do you any good, see if it doesn't! I'm going to have a wonderful life *my* way – I'll have a big house and a handsome husband and plenty of money – and you'll be the poor miserable holy holy spinster sister left behind looking after the ancient parents. That's what you'll get for being so good! Nothing worth having!'

Hannah swallowed hard. It was probably true. With her older brothers and sisters married, and Belle determined to marry Hughie when he came back from the Klondike, she would be the only one left. 'Honour thy mother and thy father...' The fifth commandment sounded strongly in her mind. Yes. That came first, she reminded herself. Her place was with her parents. Though her heart, her poor hopeless heart, longed for love and marriage, and love and marriage with one particular special man at that.

Sadly Hannah looked at Belle's angry face. She had no answer for her.

CHAPTER 6

'Was this the best you could do?' Geordie complained as they set their bags down on the deck of the ship that was to take them from Liverpool to Nova Scotia in Canada.

A large cargo hold down in the bowels of the ship had been converted to provide accommodation for passengers. Rows of bunks had been roughly fashioned along the sides and there was an open area in the centre where men gathered in groups. Hughie looked around him.

'It's not so bad,' he protested. In any case, steerage was all they could afford if they were to meet the expenses of equipping themselves for the Klondike and paying for their stake.

'Maybe not for a *teuchter* like you,' Geordie sneered.

A head came up in the little group of men nearest to them and a broad Scots voice called out, 'Who's a *teuchter*?'

'I am,' Hughie said, good-naturedly accepting the epithet. Country-born and bred, and from a Gaelic-speaking family, he knew Geordie had meant the word as an insult but he was determined not to take offence. They had a long journey ahead of them.

'Where are you from?' the man asked. The voice sounded friendly.

'Wick,' Hughie replied. 'Caithnessshire.'

'Oh yes, I know it,' and a tall middle-aged man stood up and held out his hand. 'Andrew MacNab at your service. And another *teuchter*.' It was said with a twinkle.

'Hugh Mackay.'

They shook hands. MacNab held his hand out to Geordie who stood eyes narrowed suspiciously, his hand by his side.

'Ah weel, please yourself,' MacNab said. He turned to Hughie. 'There's a place wi' us whenever you need it.' And he went back to his group.

'Thank you,' Hughie said.

The friendly MacNab looked to be better company than Geordie had been. Despite his need of Hughie's mother's money for his passage, Geordie had scarcely bothered to hide his resentment at having to accept Hughie along with it. And even though he had to admit Geordie's greater familiarity with the ways of the world had come in handy several times, Hughie was not looking forward to being confined with him for ten days on board ship.

But he need not have feared. Though they bunked one above the other, Geordie spent little time with him.

'You stay with your *teuchter* friends,' Geordie told him on the second day at sea. 'They'll look after you as well as I can.' And he had taken himself off, returning smelling of drink and loudly pleased with himself in the early hours of the morning.

Andrew MacNab had welcomed Hughie into his group.

'There are around three hundred of us all told,' he told Hughie. 'Bold Scots off to make their fortune in Canada.'

'Me too,' Hughie said.

'And your friend?'

'Well, he's not so much a friend,' Hughie said carefully. 'Just someone from home.'

'Oh aye,' MacNab said. 'You maybe need to watch that one.'

But it was more like Geordie was keeping a watch on him, Hughie thought. Although Geordie had found his own companions among the wild and rowdy crowd where there was plenty of drink and a card game always in progress, he had developed the habit of circling back from time to time to where Hughie was.

He would lean against the side of the bunk and stare at Hughie for a few moments, waiting for Hughie to speak. In desperation Hughie found his mother's old Bible and kept it close so when Geordie hove into view he could pretend to be reading it.

At first Geordie mocked. 'Can't you find anything better to do with yourself?'

But when Hughie did not respond, he gave up and merely sneered. 'Good boy,' he would say, flapping a hand at the Bible.

'I'm reading,' Hughie would reply.

'I can see that,' Geordie would say and take himself away again.

Pondering this strange behaviour, Hughie decided that Geordie was simply keeping an eye on him – and the money that would take him to the Klondike.

The Scotsmen whose group Hughie had joined also appeared to keep an eye on what he was doing too.

'You read the Bible?' one of MacNab's friends asked him.

Hughie nodded. He had not exactly been reading it but it was easier to simply agree.

'Then maybe you'd like to join us in worship on Sunday?'

And because they were a friendly bunch and there was nothing else to do, Hughie joined them. Geordie sneered, of course, but since it kept him away, Hughie stuck with his new friends.

He enjoyed their company and was sad when they parted on arrival in Canada. Now he was forced back into spending more time with Geordie on board the train to Vancouver, then on the boat trip up the island-scattered west coast. Volatile Geordie's moods swung from high-flown confidence in his Klondike gold-funded future to an irritability that seemed determined to pick a fight with anyone in reach. Hughie in desperation found himself using the old Bible once more as protection.

At this Geordie's taunts rained thick and fast till Hughie found the only way to ignore them was to actually concentrate on reading the words in front of him. He was surprised and delighted to find gems of wisdom in it. '*A soft answer turneth away wrath*' came in useful more than once and Hughie discovered there was solace to be found in the pages.

But then the first sight of Skagway chased away every thought but the gold he had come so far to find. Skagway was an anarchic tent-town with a saloon on every corner, and thronged with folk whose only focus was making a fortune from Klondike gold.

'I don't know what my mother would think,' Hughie had murmured as he stood gazing around him in amazement.

'I do,' Geordie said, now in high spirits. 'But you don't need to worry. She's not here to see you. You're your own man now!'

The town's primitiveness, dirt and lawlessness spoke of the frontier and the thrilling adventure they were launched upon.

'It's the experience of a lifetime,' Geordie told him expansively. 'A new beginning! This is where life really begins.'

CHAPTER 7

'So we have a letter from Liverpool,' Mr Reid said, turning the envelope round in his hand and studying the postmark.

Hannah sat next to Belle on the sofa, their mother at the tea table pouring out the tea and handing round the cups. Hannah could feel Belle's tension, her nerves coiled tight like a spring. If the letter spoke of her secret engagement to Hughie Mackay, their father would not be pleased and even Belle's wheedling ways would not be able to win him over.

The girls waited almost without breathing as their father pulled the letter out of the envelope and unfolded it. He scanned it quickly. Turning to the last page he read the salutation and signature. Then he looked up.

'I see it is from the young man who went off to the Klondike with that Geordie Sinclair.' He waited, his gaze on Belle, but she said nothing.

'It will be interesting to hear how they're getting on,' he commented. Smoothing out the folded pages of the letter, he began to read.

'*Dear Belle...*'

Well, Hannah thought with relief, that was a plain enough beginning. Nothing there to give away the secret engagement. And as her father read, it was clear that the letter continued in a matter-of-fact manner.

'*We're here at Liverpool, waiting to get on the boat to Nova Scotia,*' Hughie had written. '*The train journey was fine and it was good to have Geordie along. He seems to know just what to do.*'

Here Mr Reid muttered in a low aside to his wife, 'I'm sure he does – but maybe never the right way.' He continued reading.

'*There seems to be a lot of men raring to get out to Canada. Our boat is taking around three hundred Scotsmen. Not all are bound for the gold fields. Some are going to try their hand at ranching. Maybe I'll buy a ranch if I find enough gold!*'

'That would be a good thing for a young man like Mackay,' Mr Reid commented. 'There's nothing for him back here on the family croft.'

'Ranching?' Belle snorted at the idea when the two girls were back in their bedroom after evening prayers. 'He can think again,' she told Hannah. 'I have absolutely no intention of going out there or of being any kind of farmer's wife.'

'But it could be really good,' Hannah protested. 'A fresh start in a new country!'

Belle shook her head determinedly. 'No. I'm quite happy living here in Wick. When Hughie comes home, he'll have enough gold to set us up comfortably in our own home and we'll never need to think about work for the rest of our lives. This bee in his bonnet about ranching will surely be short-lived,' she said confidently.

But the tone of the letter had won approval from her father.

'The poor boy probably has no one else but his mother to write to.' He had smiled tolerantly at his youngest daughter. 'And yes, I know the lad had a *tendresse* for you so it's quite natural he would want to write to you and maybe impress you with all that he's doing.'

Belle blushed and her father shook his head. 'You young people! Oh well, it's not surprising, a pretty thing like you.' He looked over at his wife. 'I don't think there's any harm in it. Belle, you have my permission to write him a reply, but see that you don't encourage him in any silly ideas. Keep it to friendship. And if he wishes, he can write again. We'll be happy to hear what the lad is up to.'

Belle glowed with satisfaction. 'Yes, Papa,' she said and she slipped from her chair to kiss his cheek. He patted her hand fondly. As she settled back into her chair, she threw a triumphant smirk at Hannah.

And so a new pattern was established. When a letter from Hughie arrived, Belle was permitted to read it first but had to bring it downstairs to her father when he came home. He would then read it out to the family and any visitors who arrived for tea. It provided an interesting and unusual entertainment.

'*Vancouver!*' the next letter from Hughie read. '*The other side of this huge country! When we get to the next town, Skagway or Dyea, we have to be fitted out with what they call an outfit – all the clothes, provisions, and equipment that we'll need. They say you need enough food to last you through a long winter.*'

'It will be a lot colder there,' Mr Reid commented, looking across the room at Rab Cormack for agreement.

Over the weeks of Hughie's absence, Rab had become a frequent visitor to the house.

'Oh aye,' he said now. 'Up in the Klondike I believe the temperature goes a long way down below freezing. They could be snowed in for months,' he added with grim satisfaction.

'As if *he* knows anything about it!' Belle whispered acidly to Hannah. But when Rab turned to speak to her, Belle was once more all smiles and he beamed at her encouragement.

'Can't you leave him alone?' Hannah pleaded despairingly later in their room. 'You've got Hughie. Isn't that enough?'

But Belle just laughed. 'Don't be silly! I'm only playing. And anyway, Rab's never going to be interested in you. I'd just have to snap my fingers! You might as well give up now!'

Inwardly Hannah railed at the unfairness of life – but there was nothing she could do about it, except pray for Hughie's safe return and her own composure in the meantime.

The next letter from Hughie covered the boat trip from Vancouver up the west coast of Canada.

'*It is so beautiful you can't imagine,*' Hughie wrote. '*We must have covered a thousand miles.*'

After the sea journey, the choice overland was via Skagway or Dyea, and the long hard slog up to Dawson City. This was the last letter for several months.

'But aren't you worried about him?' Hannah asked Belle. 'We haven't heard from Hughie for a while.'

But Belle was unconcerned. 'He won't be able to write till they reach Dawson City, I shouldn't think. And anyway, his letters weren't very interesting. Once he's found some gold, that will be worth writing to me about!'

And Belle had smiled, a sharp, gleaming, greedy smile.

CHAPTER 8

'*Four sacks of flour, forty pounds of rolled oats, twenty pounds of candles.*' Geordie read out the list they had been given. '*One hundred and fifty pounds of bacon, ten pounds of tea...*' He flung it down in disgust. 'This is women's business!' he complained. 'Why do we have to bother with all of this?'

Hughie gritted his teeth. *Just a little longer*, he told himself. Once they reached the Klondike and found enough gold for Geordie to pay him back for his initial expenses, they could go their separate ways. And Hughie was determined that his would take him as far away from Geordie as fast as possible.

But for the time being they were both eager to get started up the trail to Dawson City. Geordie was impatient with any setback so Hughie was not surprised that he balked when faced with what he considered a woman's shopping list.

'It's the law,' the Skagway shopkeeper told them. 'Too many folk went up to the Klondike unprepared last year so now the Mounted Police won't let you through without a full outfit to last twelve months.'

'All of this?' Geordie demanded. 'We have to get everything on this list?'

'That's right,' the shopkeeper answered with a smile. 'One outfit for each of you.'

'Huh,' Geordie growled suspiciously. 'It's good for you, isn't it? Not so good for us.'

'That's true,' the shopkeeper said peaceably. 'It's been good business for the town, but you won't think anything of the outlay when you're digging up big nuggets of gold in a month or two. Think of it as a wise investment.'

Geordie's eyes narrowed greedily and he picked up the list again, turning it over to read: 'One gold pan.' His face lightened. 'That's more like it!' he said. But by the time every item on the long list had been assembled, his scowl was back in place.

'This is going to take a lot of getting up there,' he complained, glowering at the mountain of goods on the floor in front of them. Boxes of dried food; tools – long-handled shovels, saws, hatchets and picks; a camp cook stove and all the kettles and pans they would need; a heaped pile of clothing – arctic socks and heavy suits, moccasins and boots; mosquito nets. So many unfamiliar items, but each one deemed a necessity by the government.

'It must weigh a ton,' Hughie said.

The shopkeeper agreed. 'That's about right,' he said. 'But if you've got the money, you can take the easy way to the Klondike. The Rich Man's Route,' he added with a grin. 'A berth on a nice comfortable steamship and the whole journey on the water.'

Geordie's face brightened and he turned eagerly to Hughie.

'We don't have the money for that, Geordie,' Hughie said, regretfully, thinking of how his mother's precious savings were dwindling already.

'Then it's overland for the pair of you,' the shopkeeper said. 'Take your pick – Chilkoot or White Pass. They both end up at the same place, Lake Bennett – and then it's on the water the rest of the way to Dawson City.' He cast an assessing eye over Hughie's sturdy figure then Geordie's weedy form. 'If you go by the Chilkoot Pass, you have to pull your goods on sleds or carry them on your backs. Your friend may do all right but I reckon you'll find it hard work. You could always pay some packers to carry for you.'

Hughie shook his head and Geordie bristled with annoyance.

'So what's the alternative?' he demanded. 'There's got to be another way.'

'White Pass. That's a wagon trail.'

'That will be the thing for us then,' Geordie said decisively. 'You're used to horses, Hughie.'

'That's true,' Hughie said. On the croft back home he had enjoyed working with horses. But when he and Geordie arrived at the Skagway establishment recommended by the shopkeeper, the only horses available for hire were a sorry sight – old nags coming to the end of their working lives. Hughie walked around, examining them unhappily.

'Oh, what's the problem?' Geordie demanded impatiently. 'If they can pull the wagon with us and our stuff in it till we get to Lake Bennett, they'll do! We're not planning on having them with us for life and if we can sell them on at Lake Bennett to folk going back down the trail, that will cover the cost.'

Hughie uneasily parted with his money but Geordie declared himself satisfied with the wagon and the horses they had managed to secure.

'The sooner we get to the Klondike the better,' he reminded Hughie, for they were not the only ones. Once word had reached the outside world of the first gold found in the Klondike, thousands upon thousands of men and women had rushed to get their hands on the bonanza, and a steady stream left Skagway every day for Dawson City and the fabled gold fields of the north. Geordie and Hughie with their wagon and horses slipped into place amongst the others on the crowded trail.

At first Geordie crowed over 'his' decision to go by the White Pass. The first few miles were good and wide and the wagon made easy progress. But soon they were winding through the hills on a dirt road that steadily narrowed and Hughie worried that the wagon would not be able to get through.

As the days wore on the weather worsened and the trail shrank to only a couple of feet across. Geordie, in a fever to see the end of the journey and find the gold, insisted they ditch the wagon and pack their loads on to the horses.

'They can take the heavy stuff,' he said. 'We can manage the lighter stuff ourselves.'

But as the going became muddier and wetter, the rain now giving way to snow, both horses and men found it hard going. There were mud holes big enough to swallow a horse whole. In places, sharp-witted men had covered them over with split logs and charged the would-be gold miners a toll to pass over safely. In other places, slippery slate made for treacherous footing. The sharp rocks tore at the animals' legs and tripped them up. Any horse that fell was left where it lay. The column of desperate men and animals that followed simply kept going, straight over the body, till it was pounded into the earth.

Hughie, used to handling horses on the croft at home, despaired over the way the Klondikers' pack horses were treated. Overburdened, as he had to admit theirs were, the animals were pushed to the limit and way beyond it. Daily, he saw horses slip on the muddy path and break legs, or fall from the narrow trail into the gulch below. Where the drop was not so deep, some horses managed to survive the fall and could be driven back up to the trail. So when Geordie's pack horse went over, Hughie left his horse and his load at the side of the trail and climbed down after it. To his dismay, the animal lay a twisted wreck on the gully floor. It would carry no more loads.

'What are you waiting for?' Geordie shouted down to him. 'Unload it and bring the stuff up!' And without waiting for a reply, he slapped Hughie's pack horse on the rump and continued on up the trail.

Hughie stared after him in dismay. He dared not leave Geordie's outfit behind. If they went on with only the one outfit between the two of them, they would be refused entry to the mining district by the Mounted Police. Looking up, he saw Geordie and the horse disappear round one of the zig-zag bends of the trail.

Gritting his teeth, he began to unload the packs off the dead horse.

'Hey, Hughie! Is that you down there?' a voice shouted.

Hughie straightened from his task and stared up to where a small group of men had halted with their pack horses and were looking down at him, waiting for his reply.

'Is that you, MacNab?' Hughie shouted, barely able to believe his good fortune.

'It is that,' the man replied. 'Now if you'll pass those bags up, we'll give you a hand with them. We *teuchters* have to stick together!' The group of men laughed cheerfully.

'Thanks,' Hughie said with huge relief.

As he lugged the packs up from the bottom of the gulch, willing hands reached down and pulled them up. When he scrambled back up on to the trail, Hughie found himself surrounded by the Scotsmen who had befriended him on the boat. They slapped his back and exclaimed in greeting, making light of his predicament.

'No, no, we can surely help you out,' he was told and within minutes they were loading as much as they could on to their own pack horses, leaving Hughie with only his own heavy pack to carry on his back.

'*Bearing one another's burdens*,' he was told jocularly, a quote he remembered from his mother's old Bible. As he set off to trudge along the path, the men around him included him in their talk and Hughie found the hours slipped by quite pleasantly till at night he caught up with Geordie at one of the makeshift roadhouses that had sprung up along the trail.

'What took you so long?' was Geordie's greeting. 'Did you get all our stuff?'

'Your stuff,' Hughie corrected him quietly as he unloaded the packs from the backs of his friends' horses, before thanking each one as they nodded and turned away.

'It's all the same,' Geordie snapped. 'Your stuff, my stuff. We need two lots to get in.'

'Yes, I know,' Hughie said wearily, setting down the heavy pack from his back to sit alongside the other bags his companions had brought up for him.

At least Geordie had put up the tent and got a fire going, Hughie consoled himself. He fell asleep exhausted after sharing with Geordie the meal he had cooked. Late in the night he heard Geordie return to the tent from yet another card game.

Drowsily Hughie pondered Geordie's good fortune at cards. Back home, playing cards for money was frowned on but here it seemed taken for granted. It was how most of the men passed any idle hours.

And Geordie's winnings seemed to outpace any losses, though that did not make him any more popular among the other men.

In the morning, Hughie woke to find Geordie up and getting ready to leave.

'About time,' Geordie complained. 'We need to keep going. I'll put some of the extra stuff on the horse and get started.' He handed Hughie a mug of coffee. 'Your holy *teuchter* friends will no doubt help you take the rest,' he sneered.

Hughie swallowed the coffee and the sneer and rose. Together they packed away the tent, then Geordie was off, taking Hughie's horse and baggage with him.

'I'll see you tonight,' he called to Hughie over his shoulder as he slapped the rump of the horse roughly and they disappeared down the trail. 'Better get a move on. They say more snow's coming.'

Hughie viewed the mountain of goods he had been left to bring. He would never do it on his own but Geordie seemed confident the Scotsmen from the ship would help. He looked around at the stream of men with heavy packs on their backs leading laden horses on to the trail. It seemed too much to ask any of them to carry more.

'Ready to go?'

It was one of the men who had helped him the day before. And to Hughie's relief a goodly number of his helpers from the previous day were willing to take most of the bags, leaving him to shoulder the rest and trudge along the next section of the trail as the snow came down steadily.

This became the pattern of their days – Geordie going ahead with the horse, Hughie plodding along afterwards in the ever-deepening snow. To Hughie's surprise, despite the hard work, there was a significant advantage. Instead of having to deal with Geordie's volatile moods, Hughie became part of a cheerful group of men who helped one another along the trail. Their simple practical faith seemed to make a difference to them and Hughie enjoyed their company.

At last they reached the broad frozen expanse of Lake Bennett, its shores already home to tented villages of thousands of prospectors waiting for the thaw to set in so they could cross the lake.

Geordie fumed at the delay but no further progress would be possible for several months so they were forced to set up camp and make the best of it. While Geordie once more became part of one of the card-schools in the camp, Hughie headed into the woods with the men who had befriended him to chop down trees each day.

'Now we know what the axes on the list were for!' he declared.

Happier to be working in the clean cold air than sitting in a stuffy tent, the stove that heated it burning precious fuel, Hughie cheerfully helped haul the wood back to where the whipsaws in their outfit were put to good use splitting logs into planks for building rafts and boats.

At last, in late May, the ice on the lake broke and the thaw had set in enough for forward travel to be possible. As the flotilla of hand-made craft set off across the water, Hughie folded up the tent and loaded their goods on to the raft he had built. He hoped it would be strong enough to carry them and their packs the next 500 miles.

'On our way at last!' Geordie growled, lounging against their packs on the deck.

'Aye, and this should be a lot easier than the trail,' Hughie said hopefully, manoeuvring the raft into the current.

But the clear open waters of the lakes were soon followed by ferocious rapids. Miles Canyon. White Horse. Five Fingers. The Rink. Three weeks of treacherous rocks and rapids that smashed boats and drowned men. Hughie found he needed all his courage and a cool head to navigate through the deadly waters.

'Look out!' would come the shout and Hughie would see jagged rocks rising threateningly right in front of them. Grabbing onto the ropes held by men on the rocky shore would pull them clear and then they would be gliding smoothly again on calm water before rounding a bend in the river and pitching wildly into another passage of white water. Pounded by the water and battered by the rocks, the raft struggled along with Hughie keeping a sharp lookout and steering to the best of his ability, while Geordie clung on, cursing and complaining loudly. They seemed to lose count of the days, simply glad to have survived each one.

Each hard day's travel was one day nearer to their goal, Hughie reminded Geordie. And at last they heard a shout: 'There's Moosehide!'

'What's Moosehide?' Hughie shouted across to the men in the boat nearest to them.

In answer they pointed out the big white scar on the mountain ahead. 'There! Looks like the skin of a moose. Dawson City lies beneath that mountain,' they shouted back. 'We're nearly there!'

Loud cheers went up. Geordie rose to his feet and stared across at the mountain, his eyes burning. Soon, he would be there, picking up the gold that was just waiting for him. Soon, his life would really begin.

CHAPTER 9

Now all hands plied the paddles with renewed energy as the river opened out and Dawson City came in sight. Exhausted men raised a cheer and spirits lifted as at last journey's end came within reach. All the hardship, the danger, the terrible sights they had seen and the perils they had endured were forgotten. They had succeeded in reaching the fabled gold fields.

As they neared the shore, Geordie leapt off the raft.

'Just tie it up wherever you can,' he instructed Hughie. 'You stay with our stuff. I'll go into town and get the lay of the land.'

Before Hughie could make any protest, Geordie had waved an impatient farewell and was heading away, threading his way between the rafts and boats already lining the shore. Hughie watched him go. Whatever Geordie might discover, he could not achieve anything without Hughie's money so he would be back. Unless he had won large enough amounts in his card games to fund himself. Hughie shrugged. That was unlikely. For the time being, he thought, Geordie still needed him.

Hughie guided the raft closer in, staring in dismay at the hundreds of boats and rafts already moored all around. By the looks of the makeshift shelters on their decks, they had been there some time. There was little room left for newcomers.

A man lounging on the deck of a nearby boat raised himself up on an elbow. 'Throw your ropes to me. I'll tie them off here. Your raft will be quite secure.'

'Thanks,' Hughie answered, throwing the ropes as bidden. He peered beyond the clustering boats to the shore, trying to follow Geordie's hurrying figure, but he was soon swallowed up by a crowd of other men pouring off the boats and heading into Dawson City. Hughie sighed and flung himself down on the raft to wait.

The man who had helped Hughie spat into the water. 'Come to make your fortune, have you?' he enquired dryly. 'The pair of you?'

Hughie turned enquiring eyes on the man. 'Hasn't everyone?' he asked.

The man laughed. He waved a hand at all the craft huddled up against the shore. 'That was the idea all of us had,' he said. 'But we got here too late.' He paused. 'And *you've* got here far too late. All the claims are taken. All the good creeks are staked. You'll see when your friend comes back later. There's nothing left for anybody else.'

'So why are people staying?' Hughie asked.

'Some have taken jobs in town – at the saloons and hotels. Some men work other men's claims – for money or for a tiny share of the stake. They divide them up like apple pie! Big slices, little slices.'

Hughie brightened at this. Maybe they could work for someone whose stake was too big for him to work alone and then earn themselves a slice of it where they would find the gold…

His daydream was shattered as the man continued, 'A crazy few strike out further and further into the hills, trying for a claim that hasn't been taken – but if they get one, they don't find any gold. Most folk are just getting ready to pack up and go home. There aren't the big finds any more. The bonanza's finished. You'd be as well to give up now and go home while you can.'

Despondency struck deep in Hughie's heart. Was the bonanza really over? Should he just give up and go home? Working in a saloon or labouring for another prospector would not produce the money he needed to persuade Belle's parents that he was a wealthy enough husband for their daughter. And time was a factor too. How long would she be willing to wait for him – especially if she guessed he would not be bringing home what he had promised?

But perhaps he should not give up hope just yet. After all, what he was hearing was the word of only one man, maybe someone who had staked everything on an empty claim and was now embittered and giving up. He would wait for Geordie. Geordie had a knack of turning things round to his advantage. He had seen that oftentimes on the boat and the long journey to Dawson City – even if sometimes it turned out Geordie enjoyed the advantage at Hughie's or someone else's expense. Hughie sighed. What he could do? He was stuck here and Geordie was his only hope. He stretched out on the raft in the pale spring sunshine and set himself to wait patiently for Geordie, trying to soothe the worry that had overtaken him.

As he settled his head on his pack, a thought flitted briefly across his mind. His mother's old Bible. She used to turn to it whenever she needed help or guidance, and the Scotsmen from the boat across seemed to depend on it for answers. Would it have a word for him?

He knew Geordie would mock. He did not really believe it himself but still the prompting was there so he reached into the pack and pulled out the battered little book, now very much the worse for wear, its pages discoloured from many a soaking in the rivers and rapids they had encountered.

51

Hughie turned it in his hands. He had no idea where to start reading. At the beginning? Or just open it and see? That would be the thing. He was sure he had seen his friends from the boat do that when they were perplexed or needed guidance. He closed his eyes a moment while he turned the book in his hand, then taking a breath he opened it and looked down to see what it would say to him.

It had opened in the Book of Psalms. Some words caught his eye. Psalm 127 verse 1: '*Except the* LORD *build the house, they labour in vain that build it.*' That did not seem to have anything to do with him. He was not intending to build a house – except maybe for Belle when he got home. Was he labouring in vain, he wondered idly as he closed the book and put it away. Looking for answers in his mother's old Bible certainly seemed a waste of time.

He would wait for Geordie. He could depend on Geordie. Tipping his hat over his eyes, Hughie drifted off to sleep.

It was growing dark when Geordie returned, in high good humour and smelling of drink. Hughie was not surprised. If there was a place where Geordie could get a drink and a game of cards, he would have found it. And it appeared that his penchant for cards had come in handy.

'Your friend's right,' Geordie said when Hughie told him what the man in the next boat had said. 'There's not a fresh claim to be had. But there are men who are ready to go home and some of them have claims that they're willing to sell.'

'But why?' Hughie asked. 'Surely if there's gold to be found, they would want to stay and work it? The only ones available will be the worked-out mines or the useless ones.'

'That's what you'd think,' Geordie said with a self-satisfied grin. 'But trust me. I've found a good one. I've come all this way to make my fortune, and make my fortune is what I'm going to do!'

And he explained how after walking round the town and discovering the true state of affairs, he had taken himself off to one of the saloons for a consolatory drink and a card game. There, he told Hughie, he had met a young prospector who had broken his leg during the winter.

'He's a bit of a spoiled mother's boy,' Geordie said with a sneer. 'He hasn't fared at all well here. He was up at his claim when he broke his leg. Some of the other prospectors brought him into town to see the doctor and he's been laid up at the saloon ever since where the girls have been looking after him. He's run through all his money but he's still not fit to go back to the claim and work yet. I'd say the plain truth is that he doesn't want to! He says he's seen enough of gold mining to last a lifetime!' Geordie laughed. 'All he wants to do is go home on one of the steamers now the ice is broken and the passage is clear, but he doesn't have the money for it.' Geordie grinned triumphantly at Hughie. 'See how neat it is? He's got a stake that he doesn't want. We want a stake. He needs money to get home. We've got money.' He laughed. 'You could say we're the answer to the boy's prayers!'

And he is to ours, Hughie thought, sudden hope rising out of the ashes.

'It's a good deal,' Geordie assured Hughie, his eyes gleaming. 'The stake is only twenty miles out of Dawson City so we can camp out there and come back in to town when we need anything. He's even got a cabin here for when the weather gets too bad to work. What do you say? We go for it?'

'I'd say so,' Hughie said. 'Well done, Geordie.'

'I need to get back to the saloon to finalise the deal so if you could see your way to letting me have the stake money...' Geordie held out his hand.

Hughie grabbed his pack from the deck of the raft and reached in past his mother's Bible for the remains of the savings she had given him. With high hopes, he handed them over to Geordie.

'You turn in for the night,' Geordie told him, clapping him on the back. 'I'll see to this.'

Hughie laughed with delight and relief. All would be well. Geordie had found a way through what appeared to be an insoluble problem. How could he ever have doubted him? True, there had been odd moments on the long arduous journey to Dawson City when he had glimpsed a darker side to Geordie and wondered if he could trust the man. But now Geordie had saved the day. They had a stake and a foothold in the Klondike. They would make their fortunes and he would return to Belle a rich man. Secure in his trust in Geordie, Hughie fell asleep.

CHAPTER 10

Hughie woke suddenly in the darkness of early morning. Geordie was shaking him.

'Come on,' Geordie said. 'We need to get moving.'

'What?' Hughie asked blurrily. 'What's going on?'

'We have to stake our claim,' Geordie said. 'We need to do it as soon as possible to make it legal.'

He started gathering up their packs and loading them on to a couple of mules that were waiting quietly in the darkness. Hughie staggered blearily to his feet and went to give him a hand.

'What about the raft?' he queried.

Geordie waved a hand in the darkness. 'It'll be fine here. And anyway, when we've hit the gold, we won't need it,' he declared with relish. 'We'll be going home by steamer, laden with gold, just like in those newspaper articles!'

In a short while, they had left the raft behind and were heading through Dawson City. Though the streets were dark, lights were still on in the dance hall and the saloons but Geordie kept his head down and pushed the mules to go faster. Hughie plodded on behind, his eyes wide as he took in the glimpses of revelry behind the brightly lit windows.

On they went along the riverside and into the countryside outside the town. As the sky turned white above them, Geordie consulted a piece of paper with a rough drawing on it.

'This way,' he pronounced firmly and led the way along a battered track to the right. They wound their way through stands of birch and spruce as the sun rose, the air bright with birdsong that delighted Hughie.

'Look!' he exclaimed and pointed at the crimson drifts of fireweed, the blue of lupins growing wild, and the vivid yellow of arnica and daisies. But Geordie was only interested in covering the ground as fast as they could go. So determined was he to press on that they barely stopped for food.

And at last, by early afternoon they had reached a devastated valley where the green vegetation had been stripped and the whole area was filled with mountainous heaps of earth and gravel, rickety wooden structures and windlasses on the top of each. A swift-running creek ran through, channelled off by sluices into narrow streams flowing between the mounds.

'This is it,' Geordie said triumphantly, consulting the piece of paper again as he strode over to one of the mounds. Eyes narrowing, he scouted around the site, returning with a satisfied smile.

'Yes!' he declared. 'This is it. If you'll unload the mules and set up the tent,' he told Hughie, 'I'll see to the legal requirements.' And with that he began to work his way round the site, systematically tearing paper notices off four marker poles set at regular spaces round the claim.

Already a few miners had made an appearance, stopping their work to watch the new arrivals. But when Geordie began tearing off the papers, Hughie saw that the men were putting down their tools and beginning to move forward.

'Look out!' Hughie called. Geordie turned, anger in his face at the interruption, but Hughie gestured at the onlookers.

One of the miners coming down from the top of his mine shaft shouted, 'Hey you! What do you think you're doing?'

A hostile crowd gathered around Geordie but he simply took more papers from his pocket and waved them at the men.

'My friend and I have bought this stake,' Geordie told them. 'I've got the papers here. It's legally ours now.'

Suspiciously the men came closer and peered at the papers. One of them growled, 'What happened to the boy? The one that broke his leg?'

'He sold the claim to us. He's going home on the steamer,' Geordie said. 'Decided he'd had enough.'

There was a murmur from the men.

'*Cheechako*,' one of the miners sneered, and spat. He turned away and went back to his work. The others drifted away and Geordie began nailing one of the papers to each of the four poles.

'That's done,' Geordie said, joining Hughie at the tent. 'It's legal now. We'll work it together and go half-shares on what we find, right?'

The words blazed into Hughie's mind: 'what we find'. He gazed around him in wonder. What he was looking at was a gold mine that was theirs, and the gold in it was theirs for the taking. He found himself grinning excitedly. Geordie nodded and put out his hand for a handshake.

'Partners!' Geordie declared, loudly enough for the other miners nearby to hear. The two men shook hands. 'And now we do a little work and then we get rich!' he continued. 'You'd better sort out what we'll need. I'll just take a quick look around.'

How like Geordie, Hughie thought. Within the hour he would have discovered all about this mining business and found an easier way to do it. And found out where the card-school was!

Curiosity took Hughie down the rickety ladder inside the mine shaft. It was about 20 to 30 feet deep and he could see from the blackened walls where fires had been built in the past. The smell of smoke still seemed to hang in the bottom of the shaft. One side had been dug out to quite some distance, producing most of the gravel on the heap outside, but the other side though blackened was barely touched.

'What are you doing down there?' It was Geordie's voice. 'We need to get to work out here!'

Hughie scaled the ladder out of the mine and clambered down the outside to where Geordie was waiting impatiently.

'Doesn't look like the boy did much work before he broke his leg,' Geordie said, casting a disparaging eye at the mound of gravel waiting to be washed and sieved for any gold it contained. 'But there's enough to be going on with,' he told Hughie, waving at a rickety wooden box set on top of what looked like the rockers from a baby's cradle. 'It's good we bought the claim as a going concern. The rocker and all the rest of the kit belongs to us too.'

'Belongs to us.' It sounded so good. Hughie grinned. They had arrived safely in the Klondike and here he was at his very own gold mine. Soon he would be a rich man and on his way home to Belle. Laughter began to bubble up. Maybe he would strike it rich on his very first day!

'Let's get started!' he declared and, seizing a long-handled shovel, began shovelling gravel from the mound into the box. Then he grabbed a bucket, filling it to the top from the channel that had been diverted by the miners from the nearby creek. He poured the water into the box full of gravel while Geordie operated the long handle which set the box rocking.

The base of the box was made of perforated metal that held the gravel but let the finer gold dust fall through to be caught on a purpose-made apron underneath. The two men watched with bated breath as the first load of gravel was washed and sieved. They knelt together as one to check the apron.

'Nothing!' Hughie said in disgust.

'More gravel!' Geordie shouted and went back to his post at the rocker handle. Hughie shovelled gravel and poured buckets of water. Geordie pulled at the rocker handle. And after each load, they rushed to check how much gold dust had fallen through – but with the same disappointing result.

All through the late afternoon they worked and into the dim light of early evening. It sounded simple enough but turned out to be hard work. Hughie, used to hard physical labour on the croft at home and on the journey to the Klondike, cheerfully shovelled gravel and poured water, but Geordie soon discovered that operating the long upright handle of the rocker was an exhausting and tedious task.

At first they were fuelled by excitement and heady anticipation because surely they would find gold amongst the gravel! But that first taste of the work was long and hard and resulted only in blisters on Geordie's hands, a pile of washed gravel and not a trace of gold.

Dispirited and weary, Hughie lit a fire in front of their tent and cooked a meal. As he worked, he asked Geordie about the previous owner of their claim.

'What did that miner mean when he said the boy was a *chee*…?'

'*Cheechako*,' Geordie said. 'It means greenhorn.' He shrugged. 'He was just having an adventure, a young lad playing at it. He thought it would be exciting and when it turned out differently he was glad to be offered a way to get home without doing any more work.'

Hughie was glad. It was good they had been able to help him.

'He'll be on his way home by now?' he asked.

'Oh yes,' Geordie assured him. 'Now the river's open, there will be no shortage of boats coming and going.'

Hughie served up the food he had made and they ate in companionable silence.

'I'll have a wander round,' Geordie said. 'Maybe find a game of cards.'

'I think I'll write to Belle,' Hughie said. 'She'll want to know we've arrived – and about this.' He waved his hand at the stake.

Geordie rose from the fire. 'Please yourself,' he growled and headed off into the twilight.

Hughie tidied away the pots and dishes and poured himself a mug of coffee before gathering the materials for his task. But as he sat alone by the fire, Hughie gnawed the pencil thoughtfully. Did Geordie still carry a torch for Belle, he wondered. If he did, Hughie thought, with a moment's pity for the man, he was wasting his time. Belle was promised to *him*. Hughie settled down to describing his adventures for his beloved.

The days settled into a predictable pattern of long hours of shovelling and rocking the gravel in hopes that some fine gold dust would fall through. Until at last, after weeks of unproductive endeavour, they saw the glint of gold.

Their shouts of triumph brought some of the old-timers running.

'Yep, it's gold,' one of them said when on Hughie's invitation he had checked it. 'Once seen, you'll never mistake anything else for it.'

Hughie and Geordie were delighted. They had been warned so often that all they would find was fool's gold but now the claim was producing the real thing. And gradually the tiny trickle became a small heap. Geordie divided up the amount between two buckskin leather bags at the end of each day, and when fresh provisions were required he went into Dawson City with some of the gold from each bag.

'I'll be back tomorrow,' he told Hughie as he saddled up the mule. 'Are you sure you don't want to come with me?'

'There's nothing in Dawson City to interest me,' Hughie demurred. 'Saloons and dance halls will just eat up the gold I've worked so hard to get. I don't see the point of that. I'm here to make my fortune, not spend it!'

'Please yourself,' Geordie sneered and set off into town.

But Hughie was quite happy out at the stake. He had found the miners at the nearest claims were a friendly bunch so, while Geordie was away, there was always company. The old-timers clearly had little respect for newcomers but seemed willing to make space for him by their night-time fires, filling his ears with their stories of gigantic finds. Not their own. Always someone else's.

Geordie would return late the next day with fresh provisions and the work would begin again. But then summer gave way suddenly to winter. The water at the bottom of the mine shaft drained away and winter drift mining began. Hughie and Geordie spent the short daylight hours gathering firewood, then Hughie climbed down the rickety ladder to light a fire at the bottom of the shaft against the permafrost of the undug wall. Left to burn through the night, the smoke from the fires hung over the valley and everywhere smelled of burned wood.

In the morning the fire had gone out but they had to wait for the smoke to clear sufficiently before Hughie could climb back down into the mine. His friends from the nearby claims had warned him of the dangers. There were gases that could kill a man, and at the least the lingering smoke was hard on the eyes. But the newly thawed gravel needed to be dug out and piled up outside in readiness for spring when they could start washing and rocking for the gold again.

Ice gradually closed up the creek and the rivers. Mud froze hard as stone. Temperatures dropped and the Yukon stoves in the tents were working red hot day and night. And snow swept down on the workings so thickly that sometimes it was hard to make out the other claims or the men working there.

It became increasingly difficult for Geordie to get out for his evening card games and his temper became more and more uncertain.

'Why don't you grab the next clear day and go into Dawson?' Hughie suggested. 'You could do with a day out of here.'

Geordie eyed him with calculation. Hughie was, as usual, engrossed in writing one of his long letters home to Belle.

'We both need a break,' Geordie said. 'All work and no play...'

'I don't mind being boring if it gets us home sooner!' Hughie laughed. 'And anyway, what would I do in Dawson? You know I don't drink, I don't play cards...'

'True,' Geordie said. 'I still think it would do you good to have a little change of scene.'

'I don't need it, truly,' Hughie told Geordie, but he was pleased at the thoughtfulness of the suggestion. 'I'm happy getting the work done out here. The sooner it's done, the sooner I can go home to Belle.'

Belle. Geordie grimaced. Did the boy not realise the beautiful, fickle Belle had no real interest in him, in any of them? By now she would be stringing along some other witless fool, playing with him like a cat with a ball of wool. While Hughie was out here – out of sight, out of mind.

'She's a long way away,' Geordie told Hughie. 'And you're here, working hard. Don't you think you deserve a little treat? You'd work all the better for a little break.' He watched Hughie think about the suggestion.

'Maybe,' the boy said.

Geordie nodded and left it at that. But a little later, Hughie broached the subject. 'Maybe I will come with you. I don't think I need a treat but you're right. Belle's a long way away and I've been gone a good while now. I think I'd like to get her a present... a little something made out of the gold I've found. Just as a memento.'

To remind Belle you exist, Geordie thought scathingly. The boy was so transparent.

'It's been nearly a year and a half,' Geordie said.

'That's right,' Hughie said. 'It would be nice to send her something to show...' He blushed.

'To show her you're making your fortune,' Geordie completed the sentence, and added in his mind 'and to try to impress her!' He felt a moment's sympathy for the hapless youth, so entangled in his hopeless infatuation with Belle. She would surely accept the gift and reject the lad when he got home.

'How about tomorrow if the weather's clear?' Geordie suggested.

'Tomorrow,' Hughie agreed.

~

Dawson City in daylight was like no town he had ever seen. Hughie gazed around him in fascination. The main street was rough and muddy and thronged with people, including a surprising number of women – not just the gaudily dressed dance-hall girls but women dressed in miner's trousers or leather leggings and rubber boots.

'Wives,' Geordie said. 'A lot of the men brought their wives with them.'

For a fleeting moment, Hughie conjured up a picture of Belle in this environment and as hastily dismissed it. Belle belonged at home, dressed in the finest satins and silks, mistress of her own beautiful house, and soon he would be there with her, making their dreams come true.

The saloons and dance halls he had seen doing a roaring trade at night appeared to be open and just as busy in the daytime. He expected Geordie to evince interest in those but he stuck by Hughie's side, guiding him through the streets till they found a craftsman willing to take Hughie's instructions as well as Hughie's gold.

'I couldn't give her a ring before I left,' Hughie explained.

'A ring?' Geordie was taken aback. This was not what he had expected Hughie to have in mind as a gift for Belle.

'Her father wouldn't approve so our engagement had to be a secret,' the boy explained.

Geordie stared at Hughie. He knew the boy was in thrall to Belle like so many others but he had not expected Belle to have encouraged him to this extent.

'So she's said she'll marry you?' Geordie questioned doubtfully.

But Hughie simply beamed. 'Yes,' he said innocently. 'She said if I came home with gold, she would marry me.'

'I see,' Geordie said thoughtfully and he did. Hughie coming home laden with Klondike gold would make all the difference in the world to Belle as well as to her father. And he thought of the buckskin bag of gold dust he had filled from their claim, at the cost of so much hard work, and the other one tucked away under his bedding containing the proceeds from his nightly card games. He thought of Belle back home and her cruel dismissal of his suit. Anger rose fierce and hot in him.

Had all this effort been for nothing? Was this witless youth going to steal the prize from under his nose? He had thought him merely one more in the grip of youthful infatuation with Belle, but this was different. The boy was a real threat.

Hughie was still talking. Belle this. Belle that. Geordie ruthlessly squashed his fury and made himself pay attention.

'So I thought that would be nice,' Hughie was saying.

He was talking about the design of the ring and the inscription he had asked the man to put upon it. He paused as if waiting for Geordie to respond. Geordie could not remember what the boy had been drivelling on about.

'Sorry,' he said. 'What was it you wanted that man to inscribe on the ring?'

'*Mizpah?*' Hughie said. He shrugged. 'It's from the Bible.' He had encountered it on one of the times he had been idly paging through his mother's Bible. He waited as if expecting Geordie to understand.

'So what does it mean?' Geordie asked impatiently.

'*The LORD watch between me and thee, when we are absent one from another,*' Hughie said.

'Is that so?' Geordie murmured. 'Very pretty.'

CHAPTER 11

'Oh, that is pretty,' Hannah breathed, her eyes fixed on the beautiful gold ring Hughie had sent to Belle from the Klondike. The word *Mizpah* was written in raised letters across the centre of a beautifully formed ivy leaf set on a simple, narrow gold band.

She reached out and touched the word. '*Mizpah*... That is lovely. From the Bible...'

'From some of the gold Hughie's found in the Klondike,' Belle announced. She whirled away, turning the ring on her engagement finger and holding it up where she could admire it. Twirling round and round, she sang, 'Hughie's found gold and we're going to be rich! Rich! We're going to be so very rich!'

Footsteps on the stairs announced their mother's imminent arrival. Belle pulled the ring off.

'You're not to tell!' she whispered fiercely and folded the ring in her handkerchief, tucking it away in a pocket.

'No, of course not,' Hannah replied, shaking her head that her sister could even imagine she would betray her. Belle shoved the letter that had accompanied the present into Hannah's hands.

'Read!' Belle commanded.

By the time their mother entered the girls' bedroom, Belle was sitting on the bed apparently rapt as Hannah read out Hughie's latest letter.

'*Dawson City is not like any town I've ever seen before,*' Hughie had written. '*It's a rough place but many of the miners have brought their wives along. You can tell which ones – their cabins have curtains at the windows!*'

Hannah and her mother exclaimed at that but Belle bristled. If Hughie thought she was going to join him in the Kondike he was far wrong. The agreement was that she would stay here and he would return home rich. Then they would be married. She touched the handkerchief-shrouded ring in her pocket and smiled a secret smile.

Hannah was reading again.

'*There are so many prospectors here that all the creeks are staked and many of the men that came up with us have given up and gone home. Geordie was lucky to meet up with a young lad who had staked a claim but then broken his leg and wanted to go home, so we bought the claim and his cabin in town off him.*

The work in the summer months wasn't too hard and the gravel dug out last winter produced a decent amount of gold but now the ice has set in again, and the really hard work begins.'

'Come downstairs for tea,' their mother said. 'And bring the letter. Rab and your father will be interested in Hughie's news.' She started off downstairs and Belle gestured to Hannah to follow her.

'I'll be down in a minute,' she whispered and when Hannah had left, she slipped the ring out of her pocket, admiring it again. Then she opened a drawer in the dressing table she shared with Hannah and took out a small jewellery box. Removing a fine gold chain, she threaded it through the ring, then carefully fastened it round her neck, concealing it underneath her blouse.

'There.' She patted it, satisfied. A first instalment of Klondike gold. Excellent. She went downstairs with a smile on her face, much to Rab Cormack's delight. He rose and held out a chair for her.

'Belle, my dear,' he greeted her, smiling warmly at her.

'Why, Rab,' Belle said in mock surprise. 'How nice to see you.' She batted her eyelashes at him.

Hannah's head came up sharply at the mockery in Belle's voice but Rab was oblivious. His smile broadened at the apparent welcome in Belle's face as she graciously permitted him to seat her.

'Belle's had another letter from Hughie,' their mother said. But even this news did not appear to dampen Rab's pleasure.

'Let me see,' their father said and Hannah handed over the letter. 'Mmm,' he murmured as he read, '*Now the ice has set in again, and the really hard work begins.*' He looked up. 'Sounds like they're planning to stay for a while.'

Hannah noticed Rab agreed cheerfully. The longer Hughie was away, the better for him, had to be his thinking. But she saw Belle lift her hand to a barely perceptible bump under her blouse. Hannah's eyes narrowed. Belle must have hidden the ring on a chain round her neck.

As Hannah watched, while their father read out the letter and their mother listened, Belle flirted with Rab and Rab smiled at Belle, and all the while Belle's hand came up to that place on her neck where Hughie's ring lay hidden.

How could she be so deceitful, Hannah raged inwardly. Rab was a good man and he deserved much better. But he was blind. Blinded by Belle.

CHAPTER 12

'I need to save what we've found, not spend it!' Hughie protested once again.

Once the weather began to close in, Geordie had managed to persuade Hughie to retreat to the cabin in Dawson City for a few days at a time. But persuading him to join him at the saloon and dance hall was a different matter.

'No. You go,' Hughie told him time and again. 'I'll stay here. I'm perfectly happy here.'

'But you'll never have this chance again,' Geordie had declared. 'Here we have a bit of money in our pockets and we're free to do what we like. Once you get home and married to Belle, you'll have to be all respectable when you're back under the watchful eyes of the town... You'll see! So don't be a miserable old man before your time! There's no need to sit in a damp chilly cabin every night when there's warmth and pretty girls down at the dance hall just waiting to keep you company, and it won't even cost you much of your precious gold!'

That was true. Every time a prospector struck gold and came into town with the first poke full of gold dust, a bell was rung at the bar summoning everyone within hearing range to come for a free drink. Drinks all round was the order of the day and to refuse was a mortal insult, as Hughie had discovered the first time he had given in to Geordie's persuasion to visit the saloon.

Brought up by fiercely teetotal parents, he was unused to hard liquor and had tried to avoid the mandatory drink but it had been noticed. Hughie was not quite sure how. He had tried to be discreet. There had been a bit of a rumpus and the miners had stood around him and watched closely as he downed his first drink. There had been no way out but to get it over with, and loud applause and cheers greeted his splutters as the fire hit his throat.

Geordie had slapped his back. 'See? That wasn't so bad. You should trust me!' And so gradually, his protests died out and he found he enjoyed the fiery liquor. After a couple of drinks in the warmth and laughter of the dance hall, a quiet night in the lonely damp cabin writing home to Belle did not seem so appealing.

He had to admit that the girls at the dance hall were both pretty and friendly, especially black-eyed Nancy who seemed to have taken a fancy to him. Each evening, Nancy would be waiting for them, and before long she would link hands with Hughie and take him up to her room. Geordie's usual response was to wave them off, laughing.

'I'll be fine down here,' he'd say and beckon over one of the other girls to sit on his knee. 'There's no shortage of company.'

And so they whiled away the worst of the Klondike winter. The only damper on Hughie's enjoyment was the arrival of a letter from Belle. Brief but full of such sweet sincere sentiment, it caused a sudden pang of guilt.

'Darling Hughie,' she wrote, 'thank you so much for the lovely ring. I think of it as my engagement ring and I wear it on a chain around my

72

neck nearest to my heart. I think of you often. I miss you so much and I hope you will soon make your fortune and come home to me, your loving Belle.'

Geordie found Hughie sitting on his bunk in the cabin, the letter in his hand, and his face troubled.

'Let me see,' Geordie said, pulling the letter from Hughie's unresisting fingers and reading it. 'So what's the matter?' he asked. 'Belle's happy with the ring. She's missing you... So?'

'But that's the problem,' Hughie tried to explain. 'Here I am being unfaithful to her...'

'Unfaithful?' Geordie asked. 'Oh, what a fuss about nothing!'

'But Nancy...'

'Look, Nancy means nothing,' Geordie told him. 'She's just doing what girls like Nancy do. You need food, you eat. You need a woman, Nancy and the other girls provide what you need.'

'Yes, but I'm engaged to Belle,' Hughie protested. 'I shouldn't...' He struggled to express his overwhelming feelings of discomfort. 'And even if I wasn't engaged to Belle, I shouldn't be doing it! It's wrong!' He waved his hand towards his mother's old battered Bible that represented all he knew of right and wrong.

'What nonsense!' Geordie said. 'You're not doing anyone any harm. Nancy knows what she's doing. And Belle knows nothing about it so it won't hurt her. Out of sight, out of mind. And she need never know either. What you get up to out here stays here.'

But Hughie was not so sure. His conscience had been pricked by Belle's letter and when it was time to go with Geordie to the dance hall that night, he went reluctantly. Stepping into the fug, he watched Nancy thread her way between the tables towards him, smiling and laughing at the miners who called to her or patted her familiarly as she passed by.

Yes, Hughie thought, his eyes suddenly seeing clearly. Nancy was who she was. The kind of woman his mother had warned him against: the strange woman from the Book of Proverbs in her old Bible who lures men to their deaths. Pretty Nancy. Friendly Nancy with her welcoming smile.

But of course she would be pretty and friendly or her lures would not be successful – and she would not continue being employed at the saloon. It was the oldest trade in the world and he was a fool to have fallen for it.

As she approached him, hands outstretched in welcome, Hughie smiled sadly. Once the veil had been torn away, he could see Nancy for what she was – a woman using her body to make a living. And he felt pity for her – a lingering affection and kindness, but most of all pity. She reached for his hands and leaned forward boldly for his kiss, but he sidestepped and gently placed a chaste kiss on her cheek.

'I'm not feeling very well tonight, Nancy,' he told her quietly. 'Please forgive me. I'm going back to the cabin.' And he turned on his heel and left, swiftly, while he had the strength to do it.

Nancy stared after him, then she turned to Geordie. 'What's the matter with Hughie? Why's he not staying?'

'Nothing that need worry you,' Geordie told her. 'You just remember our bargain.'

Nancy nodded, but she bit her lip, clearly dissatisfied with his answer.

'What's the matter?' Geordie said impatiently, turning away to grab an empty chair at a nearby table. He sat down and focused on the girl. 'You're being paid enough and he's a nice enough boy. You knew the deal. Don't go getting attached to him now!'

'You're right,' Nancy said slowly. 'I've done what you asked. But...' She sat down abruptly on the stool next to Geordie and leaned close so she could speak quietly. 'I'm pregnant. I don't know how he'll take that. I wanted to speak to him tonight but it wasn't the right time. I'm worried...'

To her amazement Geordie's face split into a broad grin. He clapped his hands together.

'This is good news!' he declared. 'There's a bonus in it for you, my girl. You've done well. Now don't you worry about a thing. Leave it to me. And don't tell Hughie yet!'

'Are you sure?' Nancy asked uncertainly.

'Yes, of course,' Geordie said buoyantly. 'I'll tell you when. Now be a good girl and get me a drink and some writing paper and a pen. I've got a letter to write.'

When Nancy returned with the drink and the writing materials, Geordie gathered them up and sought a quiet corner. He sipped his drink and sat thinking for a while, then he began to write:

'*Dear Belle,*

You'll be surprised at getting a letter from me but somebody had to write and tell you...'

CHAPTER 13

'Whatever is the matter with you?' their mother exclaimed, throwing up her hands in uncharacteristic exasperation.

Belle gave no reply but flounced red-faced with rage from the kitchen where she and Hannah had been helping their mother with the day's baking. One hand clutching the Mizpah ring she wore at her throat underneath her blouse, her shoes clattered on the stone flags of the kitchen floor as she flung across to the stairs and up to the bedroom she shared with her sister. The two women in the kitchen listened as they heard her stamping around and throwing things.

'Oh, dear,' Mrs Reid said. 'It's not our fault the only letter today was from your Aunt Peggy in Edinburgh and not what Belle wanted.'

Hannah kept her eyes on her work. The need to keep Belle's confidences a secret from her mother was proving a strain.

'It's all right,' Hannah's mother said wryly. 'It's quite obvious what the problem is. Belle is waiting for a letter from Hughie.'

Hannah nodded and concentrated on the scone mix she was working on, her father's favourite.

'I must admit I'm surprised,' her mother said. 'It's been over a year and a half since the boys left town. I would have thought Belle would have lost interest in Hughie by now. Especially with Rab Cormack making such an effort to court her.'

Hannah winced. Rab Cormack's devotion to Belle was a sore trial to her faithful heart. Each night in the bedroom they shared, Belle whispered her dreams for the future – dreams of luxury and wealth funded by Hughie's Klondike gold. Yet she came downstairs every afternoon dressed in her best and sat in the parlour, accepting the gifts Rab Cormack brought – fine gloves, chocolates, flowers – and his adoration. The poor man was completely caught in her web.

'I knew Hughie was one of Belle's admirers,' her mother continued. 'But I thought it was nothing more than that. Just one more young man who thinks he's in love with Belle.'

She waved a hand in the direction of the angry sounds coming from the bedroom the girls shared. 'Is it possible that I've been wrong and Belle's affections are engaged?' She looked at Hannah with gentle enquiry. 'Maybe you should tell me what you know?'

Hannah squirmed and her fingers dug into the dough she was kneading. She had sworn to Belle that she would keep her secret but she owed her mother obedience. Her tender conscience already suffered from this agreement, but how could she break her word? Maybe some of the truth would suffice? She took a deep breath.

'I think Belle and Hughie had an… understanding before he left,' she said.

'Yes?' her mother encouraged.

Hannah thought of the way Belle continued to flirt with Rab Cormack each afternoon.

'I'm not sure how serious it is on Belle's part,' she added.

Her mother nodded.

'I… I think maybe she likes the idea of marrying a rich man, and since Hughie's found gold… Well, I think it's really the news about the gold she's most interested in. That's why she wants to get letters – reports about the gold, I suppose.' Hannah closed her eyes as the unpretty truth about her sister emerged from her lips.

'Ah,' their mother said sadly. 'Yes. I see that. Poor Belle has never had your approach to life. She likes the pretty things and she'll need a rich man to provide them.' She pondered a moment, then asked, 'And the present Hughie sent to Belle?'

Hannah gulped, her eyes flying to her mother's face.

'Yes, my dear,' her mother said with a smile. 'I noticed. She's wearing it round her neck under her blouse.' She laughed gently. 'I'm not blind, you know!' She watched the guilty flush rise in Hannah's cheeks. 'Tell me, my dear. You know I'll find out in the end and you'll feel much better once you've told me.'

Hannah sighed. 'Yes, I suppose so. It's a ring. He had it made out of some of the gold he's found.'

'What kind of a ring?'

'It's got an ivy leaf on it…'

'Is that so?'

'And the word *Mizpah* in raised letters on it,' Hannah told her.

'Well, that's interesting,' her mother said thoughtfully. 'I wonder if the boy knows what it means?'

'Well,' Hannah began, 'it's what sweethearts put, isn't it? Something about God being with them while they're apart.'

Hannah's mother smiled. 'Get my Bible, my dear, and I'll tell you what it says and what it really means.'

Hannah went through to the sitting room and brought back her mother's big black Bible from where it customarily sat beside her chair. Hannah laid it on the table in front of her.

'It's from Genesis,' her mother said, paging through the Bible. 'Somewhere here. Ah yes, here it is: Genesis 31:49. "*The* LORD *watch*

between me and thee, when we are absent one from another." That's
what *Mizpah* means.'

'But isn't that what I said?' Hannah asked.

'Almost, but you need to know the story to understand what it
really means.'

Hannah settled down beside her mother at the kitchen table. She
loved it when she told stories.

'It's all about old Jacob,' her mother began. 'He was a bit of a
trickster – remember how he cheated his brother Esau out of his
birthright? And then he met his match when he encountered Laban
– who substituted Leah for Rachel as Jacob's wife after Jacob had
worked for him seven years just to be allowed to marry her.'

Hannah nodded. The Reid family's morning and evening prayers
always included reading from a passage of scripture and Hannah had
taken to reading the Bible for herself as she grew up.

'Well, this bit of the story happens when Jacob has decided it's
time to go home,' her mother continued. 'Jacob and his wives and his
children, and all the flocks and wealth he has accumulated thanks
to his time with Laban. It had all got a bit awkward but Jacob was
determined to go home.'

She paused and Hannah waited as her mother put her thoughts
into words.

'Laban and Jacob, both being a bit tricky, they needed to
come to some sort of agreement that they might keep and stop
playing games and tricking one another. So Jacob set up a big
stone and got everyone to gather stones around it, as a witness to
their agreement, and he called it Mizpah, saying "The Lord watch
between us".'

'So it had nothing to do with sweethearts?' Hannah asked in
surprise.

'No, my dear,' her mother said. 'It was about two men who couldn't trust one another and had to ask God to keep an eye on them both to keep them in line.'

'Oh,' Hannah said thoughtfully. 'That's very different.'

'It is indeed.' Her mother closed the Bible and smoothed its worn leather cover.

'You don't think Hughie knows that Belle needs keeping an eye on?' Hannah asked, the picture of Belle flirting with Rab Cormack just the afternoon before clear and sharp in her mind.

'I don't know, my dear,' her mother said. She rose and opened the oven door to check how the day's baking was getting on. Satisfied, she came back to her chair by the table. 'We don't need to mention any of this to your father. Belle should be fine by the time he gets home. And you'll need to get those scones ready.' She pointed at the dough Hannah had been kneading.

'True,' Hannah said and rose to return her mother's Bible to the sitting room. When she came back to the kitchen, Belle had reappeared. She flung herself down at the table and watched Hannah roll out the dough and cut out the scones, placing them on a floured baking tray.

Belle's mouth turned down discontentedly and she drummed her fingers on the table. Hannah, attempting to wipe the table clean after the scones were in the oven, had to wait till Belle was aware of the cloth inches from her fingers, then she removed them with ill grace.

A sudden knock on the door broke the tense silence in the kitchen.

'Hannah, go and see who that is,' her mother commanded.

Glad to escape the uncomfortable atmosphere, Hannah removed her apron and hurried to the door.

'Who was it, my dear?' her mother asked when Hannah returned. Wordlessly Hannah held out the letter the postman had delivered.

'A letter!' Belle rushed at it but her mother held her back with one hand and examined the letter.

'Yes, my dear, it's from Canada and it's for you, but I don't recognise the handwriting,' she said. 'It's not from Hughie. I do hope that nothing's happened...'

Before she could finish the sentence, Belle had snatched the letter from her hand. She tore it open and began to scan the contents.

'*Dear Belle,*

You'll be surprised at getting a letter from me...'

'Who is it from, dear?' her mother enquired but Belle did not hear her, so absorbed was she in what she was reading. Her face turned a sudden bright red and hot tears started from her eyes.

'No!' she cried. 'No, no, no!' She flung the letter into the fireplace and ran from the room, howling as if in pain.

Hannah moved quickly and seized the letter from the grate, blowing on it to put out the flames. It was barely charred. She looked questioningly at her mother.

'Let me see that letter.'

She sat down in her chair by the table. Hannah handed her the letter and positioned herself behind her shoulder where she could read it too.

'*Dear Belle,*' the letter began, '*you'll be surprised at getting a letter from me but somebody had to write and tell you what your precious fiancé is getting up to. He seems to have forgotten all about you and his promises to make his fortune and bring it home to you. We've struck gold in respectable quantities but Hughie is spending it all on drink and the dancing girls at the saloon. In fact one of the ladies out here is now pregnant and expecting him to marry her.*

I thought you should know.

Your respectful and concerned friend,
George Sinclair.'

'Oh dear,' Mrs Reid said. 'This is bad. Fiancé, is it? I would never have guessed Belle would let it get that far. I don't suppose she was planning to tell us...'

'Till he came back rich,' Hannah supplied.

Her mother raised her eyebrows questioningly.

'She told me,' Hannah confessed. 'The night before he went away.'

Her mother's eyes fixed sadly on her, and Hannah bowed her head.

'I'm sorry,' Hannah said. 'But she made me promise...'

'I see,' her mother said. 'One sin leads to another, my dear. I think I need a cup of tea and a little time with the Lord. And maybe you do too.' And she rose to put the kettle on. But before she could make the tea, Belle reappeared, red-eyed, her face set, her lips thin. She was wearing her outdoor clothes.

'I'm going out,' she said. 'For a little walk. I won't be long.' There was a letter in her hand.

When she returned and joined the family for tea, her mother's sharp eyes noticed that the little bump of the Mizpah ring was no longer evident under her blouse. And her flirting with Rab Cormack had a heightened, almost feverish quality.

Something would have to be done.

CHAPTER 14

Hughie Mackay sat hunched over the little stove in the cabin on the edge of Dawson City, at his side a whiskey bottle he was in the process of emptying.

He held a letter in one hand but his eyes did not see the words. He was gazing fixedly at the ring he held in his other hand – the ring made for Belle from the first of the gold he had found. The ring she had now returned to him with this letter.

'*I never want to see you or hear from you again,*' Belle had written. '*As far as I'm concerned, there has never been anything between us. You can stay in Canada for ever with your dance-hall girl and your baby. Marry her instead of me. I don't want you!*'

Hughie struggled to make sense of it. What was all this nonsense? So yes, he was friendly – well, he had been more than friendly – with Nancy from the dance hall but as Geordie had said, it did not mean anything and he would be going home to Belle once he had got enough gold.

But how did Belle even know about Nancy? Surely they were far enough way – 'out of sight, out of mind' as Geordie had joked. What he did up here in the Klondike stayed up here in the Klondike. That's what Geordie said. There was no need for Belle ever to know about it.

But he had had a crisis of conscience about it and he had fretted about it. When Geordie realised what was bothering Hughie, he had reassured him.

'Don't you worry,' Geordie had said. 'You're not hurting anybody. You're just having a little fun. And don't you deserve it after the hard work you've been doing?'

And that was true. Hughie had put in long hours of hard physical labour to wrench tiny amounts of gold from frozen-solid lumps of earth and gravel, all the time working in terrible conditions. Surely he deserved to have a little fun?

He glanced at the letter. There was something more, something shocking in the letter. Something he knew nothing about. He scanned Belle's words, stopping when he got to the mention of 'the baby'. The girl could not be pregnant, could she? Surely in her line of business she would know how to avoid such a thing? And anyway, would she not have told him?

And so how did Belle know before him? How did Belle know any of this? Hughie struggled to make sense of it all. Finally he came to the conclusion that there was only one person who knew the answer and that was Nancy herself. He emptied the last of the whiskey down his throat. Then he staggered to his feet. He would go to the dance hall and get the truth out of Nancy. He threw the empty whiskey bottle on the floor. The ring followed it with a dull clink.

Dragging on his heavy mackinaw and thick fur cap, he pushed the door of the cabin open. The morning was grey and cold with more snow threatening but it was not far to the dance hall where Nancy worked. He had been out already, queuing to get his letter, rather than returning straight away to the workings with Geordie. But then he had been sober. Before he had read the letter. Now he was lost in a haze of alcohol and confusion.

Hughie lurched down the rough street and into the smoky fug of the dance hall. He stood unsteadily in the entrance, scanning the crowd for Nancy, heedless to the murmurs around him.

'Hughie darling.' Nancy appeared at his side and smilingly took his arm. 'I haven't seen you for such a long time.' She led him to a stool by a table in a corner out of the way. 'Here, we can be comfortable.' As she leaned over him, she smelled the drink on his breath and straightened, looking at him carefully. 'Are you all right?' she asked.

'All right?' His eyes tried to focus as he struggled to remember why he was there. As memory hit, his voice rose to an outraged howl. 'No, I am not!' He hauled himself to his feet and stared in outrage at her.

'Hughie!' Nancy tried to pacify him, but he threw off her hands and grabbed her by the shoulders, forcing her down on to the stool. He leaned drunkenly over her, staring into her face.

'I want to know…' he began, tripping over the words. He stopped and started again more slowly. 'What I want to know is…'

'Yes, yes,' Nancy tried to soothe him. 'Whatever you want…'

'Don't you try to cozen me!' Hughie roared at her in uncharacteristic fury. 'Tell me the truth! I want to know! Is it true?'

By now a crowd had gathered around them, watching open-mouthed as Hughie, usually the most mild-mannered of men, began to shake Nancy till the tears came to her eyes.

'I'll tell you,' she protested. 'I'll tell you…Whatever you want to know, I'll tell you.'

'Is it true?' Hughie demanded. 'You're expecting, and the baby's mine?'

Nancy gulped and nodded. The crowd around them went silent.

'Say it,' Hughie commanded. 'Say the words. I need to hear it.'

Nancy's voice shook. 'Yes, I'm pregnant and the child is yours. But...'

'And you told Belle.' It was like the voice of judgment. 'You told my Belle,' Hughie repeated in disgust and threw the weeping girl roughly from him.

But she clawed her way up from the sawdust floor and reached out to him.

'No, Hughie. I never did that! How could I?' she pleaded. 'I wouldn't know how to reach her...'

Hughie turned back to Nancy, drunken puzzlement on his face. He swayed on his feet, his brow furrowed with concentration.

'No,' he said slowly. 'You wouldn't, would you?'

Relieved, Nancy nodded and fumbled her way up from the floor, keeping a watchful eye on Hughie. He was staring at her as he tried to puzzle his way through his confused thoughts.

'But someone told Belle...' he muttered.

Nancy's eyes widened and she looked around for a way of escape. But Hughie's hand snaked out and held her in place.

'If it wasn't you that told Belle, then who did?' he asked.

Nancy shook her head, tears running down her face. The only person she had told was Geordie and he had told her not to tell Hughie...

'Oh, no,' Hughie said, stepping closer. 'You said you'd tell me everything.'

He reached out and grabbed her round the throat, pushing her down on to the floor again. He leaned forward and thrust his face close to hers, searching her eyes.

'So who did you tell?' His voice was coldly dangerous. 'Tell me...'

Nancy swallowed hard. 'Your friend,' she whispered. 'Geordie Sinclair.'

'My friend,' Hughie repeated. 'Geordie Sinclair.' He glowered at the girl in drunken confusion. 'So why did you tell him? Why did you not come to me first?'

Nancy tried to curl into a smaller ball as Hughie's great hands reached down to her shoulders to shake the truth out of her.

'Hughie!' she pleaded. 'Please!'

'Now, now, that's enough of that.' Big Eddie McArthy, the owner of the dance hall, appeared at their side. 'Leave the girl alone.'

Hughie turned maddened red eyes upon him and bunched his hands into fists. But Eddie just waved a hand and two burly men appeared at his side.

'Leave it,' he advised Hughie.

'I want to know the truth,' he said.

'Well, you know it now,' Eddie said. 'The girl's told you what you want to know.'

Hughie forced his thoughts into a semblance of order. What had Nancy said? 'Geordie Sinclair,' Hughie murmured the name to himself. 'Geordie Sinclair did this. He told Belle.' He dragged himself upright and pointed at the girl. 'I'll deal with you later. But first, I'll deal with my friend!' It was said with a bitter laugh. 'My very good friend, Geordie Sinclair.' Hughie lurched towards the door. 'And when I find him, I'll kill him!'

'That isn't the way!'

'Don't do it, Hughie.'

'He's not worth it!'

The men surrounding him protested and tried to stop him.

'You don't want to go out in this,' one of them said, gesturing to the dance-hall windows. The threatened snow had begun to fall.

'Oh I do,' Hughie insisted. 'I know where he is. He's at the workings. I'll find him.' And he pushed his way through the crowd of men who tried to stop him.

'This is madness, Mackay,' a man shouted at him. 'Leave it till he comes back in the morning.'

But Hughie would not listen. 'It won't wait,' he declared. 'It needs sorting out now!'

He struggled with the wind-blown snow to get the dance-hall door open and pushed his way through. Hunching his shoulders, he staggered into the driving whiteness.

Inside the dance hall, concerned murmurings ebbed away as the miners returned to the bar for more drinks. The barman passed a shot glass to Nancy.

'You'll be needing that,' he said. 'What are you going to do now?'

'What can I do?' she said sadly. She took a gulp of the fiery liquid. 'Wait and see what happens.'

CHAPTER 15

'I really should put this apron in the wash,' Hannah's mother said as she reached for it from the hook behind the kitchen door. 'Oh, what's this?' She pulled an envelope out of the pocket and studied it with surprise. 'It's Peggy's letter! I never did get round to reading it!'

In the days following receipt of Geordie Sinclair's letter, life at the Reid household had been fraught. Belle had worked herself up into such a pitch of hysteria that the doctor had to be called.

'Say nothing,' Mr Reid had said, but somehow the reason for Belle's nervous state had leaked out and around town. As a result, there came a stream of nosy visitors which drove Belle up to her bedroom declaring, to her mother's despair, that she would never, ever, come out again.

Now Mrs Reid sat down with the letter she had taken from her pocket.

'Hannah, pour us a cup of tea and we'll see what your Aunt Peggy has to say.'

Hannah settled down comfortably across from her mother.

'It's very lonely here now dear Jack is gone...' Mrs Reid began to read. 'Ah, poor Peggy,' she commented.

'It's such a pity she's so far away,' Hannah said. 'If she lived nearer we could visit her and she could come to us, then she wouldn't be so lonely.'

'That's true,' her mother said approvingly. 'But Edinburgh is so far away...' She looked at Hannah thoughtfully. 'I wonder...' And as she read the rest of the letter aloud to Hannah, it was clear that her mind was busy with something else.

'I'll need to reply,' she said when she finished. 'But first...' She looked up and said decisively, 'Hannah, go and get your sister.' As Hannah began to protest that Belle would not be willing to come downstairs, her mother cut in. 'Hannah. Tell Belle she is to come down. Now.'

When Belle appeared in the kitchen, Mrs Reid made no comment on the red-rimmed eyes and the tragic face. Instead she held up the letter and said briskly, 'I've had a letter from your Aunt Peggy. She is having a hard time on her own now Uncle Jack has died. I've been thinking and I wonder, Belle dear, if you would like to go to Edinburgh to keep her company for a little while?'

Belle was startled out of her misery. 'Me? Go to Edinburgh? To stay with Aunt Peggy?'

'I'm sure she'd be glad of your company,' her mother said. 'And perhaps a little change would do you good. What do you think?'

'But what would I do there?' Belle asked mutinously.

'I think your aunt would be glad simply to have you stay, just for company in the house. You wouldn't have to do any work. I'm sure she has help,' her mother told her. 'And I was thinking,' she continued, 'Edinburgh has a number of high-class dressmaking establishments. I wonder if we could arrange for your apprenticeship to resume there? You would be sure to get much better training in Edinburgh than here in Wick. What do you say?'

During the past year, Belle had been apprenticed to a local dressmaker. But there had been some upsets in the workroom. Jealousy, Belle declared. Their father had managed to get the apprenticeship dissolved on the grounds of Belle's delicate health and she had spent the intervening months at home waiting for the return of Hughie Mackay and her expected marriage.

As Hannah watched Belle, she could see the conflicting emotions warring in her face as she thought over this opportunity. The story of proud Belle Reid's betrayal by her secret fiancé had damaged her reputation as the town's most eligible beauty. Aunt Peggy's loneliness offered a respectable reason for a swift departure of the shamed girl to Edinburgh. By the time she returned, her unfortunate relationship with Hughie Mackay would be forgotten.

'Maybe,' Belle said thoughtfully. The tragic look vanished from her face, replaced now by canny calculation. 'Edinburgh, yes. I think that might be a good idea.'

And Hannah suddenly thought how much happier the house would be without Belle. And when Rab Cormack came to visit, there would be no Belle to flirt and toy with him. There would only be herself. Her heart lifted. With Belle in Edinburgh, maybe – just maybe – there would be a chance for her!

Hannah and her mother exchanged satisfied glances but Belle, unseeing, wandered back to the door.

'I'll need to think about my clothes.'

Sudden energy took her stamping back up the stairs.

~

Another cold dark morning standing on the railway station platform waving someone goodbye, Hannah thought. But this time she was the one trying to hide the smugly satisfied smile as the train took a rival away.

It felt like an answer to prayer but could she really whisper a thank-you to God? She would wait till the train pulled out and Belle was irrevocably on her way to Edinburgh.

Hannah turned to the man at her side but Rab's eyes were fixed on the figure at the carriage window. Belle, elegant in her travelling costume, made as pretty a picture as usual.

When he had heard of the arrangements for Belle to join Aunt Peggy in Edinburgh, Rab Cormack had been shocked.

'Edinburgh?' he had protested. 'But why?'

Mr and Mrs Reid had exchanged speaking glances and Mrs Reid had taken it upon herself to reply, quietly but firmly.

'My sister was recently widowed and she is taking it hard. She is needful of companionship and support. Belle can provide that. At the same time, Belle will benefit from a better dressmaking training in Edinburgh than she can get here. It is a good arrangement for them both.'

'But why not Hannah?' Rab had asked, bringing Hannah's head up with reproach in her eyes.

Her mother patted her arm soothingly. 'Hannah's place is here. She is indispensable to us in the house and in the dairy. No, Edinburgh is a wonderful opportunity for Belle and I'm sure she'll make the best use of it.'

Father, still hopeful of an alliance between the two families, had put in, 'Edinburgh's not so far away. Surely a prosperous man like you can get down there from time to time?'

Rab had brightened at that, much to Hannah's annoyance. Fancy putting ideas into the poor man's head!

'That's true,' he had said. 'In fact, I've an idea for the business that would need a few trips down south.' He had even smiled then.

He was not smiling now, his mouth turned down and his poor devoted heart displayed for all to see as he gazed like a left-behind puppy at the girl in the carriage. This time when a wicked puff of steam caught Hannah's ankles and she jumped back, he did not even notice.

She sighed, then caught herself. Surely once Belle was gone… *Oh, let that whistle blow*, Hannah begged silently. *Let the train just go!* Once Belle was gone, surely he would start to notice her instead. Oh, surely he would notice her!

But when the train finally drew out of the station taking Belle with it, Rab turned on his heel, face downcast, eyes unseeing, and made to walk away on his own.

'Wait for me!' Hannah called and hurtled after him, slipping her hand into his arm. Surprised, he looked down at her determined little face, searching the grey eyes that gazed up at him.

He sighed, then patted her hand. 'Come on then,' he said with resignation. 'Better get you home.'

CHAPTER 16

The snowstorm continued throughout the night but, during a brief lull, in the cold light of morning, Geordie Sinclair walked into the dance hall.

Nancy, dozing by the fire, woke to find him shrugging off his mackinaw. She rose hurriedly and grabbed his arm.

'What happened?' she demanded. 'Where's Hughie? Did he find you? Geordie…!'

He shrugged her off. 'Get me a drink,' he grunted. 'I'm perishing.' He threw his heavy mackinaw on the floor and sat down on the stool Nancy had vacated by the fire, ignoring the attention he was receiving from the other miners who had holed up in the dance hall during the storm. She stood over him for a few moments, then seeing she would get nothing out of him, hurried over to the bar.

'What's he doing here?'

'Ask him where Hughie is.'

Nancy brushed aside the questions and the comments as she wove her way through the tables.

When she brought back the drink Geordie tossed it back in one swallow, handing the glass back to her with a nod towards the bar counter. Anxious and angered but knowing better than to defy him, Nancy went back for the refill. It went down at the same speed.

She pulled over a stool and perched next to him, watching and waiting. When she judged he was beginning to thaw, she leaned closer.

'Tell me,' she murmured urgently in a low voice. 'Did Hughie find you? What happened? Where is he?'

'Hughie?' Geordie declared in a loud voice. 'Was Hughie going to come out to the workings to find me?'

A low angry murmuring began in the room. They had all seen Hughie and heard his threat.

'Yes!' Nancy persisted. 'So did you see him?'

'No,' Geordie said, raising his voice so everyone could hear him. 'I haven't seen Hughie. I've been at the workings all night. The storm closed in so I thought I'd best stop there. No.' He shook his head. 'If he had any sense he'll have gone back to the cabin. No one came out our way last night.'

'But…' Nancy protested. 'He said…'

'Shut up,' Geordie hissed fiercely and she quailed at the blackness in his eyes. 'Yes,' he said loudly. 'That will be it. The storm was far too bad for him to come to the workings last night. He'll be fast asleep back at the cabin.' He looked around the assembled throng to make sure everyone had heard. 'Now I could do with a bite to eat…' And he settled down by the fire till Nancy brought his food. Then he concentrated on the stew and beans, only looking at Nancy to demand further refills of whiskey.

Finally he rose and stretched. Pointedly he looked out of the window where snow could be seen coming down again thickly.

'Too comfortable here,' he said in a slurred voice and slid down in a heap on the crumpled mackinaw beside the fire where he began to snore. The miners laughed. It was a sight they were familiar with.

'Geordie!' Nancy began in a shrill voice.

One eye opened and Sinclair glared up at her. 'You shut up if you know what's good for you,' he hissed so only she could hear him. 'Be a good girl and do as you're told and everything will be all right. I'll look after you.'

And Nancy had to be content with that.

~

It took three days for the blizzard to finally blow itself out. Three days in which Geordie Sinclair remained at the dance hall, sleeping by the fire, spending his gold on food and drink and presenting an unworried face to the world. Nancy on the other hand was on tenterhooks and pestered him continually till the violence of his responses frightened her and she backed off.

When the next morning dawned clear, the other miners who had taken shelter in the dance hall declared their intention of making a move.

'After breakfast!' they insisted. Heaping platters of pork and eggs and beans were brought and the miners emptied out the last of the gold dust in their pouches to pay for their food. Washing the feast down with hot coffee, they discussed their hopes for the day. Keen prospectors, a day when they could work was not one to be missed.

'I'll go to the cabin first,' Geordie Sinclair announced. He threw a glance at Nancy who had come downstairs to serve the men their food. 'I'll warrant Hughie slept through the storm safe and sound. I'll go and rouse him out so we can get some work done.' His scowling

99

face warned Nancy to keep her tongue silent. She nodded worriedly and watched him depart.

True to his word, Sinclair collected his mule and headed off through the deep snow in the direction of the cabin he and Hughie shared. The other miners departed for the workings out by the river. Nancy carried the dirty plates to the kitchens and left them there for the kitchen staff to deal with, then took herself back to the main room where she nursed a tin mug of coffee by the fire. One of the other girls joined her.

'What's the matter with you?' she asked.

Nancy threw her a warning glance.

'There's nobody here,' the girl said. 'So what's the matter? Fallen out with your friend?'

Nancy shook her head. 'No. It's nothing…' She took a long gulp of the coffee and fell back to staring into the fire.

The other girl rose with an irritated shrug. 'Suit yourself,' she said. 'I was only trying to help.'

'Help!' Nancy muttered darkly. 'I think it's too late for that.'

She remained by the fire for the rest of the morning, glancing up each time someone entered the dance hall then returning to her reverie. As the sun rose and men cleared a pathway through the snow down the middle of the street, more customers began to arrive and Nancy was called on to serve drinks and food.

She had just returned to the kitchens with a tray full of dirty plates when there was a loud hubbub that had her rushing back to the main room. Two miners, their heavy mackinaws and boots snow-encrusted, clearly just come from one of the farther workings, stood in the centre of the room.

'Dead.'

Nancy caught the word as she plunged into the room. She stopped short, fear in her throat.

'Who's dead?' she whispered but they heard her and turned her way. The crowd between them broke to leave a pathway.

Nancy swallowed hard. 'Who's dead?' she asked again in a choked voice.

'See for yourself,' one of the men said harshly. 'He's out there in the wagon.'

There was a jostle of men pushing to get out of the door to go and see. Nancy walked slowly, as if sleepwalking, to follow them. By the time she reached the door, some were on their way back.

'You don't need to go out there,' one man said, standing in her way.

'Who is it?' she asked, the fear alive in her eyes.

He nodded as if in agreement. 'Hughie,' he said. 'It's Hughie Mackay.'

Nancy turned to the two miners who had brought Hughie's body. 'What happened? Where did you find him?' She searched their faces and added, 'Was he caught in the blizzard on the way out to the workings? Is that what happened?' she asked in sudden hope that Hughie's death had been simply a tragic accident.

They exchanged glances.

'Well, you could say that,' one said.

'That's what Sinclair hoped for,' the other added.

Uproar followed this announcement.

'What do you mean?'

'What's Sinclair got to do with this?'

'Look at Hughie's head,' the first miner said. 'He took a hit with a shovel.'

'We were at the workings,' the second miner said. 'The weather was too bad to come back into town so we thought we'd just sit it out. We heard the noise when Mackay came up, shouting at Sinclair.'

'We took a look out and saw Sinclair coming out of their claim with a shovel. Whatever Mackay was saying won him an answer with it.'

'Laid him flat,' the first miner said.

'Sinclair took one look, dropped the shovel, grabbed the mule and lit out of there. Left Mackay lying there in the snow.'

'He never saw us,' the first miner said. 'Wouldn't in that white-out.'

'He left Mackay to die in the snow,' the second miner added. 'If we hadn't seen what we did, anyone would have thought…'

An angry rumble began in the crowd.

'Where's Sinclair?'

'He's got to answer for this!'

'Let's go get him!'

And the crowd began to surge away from the dance hall, an angry mob baying for Geordie Sinclair's blood.

CHAPTER 17

The wind tore at Belle's umbrella as she struggled along Shandwick Place. Her skirts whipped round her legs and she felt as battered by the gale as she did by her current situation.

It was really all too bad. She had trusted Hughie Mackay. Surely
she had got him securely attached to her before he went away?
She knew nice girls did not allow much more than a kiss and a
squeeze till the ring was on their finger. She shrugged inwardly.
Well, she had never been a nice girl. And since she was going
to be married to Hughie, it did not seem so wrong to anticipate
their nuptials if it would bind him to her irrevocably. As she had
thought it had.

But she had been wrong. All that effort, all that acting the
unsure maiden so he would feel responsible… and now it
appeared that 'out of sight' was indeed 'out of mind'. She should
never have let him out of her sight.

But he would have been no good to her if he had stayed in
Caithness, she reminded herself. His family were crofters,

scraping a poor living, and Hughie had no prospect of doing any better himself. Till Geordie Sinclair came up with the Klondike scheme.

It had seemed like the answer to prayer. Except of course she did not pray. Belle had no time for such nonsense. You had to make your own way in the world. Reach out and take what you wanted for yourself. Make the things happen that you wanted.

Her mouth tightened further, her hand clenched on the umbrella. It had not worked! She could not understand it. How could it have gone so badly wrong?

Hughie should have gone off to the Klondike for a couple of years, found large quantities of gold just as the newspaper articles described, and come back a rich man to carry off his real prize: herself. They would have been married and be living in fine style for the rest of their days. She would have had servants and a big house. Beautiful clothes in expensive fabrics that someone else would have made, coming to the house for the fittings, pricking *their* fingers on the endless pins and the tedious hand-stitching.

Instead here she was, exiled to Edinburgh to live with miserable Aunt Peggy, little better than a servant in her house, fetching and carrying and listening to her sighings and moanings. And during the day, working her pretty hands to the bone in the workroom in Shandwick Place, her delicate fingers scarred with myriad pinpricks as she laboured at the menial tasks involved in outfitting prosperous Edinburgh ladies with expensive dresses to adorn their well-fed figures. Belle snorted in disgust. Hardly a one had as good a figure as herself!

She had thought being apprenticed to a fashionable dressmaking establishment in Edinburgh would be the pathway to a better future. If she could not marry her way to riches, surely her father would set her up in her own business on her return. Her Edinburgh training would enable her to employ other people to do the boring work while she greeted her clientele and gave them the benefit of her knowledge of fashion and style.

A sudden gust of wind blew her umbrella forward and Belle staggered, trying to keep her grip on it. It dipped in front of her so she could not see where she was going and for a moment she almost lost her footing. Her stumble threw her in the path of someone hurrying towards the entrance of the workroom from the other direction. They collided in a tangle of umbrellas.

'I'm so sorry!' It was a male voice with a pleasant Edinburgh accent.

A sharp reproach was on the tip of Belle's tongue but she swallowed it quickly as she recognised the voice. It belonged to Adam Finlayson. Son and heir of the owner of the establishment where she worked, he ran the tailoring and dressmaking workrooms for his father. Belle managed a breathy apology.

'Oh no,' she said. 'I'm sure it was my fault really.'

As they extricated themselves and untangled their umbrellas, she peeked up at him through her lashes.

'Why, Mr Finlayson! I didn't see you there. Such a terrible day to be out.' She tried a winning smile and was gratified at his response. He lifted his hat politely as to a social equal and not a junior employee. Belle preened.

'Miss…?' he queried, openly appraising the girl before him.

'Reid,' she provided with another smile. 'Belle Reid.'

Adam Finlayson's answering smile hinted at awakening interest. 'Miss Reid,' he said. 'I'm pleased to meet you.' And he pushed open the heavy black-painted door for her so she could step into the hallway out of the gale.

'Why, thank you,' Belle said. She took a moment to study him and noticed he returned the favour. He was a stocky young man with mousy brown hair. Not her type at all. But he was looking at her with interest. She managed a demure downcast of her eyes.

'I must go,' she said. 'I mustn't be late!' and she tripped up the stairs to the room where the girls worked, letting her skirts swish round her ankles. A quick glance showed he was watching.

'Cat got the cream?' one of the girls said sourly as Belle hung up her coat and hat in the cloakroom.

She swiftly switched off her satisfied smile. It would not do for any of *them* to get ideas. As for her, maybe things were beginning to look up. Adam Finlayson might not be much to look at, but he would be a fine catch. A suitable triumph for a girl who had been sent to Edinburgh in shame after being betrayed by that no-good Hughie Mackay.

And as the morning wore on, as Belle pinned and stitched in the light of the tall windows that lined the workroom, her mind took flight, painting pictures of a different future. The house and servants, the fine clothes and comfortable lifestyle remained the same, but now it was transported to Edinburgh. Morningside, she decided. That would be the best. And the man in the background providing what she wanted was no longer Hughie Mackay but Adam Finlayson.

It would not take much doing, Belle considered, and she began to plan her campaign.

106

CHAPTER 18

Knowing how ugly things could turn when a crowd of miners took the law into their own hands, Nancy slipped up to her room. She hastily put on her warmest cloak and outdoor boots. Then quickly checking no one was watching, she scurried down the back stairs and out into the alleyway that ran behind the dance hall. Hurrying as best as she could in the deep soft snow, she made her way to the cabin Geordie Sinclair had shared with Hughie.

'Geordie!' she shouted as she banged on the door. 'Geordie, it's me! Quick…'

The door was pulled open. 'What are you doing here?' an angry-faced Geordie Sinclair demanded.

'Geordie, they've found Hughie!' she told him, standing on the doorstep, shivering in the cold.

'So?' he asked coldly. 'What's it got to do with me?' He turned to go back into the cabin.

'They saw you,' she blurted out. 'Two miners at the next claim. They saw you…' Her voice faltered as he turned back and she saw his face.

'They saw what?' The words came out in a threatening snarl.

Nancy hesitated.

'Tell me.' Geordie took a step towards her.

'They saw you hit Hughie with the shovel, and leave him in the snow,' Nancy got out in a rush. 'They've brought his body into town. And now there's a mob on their way! They want… They want justice for Hughie.'

Quick calculation darted across Geordie's face.

'So what are you doing here?' he demanded.

'I came to warn you. So you could get away…' Nancy faltered to a stop.

Geordie's eyes narrowed. 'Good girl,' he said. 'I'd better get going then.' He dived back into the cabin, swiftly gathering up bulging saddlebags and a large pack. He started towards the mule hitched to the wall outside.

'There he is!'

'Get him!'

Loud voices approaching told them that the angry crowd had caught up with Nancy. Now the enraged men surged down the alleyway towards the cabin, the chilly air filled with their shouts and threats.

'Murderer!'

'You won't get away with it!'

Geordie quickly slung the saddlebags on to the mule.

'Grab him, boys!'

Then one of the men held up a hand. 'Hold it a minute. There's something not right here.'

The shouts were silenced as the crowd waited for what he had to say.

The man stepped forward and prodded the pack.

'That's not yours, Sinclair,' he said decisively. 'I'd know it anywhere. I made it last winter.'

Geordie's eyes fixed on the speaker.

'Where did you get it?' the man demanded.

But Geordie had no chance to answer as the crowd, balked of their prey, grew restive and started murmuring.

'What's this about?'

'We're wasting time!'

But Geordie's accuser stabbed a finger at him. 'The *cheechako* you bought the claim from. That pack was his! He bought it from me with some of his first gold. And he'd never have gone away without it.'

Now the crowd were attentive again. All eyes were focused on Geordie.

'So how come you have it?' The man's voice was accusing. 'And what happened to the boy?'

For a moment, Geordie remembered the boy with the broken leg limping with him down to the river 'to check out the boats for his journey home' – a journey that would never happen. Geordie had checked that the boy could not swim. There had been a splash. He had waited a while on the riverbank till the noises of the boy's last pathetic struggle stopped, then he had returned triumphantly to Hughie with the good news that the claim was theirs.

He shrugged. Why spend money when you didn't need to? That money was now safely in one of the saddlebags, added to his share of the gold from the claim, and Hughie's. Hughie wouldn't be needing his gold now.

As Geordie eyed up the men ranged against him, Nancy suddenly shivered, drawing his attention back to her. He smiled, turning to her, and suddenly seized her wrist in a hard grip. From a deep pocket in his mackinaw he took out a revolver and slowly and deliberately he put the gun to Nancy's temple.

He turned his head so he could look at the crowd.

'Anybody move and the girl dies,' he said calmly.

CHAPTER 19

He was there again, lounging in the big armchair, legs stretched out by the fire, comfortably taking tea with her mother and father. Hannah sighed. She knew he was only visiting because it brought him closer to Belle. Lingering in the doorway, she allowed her eyes to feast on Rab Cormack's relaxed rangy figure. How she longed for him to turn and smile at her, as if he had come to see her.

'Are you coming in, Hannah, or are you going to stand there all day?' Her father's sharp voice interrupted her daydream.

Hannah blushed as all eyes – including Rab's – turned to her. Yes, there was that lovely smile, but it was an amused smile, as for a naughty child, not the warm welcome of a lover that she so desired.

'Tea?' her mother enquired.

'Yes, please,' Hannah said and carefully chose a seat at a little distance from Rab, from where she could indulge herself in simply looking at him.

The conversation resumed. It was, as she had expected, all about Belle and how she was doing in Edinburgh. Mother provided snippets from Belle's latest letter. Not that Belle wrote frequently, and that was a cause of disquiet for her parents. This was also not something that would be spoken of in front of Rab Cormack. Mother and Father were clearly continuing in their attempts to encourage a match between the pair.

Hannah sighed again but this time her mother picked up on it.

'What's the matter, love?' she asked.

Hannah shook her head. There was no way she could reveal what was in her thoughts. Resolutely she picked up her cup and drained it.

'Just a little tired,' she said and offered her cup for a refill. 'I was up early with the cows.' Which was true. But it was true every morning.

Rab glanced across at her, an eyebrow raised, but she ignored it. He was not interested in her and that was an end to the matter. If he was foolish enough to be besotted by Belle, then no doubt he would continue in his folly. Until Belle, being Belle, showed her true colours and he would get hurt.

Then, Hannah told herself, she would be there to pick up the pieces. The lovely daydream filled her mind. Belle flouncing away, sharp words having been said. Rab standing looking horrified as he realises his idol has the most ugly clay feet. His heart breaking, he turns and there bathed in golden light is Hannah, radiantly beautiful.

'My darling,' she says...

'Hannah!'

She steps towards him, arms open wide...

'Hannah!' It was her father's voice that cut across her daydream. 'Your mother asked you a question.'

Hannah came back to herself with a start to realise that once more all eyes were on her. A furious blush flooded her cheeks. She blinked quickly to wake herself up.

'I'm sorry, Father. What did you say, Mother?' she hastened to placate them.

Her mother was shaking her head. 'You were far away. You *must* be tired. I was asking did you have any message for Belle? Robert is going down to Edinburgh next week. He has business there and he thought he would look in on Belle and see how she's doing.'

It felt like a dagger plunging straight into her heart, the pain sudden and unbearably sharp. Hannah fought for control, forcing back the tears that threatened to express her shock. She had known this had to happen. Her father had suggested it a while back. But she had forgotten, or pushed it out of her mind. And now she had to face it. Hannah glanced across at Rab and noted the slightly sheepish look on his face. And well he might, she thought. Of all the obvious contrived....

Men!

She pulled herself together. This was simply something she would have to get used to. He was a fool over Belle and would be till he saw sense. And that was not in her hands. There was only one thing to do and that was to pray.

Lord Jesus, give me the patience to wait this out. You know my feelings and You know Your plans for each one of us. Hannah made herself relax. It was all in the Lord's hands. Nothing had changed, she told herself firmly, so there was no need to react. She swallowed hard and answered her mother's question with hard-won equanimity.

'No,' she said. 'No, I don't think I've any particular message for Belle.'

She could hardly share the message she would really like to send to her sister!

CHAPTER 20

'What are you doing here?'

It was not the reaction Rab had expected and certainly not the welcome he had hoped for. In the months after Belle's precipitous departure from Wick, Rab had patiently bided his time till he thought he could decently visit the family and find out exactly what was going on.

And the news had gladdened his heart. There had been a major falling-out between Belle and Hughie Mackay. Rab had managed to prise the whole story out of Belle's father. He discovered there had been a secret engagement between Belle and Hughie.

'Romantic nonsense!' Mr Reid had said. 'They were just a pair of bairns!'

That blackguard Geordie Sinclair had written to Belle to break the news that Hughie had been unfaithful to her, that there was another woman in Canada. And Belle, unsurprisingly, had broken off the relationship.

Rab shook his head in disapproval. But Belle was young and knew no better. He could forgive... In truth, he thought he could forgive Belle anything...

Even this furious, fashionable young woman standing in front of him. This was not the Belle he remembered. No smile lit her pretty face. Instead it was marred by surprising hostility. Rab reminded himself that she was a young girl. Perhaps her heart had been broken by Hughie's betrayal and no man would be welcome till her heart was fully healed. Yes, that would be the thing. As an older, wiser man who truly loved her, he would forgive and show forbearance. She would come round.

He smiled. 'Hello, Belle,' he said, taking it slowly. 'I was in Edinburgh so I thought I'd just drop by and see how you are doing.'

'Well, you've seen,' she said snappishly and went to close the door of her aunt's house in his face.

'Your mother and father...' he tried again.

The closing door paused. Belle peered round the edge, her face still cross.

'Did they send you?' she demanded. 'Well, you can tell them from me they needn't bother. I'm doing fine here. Now you can go away and don't come back.' The door slammed shut.

Rab rocked back on his heels, thinking hard. The poor girl must be more hurt than he had realised. Ah well, he thought, a lovely soft-hearted girl like Belle would take such a betrayal hard. He would just have to play his cards carefully, taking his time. It was disappointing though...

He replaced his hat on his head and turned away, paying no attention to the nattily dressed young man sauntering confidently along the street towards him. By the time Rab had turned the corner into the next street, Adam Finlayson had reached Belle's aunt's house where he rapped confidently on the door.

The door was wrenched open to reveal a cross-faced Belle. Sharp words started on her tongue. 'I told you...' Seeing who was at the door, her face instantly transformed into a welcoming smile.

'Adam,' she beamed at him. 'How lovely to see you. I'll just get my hat.' And within moments they were walking arm in arm down to where Adam had left his carriage.

'I thought you might enjoy going to the music hall tonight,' Adam told Belle as he handed her into the carriage. 'Then supper and afterwards...' His smile was knowing.

She lowered her eyelashes for a moment, then looked boldly into his eyes.

'Oh yes,' she said. 'Yes.'

CHAPTER 21

'What are you doing? Geordie!' Nancy cried with fear, the gun cold against her temple.

Geordie ignored her, staring round at the hostile crowd.

'You don't want the lovely Nancy to die, do you?' he asked. 'It wouldn't worry me. After all, what's one more?' He waited for the angry murmuring to subside. 'So why don't you let me go, peacefully?' he offered calmly.

A roar of outrage greeted his proposal but Geordie simply stood and waited.

'All I want is a sled and enough provisions to get me out of here. That's the way we do things up here,' he mocked them.

'You're lucky we don't just string you up here and now,' one man said.

'What, and have my blood on your hands – and Nancy's?' Geordie taunted. 'She'd be dead before you could touch me. No, it's much tidier my way.'

It took less than an hour for a sled and provisions to be fetched, and the mule hitched up. Still holding the gun to her temple, Geordie pushed Nancy to a seated position on the sled and loaded the saddlebags behind her. He turned back to the watching crowd.

'Send someone to the dance hall and get one of the girls to pack Nancy's things. She's coming with me. As surety. So none of you get any ideas about coming after me.'

'No!' Nancy cried. 'Geordie! Let me go! Please let me go!'

'Oh no,' he said. 'You're coming with me, for as long as I decide I need you.'

The crowd stirred restlessly but they did as Geordie said and soon a large carpetbag was handed over.

Nancy stifled a sob as Geordie led the way out of Dawson City.

'Good riddance,' he said as the last sight of the town disappeared behind them.

'Please, Geordie!' Nancy pleaded. 'Please let me go! I'm no use to you. I'll just slow you down.'

'Oh no,' Geordie said. 'I have a plan – and I'm going to need you to make the plan work!'

'So where are we going?' Nancy asked in a whisper.

Geordie laughed. 'Manitoba,' he said. 'Your precious Hughie has rich relatives with a ranch there. We'll tell them that I'm Hughie – they'll never know the difference – and you're my wife. They'll be thrilled to see us – they're an elderly couple with no children.' He pointed at Nancy's belly where the pregnancy barely showed. 'That child will open the doors for us. We'll do very well!'

Geordie leaned in close to her, his face frighteningly calm. 'You hear me?' he asked. 'You play along and you'll be just fine. I'll look after you.' He straightened up. 'I told you I would.'

Nancy swallowed hard. All around was wilderness. High mountains, and deep snow as far as the eye could see. Geordie had driven the mule onto the thick ice of the river, and was intent on putting as much distance as he could between them and Dawson City. Nancy knew she could not walk back there.

Geordie watched the thoughts tumbling across her face.

'Well?' he demanded. 'What do you say? We can do this the hard way – or you can co-operate and it won't be so bad for you.'

A hopeless sob started in Nancy's throat. She could not see that she had any choice. She looked at Geordie. He had already killed two men. So long as she was some use to him, he would let her live.

She nodded.

CHAPTER 22

He was not happy. Despite the new-baked scones dripping with melted butter and topped with the sharp fresh crowdie Hannah had made that morning. Despite the warm welcome he had received from the Reid family. It was very clear that Rab Cormack was not his usual cheerful self.

'You've been to Edinburgh?' Hannah's father finally prompted.

'Yes. I have.'

They waited but it appeared he had nothing further to say on the matter.

'More tea?' her mother enquired.

Rab's head came up as if he had to give it thought. 'Ah, yes. Please.' He held out his cup to be refilled, then set it down absently.

'The business you went to see to?' Hannah's father persisted. 'That was satisfactory?'

Rab roused himself to respond politely. 'Yes, indeed. The firm we're dealing with there seems very competent.' He nodded. 'Yes, that was all fine.'

Finally her mother asked the question they were all waiting for. 'And did you see Belle?'

Rab looked up to see all eyes upon him.

'Yes,' he said and took a large bite of scone. But Mrs Reid was not to be deterred.

'That's nice,' she murmured. Hannah saw something in Rab's face as his eyes came up involuntarily and he began to choke on the scone.

'Take a sip of your tea,' Hannah's mother instructed.

His teacup rattled alarmingly in its saucer and Hannah watched as a parade of emotions flitted across Rab's face. When the choking appeared to have stopped, Hannah's mother asked, 'And how was she?'

'Fine,' he finally managed to say and reached for another scone which he proceeded to chew with great concentration.

Hannah's mother and father exchanged glances. It was clear whatever had happened in Edinburgh had not made Rab happy and was not something he was willing to share with them.

I'd like to wring her neck, Hannah thought fiercely. There were times when she could hate her sister. The poor man looked so sad and beaten. What on earth had Belle done to him? Whatever it was, it was clearly troubling him.

When at last he rose to go, Hannah's father accompanied him to the front door. Curious, Hannah used the excuse of carrying the tea tray through to the kitchen to enable her to linger a moment in the corridor and listen.

'Don't give up,' she was horrified to hear her father advise Rab. 'She's young. It's maybe taking her a bit longer than we thought to get over it. Don't take it to heart.'

And Rab squared his shoulders and turned to face Mr Reid. 'You're right,' he said. 'She's young and I'm older and wiser. I can wait.' And with that he was gone.

Hannah's heart plummeted. Was there no making him see sense?

'Hannah?' her mother called.

Hannah jumped guiltily and hurried into the kitchen to join her. Her mother took the tray from her and started the washing up in the big sink in front of the back window. Hannah took a tea towel from the rail on the front of the big oven and started to dry the crockery they had used. The two women worked in companionable silence. But as they tidied away the tea things, Hannah's mother said, 'Poor man.'

Hannah allowed herself a quiet snort.

'He is though,' her mother continued with a reproachful smile. 'He'd be a fine husband for our Belle. She would be back here in town where I could keep an eye on her. Rab's building up his family business so she wouldn't have to scrimp. And he's old enough to keep her in line.' She paused, thoughtfully. 'But it appears she's off on another escapade.'

She took a letter out of her apron pocket and carefully smoothed it out. 'It came this morning. I didn't like to tell your father and I wasn't going to read it out in front of Rab.' She sat down at the table and popped the wire-rimmed spectacles she now needed on her nose and began to read:

'*Dear Mother and Father,*

We're fine here in Edinburgh. I'm doing my best but Aunt Peggy is still being miserable. Her friends come round and all they do is encourage her to moan. I think she's decided there are advantages in being the grieving widow.'

Here their mother stopped and tut-tutted at her daughter's acerbity. She went on,

'*I'm getting on fine at the workroom. The other girls don't like me but that's only to be expected. Jealousy, especially now that I'm walking*

out with Mr Finlayson, the owner's son. He's a fine young man and I'm
sure I'll have good news for you about that soon.

> *Your loving daughter,*
> *Belle.'*

Trust Belle, Hannah thought. *Always an eye to the main chance.*
And the owner's son would certainly look a likely catch for a young
woman determined to have the good things of life.

She thought of Rab Cormack's sad face and echoed her mother's
earlier words.

'Poor man.'

Her mother looked up sharply. 'Which one?' she asked and in a
moment the two of them were laughing.

'Both,' Hannah finally managed to get out. 'Both of them!'

CHAPTER 23

'And what time do you think this is?'

Mrs McEwen, the workroom supervisor, was planted squarely in Belle's path as she hurried through the door and into the workroom. A large woman wearing a lilac blouse that clashed with an angry red face, Mrs McEwen pointed to the big clock on the wall.

Belle pretended to scrutinise it before answering, 'Why, Mrs McEwen, it looks like a quarter past eight.'

'And why weren't you here on the dot of eight o'clock with the other girls?' she demanded.

Belle's eyes narrowed in fury but she held her temper in check. It was maybe early days to be saying that she was no longer one of the other girls. That one day very soon she would be their boss and able to suit herself as to what hours she chose to work. They all knew she was walking out with Adam Finlayson. She had made sure of that. And surely they knew it was only a matter of time before a formal announcement was made?

'Well?' Mrs McEwen demanded. 'What's your excuse this time?'

Belle focused on the woman's angry face. In the months Belle had been there, she had become an implacable enemy, always picking on her. She seemed to take special pleasure in pointing out where Belle's work was not up to scratch. She commented unfavourably on Belle's attitude. And now, this past week, she had been waiting every morning, watching like a hawk as Belle managed to slip in by the skin of her teeth just on time.

But not this morning. This morning Belle had slept late. And that was not surprising. She had been out with Adam Finlayson most of the evenings in the week, ending up at his flat till the wee small hours – consolidating their relationship, she thought with a tiny smile.

'And what do you have to smile about?' the woman snapped sourly.

If only you knew, Belle thought. She looked calculatingly at the woman. When she was Adam's wife, Belle was confident that she would be running the business alongside him, putting to good use her undoubted sense of fashion and style. And when that happened, she certainly would not want this woman working for her. Mrs McEwen would have to go, and the sooner the better. Maybe a word in Adam's ear…

Belle smiled as sweetly as she could manage.

'Oh dear, Mrs McEwen,' she said. 'Our clock must have been slow. I'm so sorry. I'll make sure that doesn't happen again.'

And she took herself off, calmly and unhurriedly, into the cloakroom to hang up her coat and hat, then she returned to her place at the work table with the other girls with a serenity that clearly puzzled the woman.

'You see that it doesn't,' Mrs McEwen called after her. 'Or Mr Finlayson will have to know.'

Belle smiled. *Oh yes*, she thought, *Mr Finlayson will have to know, but not what you think.* She smiled and settled to the day's tedious tasks. *Not for long*, she promised herself. *Not for very much longer.*

CHAPTER 24

Nancy shivered as she hunkered down amongst the baggage on the back of the sled. Yes, Geordie had a plan. But first they had to get out of this wilderness. Despite the almost constant snow and the freezing cold, he remained in remarkably high spirits.

'Not long now!' he kept saying.

Nancy remembered nostalgically the comfortable trip up the Yukon River in the luxurious steamboat with the other girls fluttering around excitedly. It had been good business too, for the boat was filled with men with enough money to use the 'Rich Man's Route' and a bit left over for female company. The only traces of those carefree days were her silk dresses packed away in the carpetbag beneath her head.

Overland on a now frozen Yukon River, on a sled pulled by a mule in driving snow, was not Nancy's idea of travel but she soon learned better than to complain. Geordie's temper was short and swiftly demonstrated in savage blows that reduced Nancy to frightened silence.

At last, he pulled up outside a snow-covered tented settlement.

'This is No Man's Land,' he told her. 'White Horse Pass, between Canada and the United States of America.'

The two countries' flags fluttered on either side of the settlement and there were formalities to clear with customs. Nancy was surprised to hear Geordie pass her off as his sister. He returned to the sled, well satisfied.

'From here we travel like civilised people,' he declared and to Nancy's amazement led the way to where a noisy group of people were disembarking from three railway carriages pulled by a small compound locomotive – combination express, mail and baggage car.

'This will take us the twenty miles down the hill all the way to Skagway,' he told her as he hauled their packs and bags off the sled and passed them into the baggage car.

Nancy looked around in surprised delight. 'The White Pass and Yukon Railway Company,' the signs said.

'This wasn't built when we came up and they're still working on it. But it will do the job for us,' Geordie said with satisfaction.

The smart carriages were simple but comfortable and once they were settled into their seats, Nancy gazed around her with interest, an interest openly returned by the male passengers. Geordie's eyes narrowed as he watched. It occurred to him that the girl could make herself useful before they reached Hughie's relatives. He smiled.

'What?' Nancy asked suspiciously.

'Wait and see,' Geordie said, pleased with himself. He had not lost his touch. Everything would work out well for a clever man like him.

With much blowing of whistles and clouds of smoke, the locomotive began its journey down the mountainside, crossing deep ravines on flimsy bridges. One switchback slowed the train almost to a stop, so the passengers were able to see the river rushing down beneath the train and plunging into the deep narrow gorge.

'Oh!' Nancy cried and pointed. Down below the train was spread out the town of Skagway, and just beyond, a harbour busy with ships.

Geordie nodded his head in satisfaction. Yes, all was going according to his plan.

CHAPTER 25

'Off you go now,' Hannah told the boy standing in front of her.

A quick glance told her that his bare feet were less blue than when he had arrived at the door, but he was still a pathetic sight in his threadbare coat and thin scarf. The colour had come back into his cheeks a little so maybe she could bear to send him back outside.

He had come to fetch the milk for his mother but Hannah, soft-hearted as ever, had taken him inside the door and handed him a scone slathered thick with yesterday's crowdie and a mug of buttermilk.

'Get these down you,' she had directed him, standing in the doorway with her arms folded so she could watch and make sure that he got the benefit of them and did not simply add them to the provisions he had gathered for his family. Hannah reckoned that was what he had been doing these last few weeks with the odd scone she had managed to press on him.

The boy had stood before her, guilt and confusion written clear across his face.

'You are not leaving here till you've done what I say,' Hannah told him firmly. 'Just get them down you.'

Finally the boy capitulated and gulped down the scone and the milk as if he were starved. Which he probably was. Or close to. His family were among the poorest in town. His mother kept producing babies, more mouths to feed, while her husband, poor man, had been injured in a farm accident that meant he could not work to provide for them. But they were a proud family that would not accept handouts. All the more reason to surreptitiously feed this oldest lad so he would be strong enough to work and support them.

'Wipe your face before you go,' Hannah told him. 'And there's no need to say anything to anybody. Got that?' She stood aside.

The boy nodded and made his escape with the jug of milk he had come for.

'We'll never make our fortune if you keep giving things away, Hannah.'

Hannah turned to find her mother standing in the doorway.

'He was blue with cold,' Hannah protested. 'And I should think he's letting the younger ones eat his food.'

Her mother came over and patted her shoulder affectionately. 'I'm not criticising you,' she said fondly. 'You did right and I'm glad. We should share what we have. The good Lord has blessed us...'

Hannah sighed. She had thought Belle's departure for Edinburgh was a huge blessing from the Lord. No longer hidden in Belle's shadow, she had thought Rab Cormack might see her for herself and realise that her good honest straightforward love was worth having.

But no. The silly man was still besotted with Belle. And despite Belle's harsh rejection of him and her current decided preference for the rich young heir to the tailoring establishment in Edinburgh where she was doing her dressmaking apprenticeship, Rab was still running up and down to Edinburgh at the least opportunity to see her. And be turned away again.

And each time he would come to their house, tail between his legs, his face a picture of misery. And each time he would be comforted by her mother and encouraged by her father.

'Just bide your time,' her father was wont to say. 'She's young yet. She'll come round.'

Just watching Rab go through the torments of his hopeless love for Belle put Hannah through agonies. How she longed he would turn to her for comfort, but it seemed she was invisible to him.

Why, the last time he came to the house before his most recent trip to the capital, he had politely asked her father and mother if there was anything he could bring back from Edinburgh for them. And when her mother had turned to her and asked if she needed anything, Rab had almost jumped as if she had suddenly materialised out of thin air.

She sighed. Her father had counselled Rab to wait. Waiting was all that Hannah, in her turn, could do too. But it was so hard…

CHAPTER 26

'But Mrs McEwen is a valued employee,' Adam Finlayson protested. 'She's been with the firm longer than almost anyone else. And she's our finest cutter.'

Belle let her silence speak, her mouth shaped into a little moue of disappointment, as she settled herself back against the soft pillows at the head of the big mahogany bed in Adam's flat.

'My father...' Adam began.

'You know your father pays little attention to the business these days, not now that he knows he can depend on you,' Belle spoke admiringly and Adam preened. 'I'm sure you're respected as much as ever he was...' She let the pause lengthen, before adding, 'by nearly everybody.'

Adam raised himself up on an elbow to stare at her, a displeased flush staining his pale cheeks.

'What are you saying?' he demanded.

'Nothing, nothing,' Belle said. She snuggled down closer to him. 'It's just how the older generation can be sometimes.' She opened her eyes wide and appealed to him with a little laugh, 'You know!'

Reluctantly, he laughed with her. But as she began to kiss and nibble his naked shoulder, he moved away slightly.

'What are you talking about, Belle?' he asked uncertainly. 'Is there some problem I don't know about?'

'Oh, you mustn't worry,' she told him. 'I'm sure they didn't mean anything by it.'

But Adam was like a dog with a bone and he refused to give up. He put Belle away from him. 'Tell me,' he said. 'I need to know.'

'I don't want to worry you…'

'You're worrying me now,' he retorted. 'So spill it out.'

'Well, I was just coming out of the cloakroom the other day when I heard people speaking. Your name was mentioned so I waited to see what it was about.'

'And?' Adam demanded. 'What were they saying?'

'Well, the man was asking how the business was going and the woman said it wouldn't be long before your father handed the reins fully over to you…'

Adam brightened. 'That's true,' he said. 'So what's the problem?'

'Well, the woman then said…' Belle turned a sad face to her lover. 'I really don't like to tell you this…'

'Belle,' Adam said warningly. 'If there's any problem, I need to know.'

'Yes, I know. It's just that they weren't being very nice about you.' Belle closed her eyes and waited for Adam's reaction.

'So?' he said. 'You can't win friends everywhere.'

'Yes, but it was Mrs McEwen who was talking to one of the travellers,' Belle protested. 'They were laughing and saying you'd soon make a mess of the business, that some of your ideas were going to be a disaster…' She gasped and covered her mouth with her hand. 'Oh Adam, I'm so sorry!'

'Which ideas?' His tone was hard.

'For the winter programme,' Belle said in faltering tones. 'That new costume...'

'Let me get this straight,' Adam said. 'You overheard Mrs McEwen talking to one of the travellers about my new design? The new costume I'm planning to launch...' His voice came to an abrupt stop. 'I must go,' he told Belle.

By now Adam was out of bed and struggling into his clothes. 'I have to put a stop to this. That costume was my key design for the winter programme. If Mrs McEwen is passing on details to rivals...'

He turned and planted a perfunctory kiss on Belle's cheek. 'Just let yourself out,' he said. 'I'll see you later.'

After he had gone, Belle stretched and smiled. She plumped up the pillows behind her head and relaxed in the big soft bed. This was a nice flat, but once they were married, they would live in a much larger flat at a better address. She allowed herself a happy daydream of her future as Mrs Adam Finlayson.

He was not as handsome as Hughie Mackay had been but he was just as easy to wind round her finger. Better still, he was a prosperous man of good standing in the city. She would enjoy life as his wife. They made a good pair, she thought with satisfaction. They understood one another.

Ah well, maybe she should get up and get herself off to work. By the time she got there that Mrs McEwen would have had her marching orders. That would teach the staff to cross Belle Reid!

CHAPTER 27

Skagway was a surprise. In the two years since it had been founded, it had grown from a rumbustious tent-town with a reputation for lawlessness into a cheerful prosperous boom-town filled with busy, happy people.

Nancy exclaimed in delight at the fine buildings as they made their way along the crowded sidewalks to the harbour where the steamship awaited them. Her lively pretty face won an interested smile from a gentleman passing by. He tipped his hat at her and she smiled broadly in return.

'Come along,' Geordie told her, taking her arm roughly and hurrying her along. 'You'll have plenty of time for that on board the steamer.'

And once on board, and installed in a comfortable stateroom, Nancy quickly realised what Geordie had in mind.

'Your fare costs money,' he told Nancy sharply when she protested. 'This is how you pay for it.'

'I'd have been perfectly happy staying in Dawson City,' she retaliated. 'I didn't ask to come with you!'

The sudden blow silenced her.

'No,' Geordie said, ambling over to the table to pour himself another whiskey. 'And don't you forget it.'

The steamship, *The City of Topeka*, belonged to the Pacific Coast Steamship Company and plied between Skagway and Seattle. Passengers arrived and departed at Juneau, Wrangell, tiny Mary Island, and Victoria, providing Nancy with plenty of work, and Geordie with a generous replenishment of his funds. As a stream of gentlemen visited the cabin, Geordie collected their money just as he had from his sister's visitors back home, and watched them sidle away afterwards.

There was always a way for a clever man to take advantage of lesser men's weaknesses.

CHAPTER 28

Belle was delighted to see that there was no sign of Mrs McEwen when she arrived at the workroom in the morning. She sauntered in, looking around with a proprietorial interest at the tables where the other women were already hard at work. One day, she thought with pleasure, this will all be mine. I will be the one who rules the roost.

Unhurriedly, she took herself to the cloakroom and hung up her coat and hat. *One day*, she thought, *one of the girls will rush to take my coat – and it will be a fur coat*, she decided. *Yes. A lovely warm long fur coat.* She lingered for a moment, imagining the feel of the fur under her hands, the warmth…

'Miss Reid!' The sharp voice of Mrs McEwen cut into her daydream.

Belle turned in shocked surprise. What was she doing here? Surely Adam had had enough time to get down here and turn her off?

Mrs McEwen's eyes narrowed. 'I think you'd better get to work,' was all she said but she watched Belle as she moved across the workroom, aware of the antagonistic glare fixed on her back. The women in the workroom had lowered their work and were watching

Belle's progress. Belle held her head up and forced herself to walk steadily to her place as if nothing was the matter but her mind was racing. So maybe Mrs McEwen had found a way to counter her story, but she had not yet won the battle and Belle was determined that she would not.

She allowed her eyes to range over the women at the tables as she walked past them. One by one their eyes dropped back to their stitching, and the busy hum of work and quiet conversation began again. Good, Belle thought. She could brazen this out.

But as the day wore on, it became plain that more might be needed. Belle became aware that she was being cold-shouldered more than usual. Even the toadies who usually clustered around her left her alone when she went through for her tea.

And at closing time, Adam was not waiting for her with the carriage and a welcoming smile. Belle hesitated on the step. Perhaps he had been delayed?

Mrs McEwen, coming out behind her, paused and commented with a sarcastic smile, 'All on your own, then?'

Belle ignored the woman and stepped out on to the street. She would take a tram back to Aunt Peggy's house and tell her that the sick friend she had been staying with these past few weeks had taken a turn for the better. There was no reason her aunt would question her.

And the story of the sick friend would be there in place when she next needed it. As she was sure she would. Adam was probably in a meeting. He had simply forgotten to mention it.

Belle tossed her head as she climbed on to the tram. There was nothing to worry about.

CHAPTER 29

'I told you,' Hannah's father was saying to Rab Cormack. 'She just needed time away from home to grow up.'

He rustled the letter that had arrived that morning and proceeded to read snippets from it.

'Her aunt says she's made friends in Edinburgh and one of them was sick so Belle went to look after her.' Mr Reid looked pleased and proud. 'There. She's a good-hearted girl. I'm sure she didn't mean to offend you. She was probably worried about her friend...'

Rab brightened and accepted another cup of tea from Hannah's mother. Hannah noted her mother contributed nothing to the men's conversation, neither any words nor her usual smiles. But in the kitchen later she made her opinion clearly known.

'It is all very strange,' Mrs Reid said to Hannah. 'It doesn't sound like our Belle at all.' She shook her head and Hannah had to agree. Belle had never been known to help anyone.

'But herself,' Hannah said, then instantly regretted the waspishness of her comment. 'Sorry, Mother, I shouldn't have said that.'

'It's true enough though,' her mother said. 'And it's true we should not say it.' She shrugged an unconvinced shoulder. 'Maybe Belle has learned the error of her ways and is showing a good-hearted side.'

And cows might fly, Hannah thought. But she was disappointed that Rab had been so encouraged by the news of Belle's good deed that he was planning another trip to Edinburgh. The innovations he had put in place in his family business were producing good results and he was keen to diversify and expand.

'My father's not so active as he was,' Rab had explained. 'In fact, my mother's a bit worried about him.'

'It's good he has you to depend on,' Mr Reid said with approval. 'And it's right for you to take on more responsibility now, while you have him around to guide you.'

'He knows the business inside out,' Rab said. 'There's a lot yet for me to learn. I just hope there will be plenty of time…'

Hannah's father had clapped him reassuringly on the shoulder. 'Aye well, it's all in the Lord's hands, but surely there will be time for a quick trip to Edinburgh?'

Rab had beamed. 'Yes, I'm sure there's time for me to get away just for a few days.'

As Hannah took herself off to the dairy at the back of the house to see to the work needing to be done there, she sighed to herself. Instead of coming into her own in Belle's absence, she seemed to have become even more invisible.

In the dairy she hung up her coat and rolled up her sleeves. There was butter to be churned and crowdie to be made. And keeping busy seemed to help. At least she was being some use to someone, she thought.

CHAPTER 30

'Good girl,' Geordie told Nancy. He weighed the day's takings in his hand. 'We'll have enough to cover our fare east. The boat docks in a couple of hours so you'd better be ready.'

He turned to leave, then looked back from the door. 'And try and look respectable,' he told her scornfully.

Nancy waited till she was sure he had gone.

'Look respectable!'

She flung herself down on the pillows and pummelled them in her fury. But then the babe kicked inside her and she stopped and drew herself back to sit, propped up by the pillows, her hand stroking her belly.

Hughie's child. She had to think of the child. On her own she would only be able to continue working for a month or two more, then where could she go? She would be destitute. Nancy sighed. She was well and truly trapped. Geordie thought he was forcing her to accompany him, to play along with his plan so he could take advantage of Hughie's relatives in Canada. But what else could she do?

She rose slowly and began to dress. The next stage of their journey, by train from Port Moody, would require warmer clothes than the dresses Geordie had paraded her in on board the steamship. And if she was to gain acceptance from Hughie's ranching relatives, most of her clothes simply would not do. They would know at a glance what she was and she and Geordie would not even get a foot in the door. Nancy shivered. He would blame her – and punish her with his fists. Nancy could feel the child stir again. She could not let Geordie hurt the child. She gathered up the revealing silks and satins that she had worn in Dawson City and here on the steamship, and stuffed them away in her carpetbag.

Respectable? She would do her best.

'Good girl,' Geordie said when he came back for her. 'Here,' he said, reaching into his coat pocket. 'You'd better have this.'

Nancy looked curiously at the ring he handed her. It was plain gold, with an ivy leaf and a strange word, *Mizpah*, embossed across it.

'What is it?' she asked.

'That?' Geordie said carelessly. 'Hughie had it made out of Klondike gold. He sent it to his girl in Scotland. As an engagement ring. They were secretly engaged, you see.' He laughed. 'And she sent it back to him when she found out about you.'

Nancy gasped. Belle, the girl in Scotland, must have sent this ring back to Hughie with the letter that had sent him to his death. She remembered Hughie's anguish – and fury – the day he had discovered Belle knew about her, and the baby. *He must have loved this girl very much*, Nancy thought sadly.

Geordie's words echoed in her mind. 'When she found out about you.' She looked enquiringly at Geordie.

'But she only found out about me,' Nancy said, 'because you told her.'

Geordie shrugged. 'It worked.'

'You wanted the engagement broken?' Nancy asked.

'And Miss High-and-Mighty Belle Reid brought down from her high horse,' Geordie said with cheerful satisfaction.

'But…' Nancy began.

'But nothing,' Geordie said, unconcerned. 'She got what she deserved.'

'But why?' Nancy persisted. 'What did she ever do…?' Her eyes widened as a completely impossible thought dawned on her. 'You loved her too, didn't you? You wanted her for yourself…'

'Leave it!' Geordie snarled at her. 'Love!' He laughed mockingly. 'What's love got to do with it?'

'But…?'

'Love has nothing to do with it,' Geordie said deliberately. 'Let's just say she made a big mistake getting on the wrong side of Geordie Sinclair. Now you'd better put that ring on. If we're going to pass ourselves off as a married couple, it will help convince Hughie's people.'

And Nancy had to be satisfied with that.

As they waited to disembark, Nancy found she was turning the ring round and round in her pocket. It felt strange. Hughie's gold from the Klondike. Hughie's gift to a girl who had thrown it back in his face. She sighed.

This – and the baby she was carrying – was all there was to show for Hughie's life. She hesitated, then slipped the ring on. She probably had as much right to it as anyone.

CHAPTER 31

A titter of spiteful laughter greeted Belle as she walked into the room set aside for the women in the workroom to take their tea break. Avid eyes watched her progress across the floor but she steeled herself to ignore them and the newspaper they had spread out on the table in front of them that was giving them so much amusement.

She concentrated on pouring out her tea and then took her cup to the window where she could look out on the street and ignore the other occupants of the room. They did not matter but Adam Finlayson did and there was the problem. Belle had been so sure she had him exactly where she wanted him, but now she was not so confident.

Maybe she had overplayed her hand with that business over Mrs McEwen? The woman was still in charge of the workroom and making her life a misery with her constant carping.

'You'll have to do better than that, Miss Reid. Unpick that seam and do it again.' And all the other girls listening. It just was not fair McEwen kept picking on her.

Adam had not said anything. He was just… unavailable. If they met in the building that housed both the ladies' dressmaking workroom and the men's tailoring room, he nodded politely – as he always did. So that was not unusual. From the start he had said that he wanted their relationship to be 'our secret'.

'Trust me,' he had said. 'The time will come…'

And so she had bided her time. But that nod of greeting now felt distant and perfunctory, no longer the public pretence veiling their intimacy. And there had been no evenings out with Adam to brighten up her life, or nights at his flat, for several weeks now.

Tea break over, the group of girls round the table got up and went back to work, but they pointedly left behind the newspaper they had been poring over. One of the departing girls gave Belle a malicious smile as she left and the others sniggered. The remaining women sipped their tea and watched. *Harpies*, Belle thought.

Determined to show no concern, she finished her cup of tea unhurriedly and then drifted across to the table where they had left the newspaper. It had been laid open and arranged carefully to display a photograph.

The colour left Belle's cheeks as she saw that the photograph was of Adam and a young woman dressed in elegant evening clothes. The caption read:

'*Edinburgh businessman Adam Finlayson attended the musical soirée held at the Usher Hall on Tuesday evening escorting Miss Margaret Elphinstone, daughter of Brigadier and Mrs Harold Elphinstone of Corstorphine.*'

Aware that the other women were watching her, Belle unfolded the paper and opened it to the next page, pretending to be reading nonchalantly. But when she reached the snippets and gossip column, Adam's name sprang out at her again.

'*Romance in the wind?*' the piece was headed.

'*We observe that Miss Margaret Elphinstone has been seen frequently in the company of local entrepreneur, Adam Finlayson. No ring on her finger yet but the whisper is that it will not be long. Both families declare themselves delighted.'*

Belle discovered she had been holding her breath. She let it out shakily. Adam? Adam was going to be engaged to a Miss Margaret Elphinstone? When had this happened? And how had her plans gone wrong?

She had to see him, talk it over. Could he not see that she would be a much better prospect that any Miss Elphinstone? She thought back to all the nights amongst the rumpled covers of his bed. He knew exactly how satisfying she could be.

Belle put the newspaper down, drained her tea and squared her shoulders. She was not defeated. There had been some misunderstanding but she could put that right. She would forgive Adam this little lapse.

She looked at the clock. Just another couple of hours. Then, instead of going back to Aunt Peggy's, she would simply go round to Adam's flat and wait for him there.

Everything would be fine. She was sure of it.

CHAPTER 32

'I'm home,' Hannah called cheerfully as she removed her hat and hung up her coat.

In the sitting-room, her mother was looking pensive, her wire-rimmed spectacles on her nose and a newspaper in her hand.

Hannah went over and kissed her mother on the cheek.

'What's in the news to make you look so thoughtful?' she enquired curiously.

Her mother gazed at her sadly. 'Look,' she said and pointed to the photograph of Adam Finlayson with Margaret Elphinstone. Hannah took the newspaper and studied the picture.

'Oh, isn't that the man Belle said she was walking out with? He looks…' Hannah came to an abrupt halt. 'Oh dear,' she said as she realised the import of the photograph.

Her mother nodded. 'And there's worse.' She took the newspaper from Hannah's hand and turned to the next page. 'There,' she said and handed it back, pointing to a short piece entitled '*Romance in the wind?*'

Hannah read it and then carefully re-read it.

'Oh dear,' she said again. 'Belle is not going to be pleased.'

The sitting-room door opened to admit Hannah's father and Rab Cormack arriving in time for tea.

'Why is Belle not going to be pleased?' Mr Reid enquired. 'What's happened?'

Hannah and her mother exchanged glances. As far as they knew, Rab was unaware of Belle's relationship with Adam Finlayson.

Mr Reid strode over to his daughter and took the newspaper from her hand. 'Let me see,' he said. As he read it, Rab went over and stood by his side where he too could read it.

'But what has this to do with Belle?' Rab asked in puzzlement. 'Who is this Adam Finlayson?'

'Nobody you need to worry about,' Mr Reid said jovially, 'and certainly not now.'

'Wait a minute,' Rab persisted. 'Finlayson? Finlayson? I know that name.' He leaned over to look again at the newspaper. '*Edinburgh entrepreneur*,' he read. 'Oh, yes, I remember. The place where Belle is doing her apprenticeship...' he began slowly. 'Don't the Finlaysons own it?'

Mr Reid nodded unwillingly.

'Adam Finlayson,' Rab repeated. 'And Belle,' he said. He looked down at the photograph, carefully reading the caption, his face still puzzled.

When he looked up, he saw pity and embarrassment on the assembled faces: Hannah's and her mother's gently pitying, Mr Reid embarrassed and decidedly uncomfortable.

'Now now,' Mr Reid said. 'It's all over now if this newspaper is to be believed.' He folded the newspaper away and gave it to Hannah with a scowl, and a nod of his head to dispose of it. 'I knew it would blow over,' he said. He clapped Rab on the shoulder and made to draw him to a chair.

But Rab was staring at him, trying to make sense of it. 'So there was something to blow over?' he asked slowly. 'And that's why she didn't want me coming to Edinburgh... because...'

'Yes, yes,' Mr Reid said brusquely. 'But that's no longer an issue. She'll be happy to see you now. I'm sure of that. When are you going down to Edinburgh next?'

'I hadn't planned anything,' Rab murmured, clearly bewildered at what he was hearing.

'Well, I think you should,' Mr Reid said. 'Strike while the iron is hot, that's what I say. I would think she will be prepared to look more favourably on you now. She may even be ready to come home...'

Rab's face brightened as he thought it over. 'Yes,' he said. 'You're right. If that man has been toying with Belle's affections, and now he's getting engaged to someone else...' He gestured to the newspaper still in Hannah's hand as she stood at the door listening in dismay. 'Belle may indeed be happy to come home,' Rab said decisively. 'I'll get down there as soon as I can.'

He quickly took his leave, the front door banging behind him.

'Well, I think that was all for the best,' Mr Reid said, coming over to stand with his back to the fireplace, a satisfied smile on his face. 'I think we can throw that paper on the fire. It's served its purpose.'

He reached out his hand for it and Hannah discovered she had been clenching it so hard, she had scrunched the page into a tight ball. She forced herself to let go and hand it over.

As she watched it turn to flames and ashes in the fireplace, she counselled herself to hold steady. Who knew what would happen when Rab got to Edinburgh? But her heart was troubled.

Hannah took a deep breath and prayed silently. *Your will, Lord. Your best will – for all of us!*

CHAPTER 33

'They're called Alexander, not Mackay!' Geordie exploded with frustration. He was using the long train journey from Port Moody to Manitoba to coach Nancy in what she would need to know to convince Hughie's aunt and uncle of their bona fides.

'But why?' Nancy asked. 'Hughie's surname was Mackay.'

'Yes, I know,' Geordie said irritably. 'But *they* are Alexander. They're probably related to Hughie's mother rather than his father.'

Nancy considered that. 'Yes, that's possible.'

'Will you just shut up and listen – and try to remember what I'm telling you,' Geordie told her angrily.

'But how do you know all this?' Nancy queried.

Geordie sighed and gritted his teeth. He remembered the long boring journey to Dawson City and Hughie's constant chatter along the way and round the fire at night. At the time he had shut his ears to most of it but now he wished he had bothered to pay more attention.

'Hughie,' he said briefly. 'He talked about them. I can't remember much so we'll have to do our best. As I was saying…'

At last the train from the west coast pulled in to Brandon in Manitoba and it was time to disembark.

159

'We don't want to look too prosperous,' Geordie told Nancy dismissively when she complained at the poor-looking horse and buggy he had purchased. 'They're more likely to have pity on us and take us in if we look a bit sorry for ourselves. In you get. It's not far now.'

The bustling town of Brandon was surrounded by good farmland and prosperous farms and Geordie's spirits rose as they trotted steadily along the road. But as the hours passed and they had not reached their destination, Nancy's nerves began to fray.

'Are you sure?' she burst out. 'Are you sure we're in the right place? You said you didn't really listen to Hughie! We could be completely lost! And anyway, what if his aunt and uncle know what Hughie looked like? You look completely different! We'll get thrown out and…'

Geordie's hand lashed out and slapped the girl harshly across the face.

'Just shut up!' he told her furiously. 'I listened enough to Hughie. We're on the right road and everything is going to be fine if you'll just do as I've told you. Have you got that?'

He slowed the horse and turned to fix her with his angry eyes.

Nancy gulped and nodded, her face tear-stained and reddened from the blow.

'Good. You just remember that,' he said. 'Then nothing can go wrong.'

By the time the Alexander homestead appeared at the end of their journey, they had not spoken for over an hour and Nancy was huddled in chilled misery on the far side of the seat from Geordie.

'We're here,' he murmured warningly to her. 'Now start looking the part.'

As the horse trotted up to the house, Geordie cast greedy eyes over the homestead. The main house was in good shape as were the bunkhouse, barns and stables that were set back behind it. Paddocks provided grazing for a handful of horses. Strong sleek animals, obviously well fed. The plume of smoke from the ranch-house chimney augured well for their reception.

As they approached, a dog began to bark and a grey-haired woman appeared on the step, wiping her hands on a large white apron. She stood her ground as Geordie slid off the seat of the buggy and stumbled towards her.

'Aunt Marie?' he asked. 'Marie Alexander?'

Sharp eyes examined him.

'And you are?' the woman asked. Her words were spoken with a French accent.

'Aunt Marie, I'm Hugh… Hugh Mackay. Your husband's nephew. My mother is…' Here Geordie faltered. He could not remember Hughie's mother's name. He had never taken that much interest. But the woman did not appear to notice. Coming closer to inspect them, she waved her hand in Nancy's direction.

'And who is this?'

'My wife,' Geordie said. 'Nancy.'

Again the sharp eyes fixed on him.

'Then you'd better bring her in,' was all she said.

Geordie hurried back to Nancy.

'Come on,' he told her. 'We're in. But you'd better mind your tongue. Don't forget what I told you. And I'm Hughie from now on. Remember.'

A man had appeared from the stables and came to stand by the head of the horse.

'Albert,' Marie said, pronouncing the name the French way. 'He will show you where to put your horse and the buggy. You can bring your bags in later.'

Dismissed, Geordie made a show of helping Nancy carefully off the seat as the old woman watched. As Nancy approached her, the woman exclaimed, 'Ah, *ma chère*, you have had a hard journey – and a *bébé* on the way too. Come in, come in. It is as well you have reached us safely.' And she took Nancy's arm and led her into the house.

Geordie Sinclair climbed back on to the seat of the buggy and clicked the reins to set the horse following Albert, a satisfied smile lurking on his lips. No woman could resist another woman in need. Surely they would do well here.

CHAPTER 34

Belle let herself into Adam's apartment building. It was a gaunt old place built solidly of huge blocks of sooty red sandstone. The big front door gave way to a plain entrance hall. A long curving stone staircase wound upwards to three narrow landings with a door at each end. Adam's flat – his pied-à-terre as he called it – was the furthest door on the third floor.

Belle climbed the stairs. The Finlayson family residence was out in the Braid Hills and Adam made his main home there with his parents. But finding the need for somewhere more private – here Belle's lip curled in appreciation – he had purchased this mansion flat, telling his parents it would be more convenient for the business when they were particularly busy and for the evening social engagements he needed to attend in town.

She reached the third landing and stood for a moment to compose herself. Then, as so many times before, she let herself into the flat with the key Adam had given her.

She found Adam seated in a comfortable armchair in the high-ceilinged sitting room reading a newspaper. Belle saw it was the same edition of the newspaper that the girls at work had so helpfully left behind for her to see. She took a deep breath. This had to be sorted out. And she would *not* lose her temper! There was too much at stake.

Adam looked up but he did not put the newspaper down or stand to greet her.

'Belle?' he said, and raised an eyebrow.

She walked over to him, holding her emotions in check. Her plan was to drop an affectionate kiss on the top of his head but his hand snaked out and gripped her wrist, holding her off. Surprised, she took a step back. Adam let the newspaper fall on to the floor and rose to face her.

'What are you doing here?' he asked. There was no friendliness in his tone, no trace of the lover he had been just a few weeks before. His demeanour was frosty. 'I don't recall making any arrangement...?' Again the quizzical eyebrow.

Belle tried for a careless show of unconcern.

'Do we need to make arrangements?' she asked lightly. She held up the key in her free hand. 'After all you gave me a key so I could come and go...'

'Ah yes,' he said, and before she could protest, he had removed the key from her grasp and slipped it into his waistcoat pocket. He dropped her wrist and flung himself back in his chair, picking up the newspaper again and raising it before his face.

Belle stood, perplexed. What to do now? She would not simply turn tail...

Adam peered over the top of the newspaper.

'Still here?' he asked carelessly. 'Well, thank you for bringing back the key...' As if in an afterthought, he held the newspaper out to her, open at the page with the photograph of himself and Miss Elphinstone. 'Because you won't be needing it any more.'

Belle glanced at the page and fury caught up with her.

'What do you mean?' she demanded angrily. 'Adam, we... You can't do this to me...'

Adam looked up again and this time he carefully folded the newspaper onto his lap, the photograph uppermost.

'*We?*' he queried insultingly. 'You didn't think you were any more than a temporary diversion, did you?' Adam gestured at the photograph. 'Now Miss Elphinstone... That's the kind of girl my family approves of. An excellent match. Everyone says so. She and I will be married before the year is out. So I'm afraid, my dear, our little *affaire* has to come to an end.'

'Adam!' Belle cried. 'You can't... You told me... You said...'

'Yes, yes, yes.' He waved her words away. 'But surely a girl like you knows that's the sort of thing men say in those situations.'

'A girl like you.' Belle heard, and understood the implication. 'Those situations.' She stared at him, hands on hips, as she realised just how wrong she had been about him. She had completely miscalculated...

Adam Finlayson picked up the newspaper again and snapped it open decisively. The interview was clearly over.

'I thought...' Belle began slowly.

'Well, you thought wrong,' Adam said. He looked over the top of the paper again. 'Seriously, my dear, you could hardly have expected anything else.'

Speechless, Belle stared at him, as all her hopes and dreams came crashing to the ground. All her strategies, everything she had done that she had thought had wound Adam round her finger, tied him to her...

With an irritated grunt, Adam stood up and dropped the newspaper on to the chair. He went over to the bureau and opened it, his back to her. When he turned around, he was holding a wad of notes in his hand.

'Here,' he said, proffering them. 'I think that's the usual thing, isn't it? Was that what you came for?'

Belle stared at him in horror. He was paying her off. As if she were a common whore... For a moment Belle thought of tearing the money from him and throwing it in his face. But now that her plans were in tatters, her practical mind told her she might need that money.

She could no longer stay at the workroom; that was clear. Mrs McEwen and the girls there would make her life a misery. But what could she do? So yes, she might need the money. She swallowed her fury and her pride, and stalked towards him, wrenching the money from his hand.

Without a word, she stuffed the notes into her reticule and headed for the door. His voice followed her.

'You earned every penny of it,' he mocked. 'And should you want to return after I'm married, I'm sure we can come to a satisfactory arrangement.'

For you, Belle thought in fury as she slammed the door and hurried down the stairs, her feet drumming on the stone. In the hallway she took a deep breath to compose herself before she stepped out into the street.

'Belle?'

Belle looked up to see Rab Cormack standing in her path, his face anxious, uncertain of his reception. That was hardly surprising. She had been deliberately cold towards him the last time she had seen him. Trying to get rid of him, she remembered, when she thought Adam Finlayson was within her grasp. But now...

'Robert!' she said, putting a smile of welcome on her face and her hand on his arm. 'What a lovely surprise!'

Maybe things were not as hopeless as they seemed. There was always Robert...

CHAPTER 35

'They're engaged?' Hannah whispered in horror. 'Rab and Belle?'

But it was plain to see that her father was delighted. Rab looked dazzled and a little sheepish, and Belle... Belle was saying nothing but looking smug. Beautiful and confident and very pleased with herself.

The couple had surprised everyone by returning together from Edinburgh in Rab's new carriage. They arrived at the front door of her parents' Wellington Street house to a tumultuous welcome. Belle's father, at first wholly absorbed in looking over the vehicle, needed to be prised away for a quiet word with Rab. He returned, beaming broadly, and slapping Rab on the back.

'Well done!' he declared. 'Well done, my boy!'

Belle meanwhile had waited till Rab had helped her out of the carriage, then she had walked to her parents' door on his arm as if she were a royal personage visiting the lower orders. Dressed in the very latest Edinburgh fashion with a fur tippet round her shoulders, she had waited till all eyes were on her before she drew off her gloves to reveal the sparkling engagement ring on her left hand.

'Oh my dear!' her mother cried and flung her arms around her. Belle accepted this effusion of emotion but retained a little distance.

'Engaged?' Hannah said again.

Belle spared her a swift glance. 'That's right,' she said. 'I suddenly realised what a fool I'd been. How dear Robert was the only man for me.' She cast him a glittering glance and he beamed besottedly at her. 'He asked me to marry him and I accepted. Why waste time?'

She leaned towards Hannah and whispered spitefully, 'So you'll need to get used to it, sister. He's mine now. You'll never have him.' She thrust a bandbox into Hannah's hands. 'You can help take my things up to my room.'

'Our room,' Hannah said rebelliously.

'Oh, I don't think so,' Belle said, imperiously. 'I'll be needing the space for my trousseau. In any case,' she said with a speaking glance at Robert, 'it won't be for long. I'll be a married lady soon.'

And taking her mother's arm, she led the way into the house, leaving Hannah open-mouthed behind her.

Hannah swallowed hard. Surely this was the worst possible thing that could happen? Belle married to Rab and living in Wick, where Hannah would have to see them every day for the rest of her life. How was she going to bear it?

She glanced at Rab, at the heightened colour in his cheeks, the excitement and wild happiness, underlain by just a trace of boyish shame as he looked at her... Or was she imagining what she wanted to see? Hannah shook herself. *Don't be so silly*, she told herself fiercely. Of course she was imagining it. The man had always been in love with Belle and today must be his happiest day.

And her unhappiest.

She reached out and touched the beautiful carriage. Although its shining black glory was marred by the dust and mud of the road, it was a fine vehicle.

'It's wonderful, isn't it?' Rab asked, coming to stand beside her and she knew he was not only speaking of the carriage.

Hannah looked up at the man she loved and felt the tears begin to choke her throat. Belle would never make him happy. Could he not see?

But no. He could not. Belle had woven her spell and caught him in her web as surely as if she were a spider and he a little fly. Hannah's heart cracked wide open in sudden terrible pain. How could she live with what he had done?

Rab was waiting for her answer.

'It's a fine carriage,' she managed, and hurried into the house.

CHAPTER 36

Geordie sat by the fire congratulating himself. Everything was going to plan. The Alexanders had swallowed their story and he and Nancy were nicely settled here. He was sure that the baby, when it arrived, would seal their acceptance.

The ranch house presided over a prosperous and flourishing business. The fertile land produced good-quality wheat which was in great demand at good prices. Bill and Marie had no children of their own so surely, as Hughie arriving so providentially in their midst, he would inherit the property and a good living with it. Maybe not what he would have chosen for himself, Geordie thought, but it would do for the time being. All he had to do was play his part a bit longer – and make sure Nancy did.

They were sitting in the cosy front room after their supper. Warm and well fed, Geordie nevertheless was monitoring the conversation carefully in case Nancy made any slip. He was pleased to see she had the sense to encourage Marie's stories about the family rather than do much talking herself.

'That wagon,' she was saying. 'Out the back.'

'The old covered wagon?' Marie asked and Nancy nodded.

Safe enough topic, Geordie thought, and let himself relax with one ear open.

'Your uncle came out from Toronto in that,' Aunt Marie said. 'Coming west was hazardous. He got himself lost a couple of times and met a few bears – not to mention my parents!' She laughed, then added more seriously, 'But nowhere as bad as what you two have come through.'

Nancy murmured agreement and catching Geordie's eye, shivered. If Marie only knew…

'You had a rough time up there in the Klondike,' Marie was saying. 'You were right to come to us, though it has been a very long journey for you.'

She patted Nancy's hand encouragingly.

'At a time like this you need to be with your family and we are your nearest family, yes?'

'Yes,' Nancy said. 'My mother died when I was a baby.' Feeling Geordie's watchful eyes upon her, she faltered to a stop. But Marie did not take it amiss.

'Ah, *ma pauvre*, of course you do not like to speak of it. Well, I will just have to do as best I can as a substitute mother to you!'

Tears started in Nancy's eyes. The kindness of this good woman was almost more than she could bear.

'There is nothing to distress you here,' Marie tried to reassure her. 'You are safe with us. In any case, the good Lord brought you to us and He'll see you through the birth of the baby. Don't you worry.'

But this simply brought more tears. Geordie Sinclair's eyes narrowed as he watched. The girl was becoming a liability. The pregnancy was making her emotional and Marie's pious talk was feeding into her weakness. Any minute now she would blurt out the whole story and they would be out on their ears.

172

As Marie gently put a comforting arm round Nancy, suddenly it dawned on Geordie that it might be only him that would be thrown out if the Alexanders discovered the truth. Marie appeared to have taken a real liking to Nancy. And Nancy was carrying Hughie's baby – the only genuine link with these people. It was *his* position that was the shaky one and that would not do.

Marie was staring at him strangely, and he realised that she expected him to do something about Nancy's distress. He felt uncomfortable under her scrutiny, as if Marie Alexander could see through him.

He shook himself. What did it matter what she thought? She was only a woman and not even… His eyes ran over her face, taking in the evidence of her mixed-race parentage. Half-breed, he sneered. A mix of the native people and the French settlers. *Métis*, he had learnt it was called here.

Well, if it came to it, he could surely deal with any suspicions she might have. Women's fancies! Aye, that's what he would say.

CHAPTER 37

The wedding was lavish. As lavish as Belle could squeeze out of her parents and Robert's parents. The ceremony was held at the Pulteneytown Manse and then a wedding breakfast followed for all the relatives and friends that could be accommodated back at her parents' house in Wellington Street.

Belle, in what Hannah felt was pure malice, had insisted she be bridesmaid. That meant Hannah could not hide away but had a grandstand view of the ceremony and Belle's triumph.

Hannah had schooled her face to quiet unconcern as she watched Rab place the wedding ring on Belle's finger, but inside her stomach churned with the anguish she felt. At the celebration afterwards, she busied herself with helping elderly relatives and the very young – anything to occupy her mind and her heart.

She kept carefully away from her mother, the only one whose perceptive eyes would see through her façade. Belle's insistence on a big wedding ensured there were plenty of seldom-seen people to chat to and Hannah, being Hannah, was the one expected to deal with awkward guests and the inevitable spills and mishaps.

She was glad of it. By the end of the afternoon she was as exhausted physically as she was emotionally. But at last it was over and Rab led Belle out to his shiny new carriage to depart on their honeymoon.

But Belle paused on the step, her bridal bouquet in her hand, as she looked over the assembled crowd come out to wave them on their way. Some of the younger girls called out 'Me! Me!' wanting to catch her bouquet as she flung it, wanting to be the next to marry.

Belle looked straight at Hannah, a cruel smile twisting her mouth. Hannah stood her ground, her face calm, hands firmly by her sides. She had no intention of catching the flowers. But as she watched Belle taking careful aim, it was clear that there was no chance of the bouquet coming her way. Belle deliberately threw it to the other side of the crowd.

Holding Hannah's eyes, she laughed triumphantly, then still all smiles, she allowed Rab to help her into the carriage and away south on their honeymoon trip.

'Well, that's that,' a great-aunt at Hannah's side declared.

'Good luck to him,' another commented. 'He's going to need it.'

'Aye, she may be all smiles today but it won't last.'

The two old ladies nodded their heads wisely.

'Ah well, time to be getting home,' they agreed.

In a short while, Hannah thought, the house would be empty of guests and she could escape to her room – the room she had shared with Belle for most of her nineteen years, and retrieved now that Belle had married Rab. She sighed. It was likely to be her room, her only home, for the rest of her life. Her heart ached, but the pain was thankfully dulled by exhaustion. And the familiarity of her old hopeless love for the man who was now her sister's husband.

Hannah looked over at her parents. Her father was clearly proud and satisfied, if uncomfortable in his brand-new wedding suit. Belle was now off his hands. Job well done. She was Rab's problem now.

Hannah's mother, elegant in her navy dress by his side, glanced across and caught her eye, a question unspoken. Hannah nodded and kept her face impassive. She was doing fine. No one must know.

She had wondered... when Rab came over to say goodbye. There was something in his expression. She hoped it was not pity. She could not bear it if he knew of her hopeless devotion to him and felt sorry for her.

She took herself roundly to task. No one knew.

'Ah well,' one of the great-aunts was saying. 'Only the good Lord knows what the future holds for those two.'

The good Lord, Hannah thought. How could she have forgotten Him this day of all days? But she had been so caught up in her misery and her need to be in control of the picture she presented to the outside world (and especially to Belle, her honest heart confessed) that she had forgotten Him. Till now.

She had been taught to pray at her mother's knee – the Lord's Prayer, said by rote, with a loud 'Amen' at the end. As a child she had come confidingly to Jesus with her requests and hurts and prayers and as she grew and learned more of Him, she had drawn ever closer to Him. Now suddenly reminded of His constant understanding Presence, Hannah did not feel so alone. The good Lord knew everything so He knew what pain was in her heart. There was solace in knowing He was with her, even on this day of all terrible days. She reached out to Him in prayer.

You do know, don't You? Hannah said in silent prayer. *And You do care. I know You'll look after me...* And then in a sudden anguish of feeling, her heart cried out, *But look after him too! Don't let her hurt him! Don't let her destroy him! I love him so much!*

CHAPTER 38

Under Marie's kindly care, Nancy began to thrive.

'But shouldn't I be doing something?' she asked Marie. 'Can't I help? I'm not used to sitting around all day!'

'You need to rest,' Marie told her. 'I've got enough help. When the baby comes, you'll have plenty to do!' And Marie ladled another helping of her famous blueberry pie on to Nancy's plate. 'Eat up! You'll need your strength!'

Nancy sighed with pleasure. Never in her life had she received such care. She only wished they were not here under false pretences. Marie and Bill were such good people. Religious people. They would probably be shocked if they knew what she was and that she and Geordie were not who they said they were – not even man and wife.

'You let slip one word and we'll be thrown out,' Geordie had warned her just the other night when they were alone in their room. 'And if that happens, don't expect me to hang around! You'll end up having the child out in the wilds on your own and you know you don't want that.'

As she recalled his threat, Nancy shivered and Marie came hurrying over. 'Are you cold, my dear? Let me get you a warmer shawl.' And the dear woman fussed over Nancy as if she were her own beloved daughter.

Tears sprang to Nancy's eyes. She had never known her mother. One of the dance-hall girls in San Francisco, she had left her infant behind when she had taken off with some fancy man or other, and one of the other girls had brought her up. When Nancy was old enough, she took her place first in the chorus line, then in the arms of whoever would pay for the pleasure.

When gold was found in the Klondike, the troupe had decided to up sticks and go there to make their fortune, plying their trade to fund their passage on the luxurious steamship from Seattle to Dawson City. And it was there in Dawson City that Nancy's path had crossed with Geordie Sinclair's. It had been, she decided, the very worst thing that had ever happened to her. He had paid for her favours for a while, then he had put his plan to her. She was to seduce Hughie Mackay.

'He's an innocent,' Geordie had told her. 'He needs someone to show him a good time and you're the girl to do it. It's a kind of a birthday present.'

And she had believed him. It had been easy money since getting to know Hughie was a pleasure. Comparatively innocent, that was true, but that made him all the nicer to know. Geordie had simply watched and waited, and when she had told him she was pregnant, he had gloated with evil delight.

Nancy, remembering, stroked her swollen belly protectively. Whatever happened, she would not let Geordie hurt this child.

But he had already used the child to hurt two other people – Hughie and Belle, Hughie's girl in Scotland. Nancy looked at the Mizpah ring on the third finger of her left hand and turned it gently round and round. Hughie had come all the way from his home in Scotland to find the gold to make that ring – and he had sent it to Belle as a token of his love, his honest, good intent. And then Geordie had brought it all crashing down and Belle had sent the ring back to Hughie.

'How she would hate to know you're wearing it now!' Geordie had said with satisfaction. The thought clearly pleased him.

Had Geordie loved Belle? It seemed a nasty twisted kind of love if it made him happy to hurt her like this.

Nancy shivered again. She knew to her cost how Geordie liked to hurt people.

CHAPTER 39

Hannah measured out the milk from the big pitcher into the white enamel pail and returned to the doorway of the dairy in the cold of the early morning. The small queue of poor folk waiting for their share of yesterday's left-over milk had dispersed by now, leaving only one familiar face. A young lad. He stood there, wolfing down his bread and jam sandwich as if he had not seen food for days.

He grinned at her and wiped his hand across his mouth. 'Thank you, Missis,' he said. 'That was good.'

'You needed that,' Hannah said with a smile. 'Here's the milk for your mother. Go on, now, and I'll see you tomorrow.'

It was a sad state of affairs, she considered, that she looked forward to a visit from this scruffy lad with the bare feet – but she had grown fond of the boy and their brief conversations by the door. He was a bright lad who just needed a chance in life. She had taken to telling him about the Lord Jesus while he ate.

She turned to close the dairy and go back into the house, wondering what more she could do for the lad. Perhaps a word with her father when he came home for tea. But no. She would not get the chance. Because Belle would be there.

Belle had taken to swanning into the house each afternoon for tea, playing the grand lady, and showing off about her wonderful life with Rab to the distinct pleasure and approval of her father.

Hannah shook her head. No, she would not get a chance to discuss anything with her father. She would need to find another opportunity. If her father would be willing to give her the time or listen to her.

She became aware that the lad had not gone. She turned back to him.

'What is it?' she asked. 'Have you forgotten something?'

'No, Missis,' he said, then added, 'You told me yesterday "*All things work together for good to them that love God*".'

'Yes,' Hannah said. 'Romans chapter 8 verse 28.'

'Do you really believe it?' the boy asked.

'Yes,' Hannah began, then slowed.

The boy simply waited. Hannah looked at him. She could understand it would be hard to believe in his situation where life was so unrelentingly difficult. She sighed. And maybe, in its own way, just as hard in hers. But still she clung on to belief.

'Faith,' she told him, 'is about believing God is good and has everything in hand even when life is hard. Believing He can make things turn out well – even when we can't see any way ahead.'

'So no matter how bad things are now, it will turn out all right?' he asked.

'Yes,' Hannah said. 'That's it exactly.'

'Good,' the boy said. 'We need it.' Then he and the white pail of left-over milk were gone.

Hannah stood gazing after him in amazement. What was that about? Yes, they had often talked together about God. She had tried to teach the boy a little. Maybe he had been listening after all, not simply enduring her preaching for the sake of his jam sandwich!

But what was it he had been querying? Oh yes, that text about all things working together for good… 'No matter how bad things are now, it will turn out all right.' That's how he had paraphrased it. How strange – and appropriate. It was just what she needed to hear. Could it be a word from the Lord? It was so unexpected she had to laugh. A grubby boy with bare feet was an unlikely angel messenger.

But she walked into the house with her heart uplifted. It would be good to be sure of that but she could not see how it ever could be. She had given her heart to Rab Cormack many years ago and she wanted no other. But now he was Belle's husband and there was no good pining. She just had to get on and make the best of it.

And pray, the thought came. Yes, she could pray for him. Poor man, the last time she had seen him he looked like he needed it. And Belle? Surely she should pray for Belle too? It would be the truly Christian thing to do but Hannah was not sure she was Christian enough to do that yet. And each afternoon, it seemed to get further out of her reach as she sat listening to her sister.

'Oh, Robert insists I only have the best!' Belle trilled over and over. It was Robert this and Robert that and surely he was her devoted slave and could not do enough for her.

Hannah was sure Belle knew she was twisting the knife in her broken heart. So each day, she dressed carefully to take tea with her mother, her sister, and whoever else arrived to be an audience for Belle. She strove to pretend serene unconcern while her heart ached – and, she had to admit, her hands itched to slap her sister!

She shook herself out of her reverie and went indoors to help with the rest of the day's chores. Stay-at-home spinster sister she might be, but she would make sure she kept busy and had as little time as possible to think. No one would know her heart was past mending.

But that afternoon came the hardest trial of all as Belle's triumph reached its greatest height. Hannah thought for sure the ladies assembled in her mother's sitting room must hear the smashing of her already broken heart into tiny fragments.

'A baby,' Belle announced with a smug smile. 'Darling Robert is so pleased!'

Hannah sat numbly as the aunts and her mother cooed and fussed over Belle. A baby, Hannah thought. A child.

Belle looked over at Hannah, malicious satisfaction in her face.

'Just think!' she crowed. 'I'll be a mother.'

Hannah heard the spiteful unspoken message: 'And you won't.' She saw Belle waiting for her response, watching like a cat with its paw on a stricken mouse for any move… But Hannah was not going to play.

She breathed in carefully and sent up a rapid prayer for strength. When she was sure her emotions were under control, she said calmly, 'How lovely. I'll have another niece or nephew.'

She reached to pass round the plate of shortbread and let the conversation continue around her. Though she tried to banish Belle's news, the thought occurred to her: just what kind of mother would her sister be? It did not bode well for the child.

And suddenly a flame of anger lit inside Hannah. Surely Rab deserved better than this for his child? And how could she bear to stand on the sidelines and watch?

Hannah sighed. There was nothing, absolutely nothing, she could do about it.

CHAPTER 40

'That's a pretty thing,' Aunt Marie said, pointing at the ring Nancy was turning round and round on her finger.

They were sitting companionably together, working on some last-minute sewing in preparation for the arrival of Nancy's baby. Marie had declared it was time for a break and some of the coffee from the enamel pot that seemed a permanent fixture on the range.

In reply Nancy held her hand up to display the ring.

'Hughie had it made out of the first gold he found in the Klondike,' she said, and then bit her lip. Geordie had told her not to speak to Marie about what had happened before they arrived at the homestead, but it was so difficult. Marie was kind and interested, balm to Nancy's soul, and she liked to chat – and ask questions. Fending them off was becoming harder by the day. Marie was a bright intelligent woman and would not be put off for ever. Today was a case in point.

'Why, that's lovely,' Aunt Marie said. 'I never would have taken Hugh for a romantic...'

'Oh, he was,' Nancy began and stopped in sudden panic. Now she had given too much away. She had been thinking of Hughie, the *real* Hughie, not Geordie Sinclair, and Hughie was in the past, not the present.

'Was?' Marie had picked up on the word. 'Did something happen to change him?' She picked up Nancy's hand and examined the ring, tracing the word that was embossed across it. '*Mizpah*,' she said thoughtfully. 'That's a strange word to put on a wedding ring. It's more something for someone you knew you were going to be parted from.'

Nancy's hand flew to her mouth.

'How did you know?' she blurted, thinking of Belle far away in Scotland parted from Hughie. 'What does it mean? Where does it come from? Is it some Scottish thing?'

'No, it comes from the Bible,' Aunt Marie said.

She stood up and went across the hallway to her bedroom, returning with a large Bible with well-worn black covers. She sat down beside Nancy and thumbed through the pages.

'There,' she said. 'The Book of Genesis. This is the first time it's mentioned. Chapter 31 verse 49. It means "*The* LORD *watch between me and thee, when we are absent one from another.*"'

'Oh that's lovely,' Nancy said. 'I didn't know...'

She watched as Marie closed the well-worn pages of her Bible and stroked the cover with her hand.

'Was the ring originally meant for someone else?' Marie probed gently. 'Someone that let Hughie down?'

Nancy bit her lip. How much dared she tell? But she needed to say something, to explain this strange ring on her finger.

'Yes,' she began slowly. 'There was a girl back home...'

'And Hughie had the ring made for her?'

Nancy nodded, glad that Marie was making it so easy for her.

'But she wouldn't wait for him? Was that it?' Marie asked.

'Not exactly,' Nancy said, uncomfortable now. She did not want to lie to this lovely lady who had been so good to her. But what could she say that would not get her into trouble?

Marie was watching her from shrewd eyes. 'Ah, I think I see,' she said. 'Hughie met you...'

'That's right,' Nancy said gratefully. 'And she broke off the engagement. She sent the ring back.'

'What are you saying?' Geordie Sinclair had come silently into the house and now he stood on the threshold watching them, a black glower on his face.

Nancy looked up in dismay. How long had he been standing there? How much had he overheard?

'I didn't say anything...' she stammered.

'I heard you speaking,' he challenged her.

Nancy swallowed hard, the fear plain on her face.

'Just silly women's things,' she whispered. 'I didn't...'

'You'd better not. You've got to think of your health. It wouldn't be good for you to upset yourself.' He paused meaningfully, watching closely as she absorbed his meaning and the colour fled from her cheeks.

'I won't. I promise, Geord...' Nancy caught herself in time as his name threatened to spill from her lips. 'I promise.'

Geordie Sinclair turned on his heel and left, slamming the door behind him.

'What was that about?' Marie asked curiously. 'He doesn't like you talking about his fiancée?'

Nancy nodded miserably. It was clear that Geordie had heard some of what she had said and now probably thought the worst. She was afraid of the punishment he would mete out when he returned and they were alone.

189

'He must have loved her a great deal,' Marie murmured.

For a moment Nancy thought she would give way to hysterical laughter. Geordie love anybody? Other than himself? That was impossible.

CHAPTER 41

'And what time do you think this is?' Belle exploded in fury. 'I'm fed up with staying here on my own...'

Rab Cormack gazed wearily at his young wife. Even in a rage, she was still beautiful, though her body was thickening with the pregnancy that she so hated. One more thing to blame him for. He sighed. According to Belle, everything was his fault.

But he had tried, his tired mind protested. He had tried his best to make her happy, working hard to bring home more money so she could indulge her desire for new clothes, new furniture, new everything for the baby. But working harder meant working longer hours and that did not please her. She complained about being left alone in the house. So he encouraged her to go to her mother's, to spend time with her friends.

'I haven't got any friends!' she had screamed at him.

He had gaped at her then. He had always assumed she was at the centre of a wide circle of adoring female friends.

'Don't be stupid,' she had told him. 'The other girls have always been jealous.'

He had accepted her word. He could understand that lesser mortals would feel inferior to someone like Belle.

'You're not happy,' his mother confronted him bluntly the other day when he popped round briefly to see her – all that he was allowed now.

And he had to admit that was true, but the worst of it was that Belle was not happy either and he had no idea what to do to make her happy. Nothing seemed to please her. He had tried bringing her gifts but too often she would fling them in his face. He offered outings in his fine new carriage but she hated her pregnant body and refused to leave the house in the daytime when people could see her.

So he had gone round to his mother's and asked for help.

'What am I doing wrong?' he had pleaded. 'Why can't I make Belle happy? I love her. I adore her. I'd do anything...'

And his mother had simply stated, 'You're not happy.'

But he had waved it away. It did not matter. *He* did not matter. Belle, only Belle, mattered.

His mother threw her hands up in defeat. 'Ah well, my son,' she said. 'You made your bed and now you'll have to lie in it.'

So he gritted his teeth and went home, learning to duck when Belle sent something sailing in his direction. He learned to keep his tongue between his teeth and remain silent when her anger spilled out into bitter words.

And he learned to cherish the rare occasions when she smiled and was his Belle again. It was the pregnancy, he decided. Women often got funny with women's things. When the baby was born, Belle would once again be the warm, loving girl who had turned to him in Edinburgh.

He treasured that memory. Belle's father had told him there might be a better chance for him so, with high hopes, he had found a reason to get himself down to Edinburgh. And yes, he was received with glad welcome.

He had to admit he had been surprised at how generous Belle had been with her favours, but he had always intended to marry her so it was only anticipation, not real sin, he told himself. She had been very welcoming, he remembered with a shamefaced smile.

It had been a long time since she had been so welcoming, he thought sadly. The pregnancy, he reminded himself. He could hardly expect...

They had returned to Wick engaged. The marriage had taken place soon afterwards. And Belle found herself pregnant soon after that.

Was that when things started to go wrong, Rab wondered. Well, it would all sort itself out, he told himself. He loved her and he had enough love for both of them. He would just keep on honouring his side of the bargain. He would be a good husband to Belle.

CHAPTER 42

'I cannot like it, *mon cher*,' Marie told Bill in the privacy of their room that night. 'The girl, she is afraid of him.'

'He has a hasty temper, that's true,' Bill agreed slowly. 'But surely...'

A short cry came from the room next door. Bill and Marie silenced and listened. They heard a soft thump and a smothered noise. Another. And another.

'I do not like it,' Marie said. 'Will you not go to the door and listen, make sure it's all right?'

Bill held his hand up. 'Hush,' he told her. 'You worry too much. They are young and...'

'And Nancy is very pregnant,' Marie told him crisply. 'No, I do not think this is love that we are hearing.'

She got up from the bed and crept on silent feet to the adjoining wall, putting her ear to where the split logs were joined.

'Ah, I cannot hear,' she complained. But a louder cry came from the next room, a cry that was clearly Nancy in pain.

'I have it!' Marie cried and pulled on her warm dressing-gown and slippers. She gestured to her husband to follow her. Loudly crying 'Nancy! Nancy!' she hurried into the hallway and knocked at the next-room door.

'Nancy!' she called. 'Is the baby coming?' She pulled open the door, making sure Bill was behind her.

Nancy was cowering on the bed. Her face was reddened from the blows she had received. Tears streamed down her cheeks and she was rocking herself to and fro and gasping in pain.

'Nancy!' Marie cried in concern. 'My dear! Let me see to you!' She turned to her husband. 'Get that one out of here,' she said, gesturing to the man who had staggered away from the bed, his face a furious mask.

'This is no place for menfolk,' Marie announced and swiftly shut the door on them, then turned to take Nancy in her arms. 'Oh my dear, whatever has happened?'

Nancy gasped as another wave of pain shot through her.

'He was angry,' she panted. 'He thought I'd told you... too much. Always when I do something wrong...' Nancy looked away, shamefaced. 'He says I'm useless.'

Marie held her close and stroked her hair. 'Oh, my dear,' she soothed. 'So he beats you, yes?'

Nancy nodded. 'Yes.'

'And today?' Marie probed. 'What was it about?'

'Today – when you asked about the ring.' Nancy held up her hand to display the Mizpah ring. 'He heard some of what I said and he thought...'

'What did he think?'

'He thought I'd told you the truth,' Nancy said hopelessly. Before Marie could interrupt, another pain hit and Nancy gasped and writhed in Marie's arms. 'He started hitting me and I couldn't make him stop. I tried to tell him the pains had started but he wouldn't listen. He just kept hitting me. He pushed my face in the pillow so I couldn't cry out – but then the pains started coming faster...' She gasped again.

Marie gently extricated herself from Nancy's tight grip. 'We must get you into bed. My cousin is a healer. I'll send for her and we'll get you through this. No more talking for the moment. You can tell me all after the baby is born. But for now you will need all your strength for delivering your child.'

Nancy nodded wordlessly and allowed Marie to get her into bed. But when Marie made to leave the room, Nancy in a panic held on to her hand.

'Don't leave me! He'll kill me, like he did Hughie. Please don't leave me!'

Marie's eyes narrowed but now was not the moment to ask questions. 'I won't leave you,' she soothed the girl. 'I'm just going to the door to get some help. Watch me...'

She went steadily to the door and opened it a chink so she could peer outside.

'Bill!' she called and when he came, she whispered quickly to him, 'There is more here than we realise. I think that man is not your nephew Hugh and he is dangerous. It would be better if he slept in the bunkhouse with the men tonight. Warn Albert and the men to keep an eye on him.'

Bill whistled through his teeth but nodded.

'And I'll need you to fetch Lisette with towels and hot water – the baby is coming. She will know what to bring. And would you please send for my cousin Christine? We may need her. The girl is very weak already.'

As the night wore on it became obvious that the women needed all their prayers as well as Christine's expertise and experience. But at

197

last, well into the next day, the feeble cry of a baby told of a successful delivery.

'You have a son,' Marie told Nancy. 'What will you name him?'

'Hugh,' Nancy whispered. 'He should be called Hugh after his father.'

CHAPTER 43

When the baby came, Rab realised, as he paced up and down, just how much he had pinned his hopes on this event. When the baby came, Belle would love him again. When the baby came, they would be a happy family. When the baby came, everything would be all right.

Oh, let it be, he had prayed fervently. Over the weeks his silent prayers had become more and more anguished and now he felt helpless indeed. *Dear Lord, please let it be all right,* he pleaded. Why did the getting there have to be harder than he could ever have imagined?

The pregnancy had not been straightforward. Belle had been horribly sick from the start and that had made her temper even worse than before. She blamed him for her sickness. When she developed cravings for strange foods, he searched high and low to procure them for her. He would have gone up and brought down the moon itself if it would have made her happy. But it seemed that nothing he could do was right.

His mother had assured him that it took some women like that. *Her* mother and sister said nothing. They seemed unsurprised. Not that he had much opportunity for conversation with them. Belle had made it plain from the start of their marriage that he was not to visit them without her.

'You're not a single man any more,' she had told him. 'And they're *my* family, so you should only visit them when I do.'

So that is what he had done. What Belle wanted. As always.

He paced and worried. Because now she was suffering unimaginable agonies to bring forth his child. So yes, it was all his fault.

At first she had howled with the pain and thrown whatever was within reach. Then she had sent him for her mother.

'Not Hannah,' she had instructed. 'I don't want her here.'

But Hannah had come too. Mrs Reid had insisted she needed her.

'I told him she was not to come!' Belle had yelled at her mother but then another contraction had distracted her. Rab was hurried away downstairs with Hannah to make a cup of tea for him. Shortly afterwards, Mrs McBeath the midwife had looked in.

'How is she?' Rab had asked anxiously.

'She's doing fine,' Mrs McBeath had reassured him. 'These things take time – and often sound a lot worse than they are!'

It certainly sounded bad enough to Rab but Mrs McBeath had chuckled cheerfully and gone on her way.

'It'll be a while yet,' she said. 'I'll be back later.'

And Rab had to be satisfied with that. His every request to be allowed to comfort Belle was denied so he continued to sit by the range or pace the kitchen floor, his ears tuned to the noises upstairs, flinching at every cry, imagining what Belle was going through. Hannah came downstairs from time to time to check that he was eating. There was a cup of cold tea on the table and a plate of sandwiches she had made – but he had no appetite for either. Till this was over. He kept pacing. Somehow keeping moving helped.

Up in the bedroom, Hannah and her mother exchanged glances. The long labour was taking its toll and Belle's outraged screams had given way to exhaustion.

'I think we need Mrs McBeath to come back,' Mrs Reid said. 'Hannah, will you go and see if you can find her.'

Hannah slipped from the bedroom only to be confronted by Rab at the foot of the stairs.

'Where are you going?' he asked, seeing her pull on her coat and hat.

'Sshh!' she admonished him with a wary look upstairs.

'What's going on?' he demanded.

'It's taking a long time and Mum thinks Mrs McBeath should be here, so I'm going to fetch her.'

'I'll go,' Rab said, grabbing his coat from the chair. 'It will give me something to do.'

Hannah looked at him with pitying eyes. 'Go on then,' she told him and watched him hurry out of the back door.

She went back up to the bedroom. 'Rab said he'd go,' she said quietly to her mother.

'Go where?' Belle's voice was exhausted but still determined.

Hannah and her mother exchanged glances. If Belle knew they had sent for Mrs McBeath, she might realise how worried they were. If she didn't already.

'Tell me!' The command, though whispered, carried the full force of Belle's personality.

'He's gone to fetch Mrs McBeath,' her mother said. 'Belle, this is going on too long. You're tired and the babe...'

'Damn the babe,' Belle replied bitterly. 'The sooner I'm rid of it the better. So the sooner Mrs McBeath gets here the better.' She slumped back on to the bed.

Brisk footsteps on the stairs told them Mrs McBeath had returned. She came bustling into the bedroom.

'Now then,' she said cheerfully. 'How are things here?'

She threw her coat off and began to roll up her sleeves. Swift examination was followed by a whispered consultation between the two older women.

'Right, Belle,' Mrs McBeath. 'We need to be giving you a bit of help.'

'About time,' Belle got out between gritted teeth.

Hannah, watching from the sidelines, saw her mother's anxiety as Mrs McBeath set herself to assist Belle in delivering the child. She caught fragments of the murmured conversation between her mother and the midwife. 'The baby ... in difficulties ... the cord around his neck...'

'Scissors!' An urgent demand.

Quickly she offered them.

Finally, the cry of a child. Weak but living.

And then Rab banging at the bedroom door fit to break it down.

'It's a boy,' Mrs Reid told him. She looked over her shoulder at Mrs McBeath who gave her a swift shake of the head. 'We'll tell you when you can come up.' And she closed the door in his face.

She turned back into the room and went to join Mrs McBeath who was bent over Belle.

'Hannah, bring the infant,' Mrs McBeath instructed. 'Give him to Belle.' She tried to pull Belle up into a sitting position but Belle was a dead weight resisting her. 'Belle,' she said sharply, 'you need to hold your baby, try to feed him. It will help.'

But Belle looked at the red-faced infant with disgust. 'Take him away,' she ground out. 'I don't want him.'

'Belle,' the midwife said warningly.

'Belle, be a good girl and do what Mrs McBeath tells you,' her mother said. But Belle just turned her face into the pillows.

Hannah watched Mrs McBeath lead her mother away from the bed.

'We've got a problem,' she murmured.

Again Hannah could only catch snatches of the words: 'placenta … only part … You need to be prepared...'

Her mother gasped and bit hard on her lip, her face shocked and afraid.

'We can try...' Mrs McBeath was saying and led the way back to the bed where she leaned over Belle, and began to gently palpate her belly. Her mother grasped Belle's hand and stroked her hair, then stepped back in sudden horror as blood began to run from the bed, narrowly missing her feet.

'Quick, get the doctor!' Mrs McBeath instructed. 'Hannah...'

'Doctor?' Belle's voice was shrill and weak. 'What's the matter? Tell me!'

The two older women exchanged glances.

'Tell me!'

'You're bleeding, Belle. Heavily. The placenta hasn't come out completely and the bleeding...'

'Say it,' Belle commanded in a weak voice. 'The bleeding?'

'If we can't get it to stop...' Mrs McBeath began. 'We need to get the doctor. Hannah, you go, and bring him back as fast as you can!'

'No,' Belle said, her eyes fixed on Hannah. 'Mother, you go. And send Rab up here quickly. Mrs MacBeath, I want a minute with Hannah first, then send Rab in.'

The two older women looked uncertain.

'Go!' Belle said, her voice rising alarmingly.

The two older women left the room, looking back with worried faces as Hannah approached the bed.

Belle waited till the door closed behind them, then, her white face fixed in a mask of spite, she hissed, 'I'm not done yet!'

'Belle!' Hannah protested.

'Belle this, Belle that,' the girl in the bed mimicked in her thin weak voice. 'What do you know about anything?' She rallied her strength and pointed at the child in the crib in the corner. 'My baby,' she said, but there was a hard mocking tinge to her voice. 'And Robert's. I gave him a child. There, that hurts you, doesn't it?'

Hannah kept her face still.

'Robert's child,' Belle repeated triumphantly. 'Well, at least he thinks it's his.'

Hannah gasped.

Belle was watching her, her gaze mocking. 'You see? You know nothing.' She took a deep breath and licked dry lips. 'Why do you think I was in such a hurry to marry him?'

'But why?' Hannah whispered.

'Adam Finlayson had had his fun and threw me over. He was going to marry that Elphinstone chit. I wasn't good enough for him to marry!' Belle hissed the words out and moved restlessly in the bed. 'Then Robert turned up. Providential,' she mocked. 'I was beginning to worry I might be pregnant so I just had to make sure… Robert will never know now whose child it is.'

Hannah's eyes opened wide as she took in the implications. She remembered Rab's shamefaced happiness when he and Belle returned from Edinburgh to announce their engagement and the marriage that followed so quickly. So Belle had made sure…

'So whose baby is it?' Hannah demanded. 'Adam Finlayson's or Rab's?'

'I don't know,' Belle whispered defiantly. 'And I don't care.'

'Oh poor Rab,' Hannah breathed.

'Poor Rab!' Belle struggled for words. 'It will be poor Rab! I shall make him promise that if I die he is never to marry again.' Her eyes lit with unholy delight. 'So you'll never have him! He'll do anything I say. I promise: you'll never have him!'

'Belle?'

It was Rab, standing at the door. He stumbled to the bed and gathered Belle up in his arms. Hannah watched in horror as the red blood suddenly poured like a torrent on to the floor.

'Go… away,' Belle whispered.

'Please, Hannah,' Rab begged.

Numbly, she walked to the door and closed it behind her. Like a sleepwalker she made her way slowly down the stairs. And etched on her mind was the picture of Rab holding Belle so tenderly in his arms. Belle casting one last glance over his shoulder at her. One glance so filled with malice.

And yes, Rab would promise. Rab would promise Belle anything.

CHAPTER 44

'Please,' Nancy begged. 'I must tell you.'

She gripped Marie's hand and tried to pull herself up on the pillows.

'I must tell you,' she said urgently. 'Before Geordie comes back. You need to know…'

She glanced over at the woman who had helped with her delivery.

'Thank you. Thank you for all you've done to help me… but…' Nancy turned to Marie. 'Can we be alone?'

Marie nodded and turned to Christine, gently requesting her to leave them for a few moments. When she had gone, Marie returned to Nancy's side and sat down beside the bed. She took her hand in hers.

'Now you can tell me everything,' she encouraged Nancy.

'You'll be… angry,' Nancy said miserably. 'Disgusted with me and angry. But it is time. You need to know.'

'Let me decide, *ma chère*,' Marie told her gently. 'You say what you have to say. I am listening.'

'My name *is* Nancy,' the girl began. 'But I'm not Nancy Mackay. Hughie and I were never married.' She watched Marie's face for the rejection she expected, but Marie simply nodded.

'Go on,' she said.

'You're not…'

'Not surprised,' Marie said quietly. 'We thought maybe that was the case.' She shrugged gracefully. '*Chérie*, it would not be the first time.' She patted Nancy's hand.

'But there's much worse,' Nancy said. 'I was working at the dance hall in Dawson City. My mother was a dancer before me and that's all I know. All I know of her and life.' She cast a quick glance at Marie, searching her eyes for understanding. 'Dancing and…' Her voice dropped. 'With the men,' Nancy whispered and swallowed hard in shame.

'But yes,' Marie said. 'I understand about these things.'

'That's how I met Hughie,' Nancy said.

'Yes,' was all Marie said.

Nancy continued, 'Hughie had come to Dawson City with Geordie, Geordie Sinclair. It was Geordie who first made friends with me.' She shivered. 'He is a bad man. He wanted to cause trouble between Hughie and his fiancée Belle back in Scotland so he told me to be friends with Hughie…' Again her eyes searched Marie's face. 'To lead him on, yes?'

'Yes.' Marie nodded her understanding.

'He was a nice boy. He was really quite innocent. I did what Geordie said I must do. I led him astray.' Nancy paused, looking back into the past. 'But then I got pregnant.' Her eyes flew to Marie's face. 'I didn't know what to do. That wasn't part of the plan… so I went to Geordie and told him and he… laughed.' Nancy shivered again. 'He said that would do just fine and I wasn't to worry Hughie about it for the time being. And I wasn't to worry myself either. It would all be taken care of.' Nancy's eyes searched Marie's face. 'I believed him. I trusted him. I thought he meant the baby... I know the other girls... There are herbs...'

Marie patted Nancy's hand. 'What happened then?'

The tears pooled in Nancy's eyes. 'One day Hughie came to the dance hall in a fury. He'd had a letter from his fiancée – Belle – breaking off their engagement and sending back the ring.' Sadly she lifted her hand and twisted the Mizpah ring round on her finger.

'Ah, I see,' Marie said quietly.

'Hughie thought I'd told Belle. But I hadn't!' Nancy cried. 'I wouldn't have done such a thing.' Tears began to slip down her face. 'He was very angry with me. He made me tell him... I told him that I had told Geordie. And he went after Geordie.'

Again Nancy slipped into memory, eyes unseeing. 'It was a terrible afternoon of driving snow. It wasn't fit to go out in. But he went. And a little later Geordie turned up at the dance hall. He pretended he hadn't seen Hughie but I knew. In my heart I knew. He stayed till the storm blew itself out – a couple of days – then he went back to the cabin they shared, saying he was sure he'd find Hughie there safe and sound. But I knew. I knew something dreadful had happened.'

Marie patted the girl's hand again to try to calm her. Hectic colour had bloomed in her cheeks and her eyes were bright with a kind of fever.

'I knew something terrible had happened!' she whispered. 'And then a couple of the old-timers turned up with their hand-wagon.' Her voice dropped even lower. 'With Hughie's body on it.'

'Oh my dear!' Marie exclaimed.

'They came into the dance hall and they told everyone. They said they'd seen Hughie turn up at the workings and Geordie come out to him. How Hughie and Geordie had fought and how Geordie had hit

209

Hughie with a shovel, then left him in the snow. Left him to die.' She swallowed hard again, her voice weakening. 'They went out and got him. But he was already dead. Geordie had killed him.'

There was silence in the room as Marie took in what Nancy had said.

'And then?' Marie asked.

'The men decided to sort Geordie out, but...' Nancy sighed. 'I went to warn him.' Her eyes appealed to Marie for understanding. 'I felt someone should. Everybody liked Hughie! But they were a lynch-mob. There shouldn't be another death!'

Marie nodded.

'So I went to the cabin. And when they arrived, Geordie pulled a gun and said he'd kill me if they didn't let us go. So they did. They fetched a sled, sent to the dance hall so one of the girls could pack some clothes for me. Geordie hitched his mule to the sled. And then they escorted us out of town.'

She looked up at Marie out of hopeless eyes. 'Geordie had remembered Hughie talking about his relatives who had a ranch – so he thought if we came here...'

'He could pass the pair of you off as Hughie and his wife.'

Nancy nodded sadly.

'And then what?' Marie asked softly. 'What was the plan after the baby was born?'

'I think he planned to stay here,' Nancy said. 'You don't have any children so he thought...'

'He thought he would have the ranch?' Marie asked.

'Yes.'

'After our time?' Marie asked. 'Or was he planning on hurrying us up a little?'

Nancy gasped in horror. 'I don't know! He never said! I swear it!'

Marie calmed the frightened girl. 'I believe you. Now I think you should get some sleep and I need to talk with my husband. Am I right in thinking you don't want to see Geordie?'

Nancy shook her head vigorously. 'No! Please!'

'I'm sure I can think of an excuse,' Marie said. She tucked the covers up around Nancy's thin shoulders. 'Sleep now and build up your strength. Don't you worry about anything.'

But she paused in the doorway, looking back. 'Tell me, Nancy, as far as you know, does Geordie still have his gun?'

CHAPTER 45

'What am I supposed to do with a baby?' Rab Cormack railed at his mother. 'And why won't it stop crying? I can't stand the noise. I'm going out!'

He flung out of the house, slamming the kitchen door behind him, and nearly ran into Hannah who was on her way to visit. She took a quick step back.

'And what are you doing here?' he demanded with a glower.

Hannah clenched her hands in her pockets to stop herself reaching out to him. How she wanted to comfort him, but she knew she could not. Must not. He was hurting so much he would lash out at anyone.

'Visiting your mother,' Hannah said briskly and stepped round him and into the house.

'Whew!' she said with a grin as she closed the door behind her.

Mrs Cormack smiled wryly. 'Hullo, Hannah. It's good to see you. I could use a cheery face today!' She sighed. 'He's taking it hard,' she continued. 'And now he's fretting about the baby.'

'Is that so?' Hannah said. 'That's a good thing surely – that he's taking an interest in the child?'

'Taking an interest!' Mrs Cormack echoed as she lifted the kettle off the range and filled the teapot. She waved Hannah to a seat by the table and set teapot and cups and saucers close to hand. Milk jug and sugar bowl followed and a plate of shortbread. She pulled out a chair and sat down with a heavy sigh.

'I wouldn't call it "taking an interest",' Mrs Cormack said. 'He doesn't seem to know what to do. The girl we got in to help was no use at all. I'm doing my best but I'm too old to look after a baby at my age. Worse, the wee one's constant crying is driving him mad.'

Mrs Cormack poured the tea and handed a cup to Hannah. She set her own cup down with a thump. 'And it's time he went back to his own house. Laid those ghosts.'

Hannah sipped her tea and listened quietly. Upstairs the crying began again.

'Oh poor wee thing,' Hannah said. 'Has he not given the child a name yet?'

Mrs Cormack shook her head. 'He just went to pieces when Belle died. It's almost as if he's blaming the baby...'

'That's not right,' Hannah said forcefully. 'And surely it's time the child was christened.'

'I know that!' Mrs Cormack declared. 'But try telling him! He won't listen.' She sighed again, heavily. 'If we're to get the child christened, it'll need a name.' She stopped suddenly. 'Will you listen to me! I'm calling it...'

'It,' Hannah supplied. 'Yes. That won't do.' She paused. 'That child needs a name or it – *he* – will never be a real person to its father... his father.' She finished off her cup of tea and set the cup down. 'He should be called after his father. Robert.'

'That was his father's name too,' Mrs Cormack said.

The two women exchanged complicit glances.

'Then that's his name,' Hannah said. 'Robert. And we'll call him… Bobby?'

'That would do nicely,' Mrs Cormack said.

The crying upstairs rose to a crescendo.

Mrs Cormack began to raise herself wearily to her feet. 'I'd better go and see to him,' she said with a loud sigh but Hannah forestalled her.

'No, no,' she said. 'I'm here now. You sit and have your tea. I'll go up and see what's the matter with Bobby.' She said the name with a grin.

Mrs Cormack subsided gratefully into her chair and reached for a piece of shortbread. Hannah gave her a quick smile and headed for the stairs.

In the little back bedroom, the infant was yelling his outrage at the world, red in the face and kicking strongly at the blanket over him.

'Now, now,' Hannah said soothingly. 'This will never do.' She leaned over the cot and picked the baby up, checking whether his nappy needed to be changed. 'Ah, I see,' she said. 'Well, Bobby, my wee man, let's get you clean and fresh first, then you'll be a lot happier.'

As one of five girls in her family, she had received plenty of practice helping with her older sister's babies so it took Hannah no time to get Bobby changed. Wrapping him in a lacy shawl, she brought him downstairs and settled herself back in her chair by the table, holding Bobby comfortably in one arm while she accepted another cup of tea from his grandmother.

The two women were deep in conversation when the back door opened and Rab Cormack returned. He stopped in the doorway, head cocked, listening. He gave a loud sigh of relief.

'Peace!' he said. 'At last!'

Then as he came into the kitchen, his eyes alighted on the baby in Hannah's arms.

'Shh!' she said, putting a finger to her lips. 'Bobby's asleep. Don't wake him.' She rocked the baby gently.

Rab took a few steps closer, peering to see the sleeping infant. For a moment his face softened, then the scowl returned.

'Good,' he said. 'Well, if you can manage him, you can have him. I don't ever want to see him again.'

CHAPTER 46

Bill could smell the drink on the man the moment he walked into the bunkhouse. The other men were giving Geordie a wide berth so he was sitting on his own, hunched on a stool by the fire. As Bill came into the room, flanked by Lou and Albert, the other men made themselves scarce.

'Well? Has she had it yet?' It was said contemptuously in a drink-slurred voice.

Bill strolled peacefully towards the fire, stretching out his hands as if to warm them. Lou and Albert placed themselves at the door, their stance watchful readiness.

Bill turned to the man hunkered down on the stool.

'Mother and baby are doing fine,' he said quietly.

'Well, good for them.' The man took a long swallow from the bottle in his hand.

'Yes,' Bill said. 'Don't you want to see them? Your wife and child?'

The man laughed.

'It's the usual thing,' Bill told him.

'Is it?' came the sour reply. The man staggered drunkenly to his feet, lurching unsteadily. 'In that case, I'd better do it.

Don't want anybody thinking...' Here he wobbled to a stop and looked at Bill out of befuddled eyes. 'What didn't I want people thinking?'

'I wouldn't know, Geordie,' Bill said quietly.

'No, you wouldn't,' Geordie replied, a crafty gleam in the whiskey-reddened eyes. But then they sharpened suddenly. 'Wait a minute. What did you call me?'

'Your name,' Bill said.

'Thass right. My name.' He swayed, obviously struggling to think about it. 'But how did you know my name?' The words came out slow and menacing. Then his voice rose to a shout: 'The girl! *She* told you! No one else knew!'

He lurched towards the door. Lou and Albert moved so they were side by side, blocking the exit to the bunkhouse. Their hands went to the guns on their hips.

'I'll kill her.' Geordie spat the words.

'Like you did Hughie... my nephew,' Bill said, still standing quietly by the fire.

Geordie swung round to face him.

'What did you say?' he demanded.

'You said you'd kill Nancy. Then that would be two people you've killed – murdered.' Bill let the word drop heavily into the tense atmosphere of the room. 'You killed Hughie – my nephew – back in the Klondike. Didn't you...' He paused, then said the name with quiet deliberation. 'Geordie.'

'I didn't mean to!' Geordie protested. 'It was an accident! We had a fight...'

'You left him in the snow,' Bill said. 'You knew he was injured. You left him to die...'

'I... I...' The words staggered to a stop.

'Yes,' Bill said. 'I – you were thinking only of yourself. And so Hughie died. And then you took Nancy hostage and thought you could pass yourself off as Hughie...'

Geordie Sinclair looked wildly around him. The other ranch-hands ringed the walls and filled the doorways. At the main exit to the bunkhouse, Lou and Albert stood, hands resting on their guns. Bill waited by the fireplace.

'What are you going to do about it?' Geordie demanded. 'You seem to have all the cards!'

'We're going to let you go,' Bill said. 'You don't belong here. In the morning when it's light, we'll put you on your horse and give you enough provisions to take you away from here.'

Surprise lightened Geordie's face, then his eyes narrowed craftily. 'And the girl?'

'The girl stays here,' Bill told him. 'With the baby. Hughie's baby. He will need his mother. They stay. You go. Alone.'

Sobering quickly, Geordie tried bargaining. 'She won't need the buggy then.'

'Quit while you're ahead,' one of the hands rumbled.

Geordie flung him a venomous glance.

'Good advice,' Bill said. 'I'm going back to the house. Lou and Albert will keep you company here till the morning. I suggest you get some sleep. Then we'll help you pack and see you on your way.'

Geordie looked round at the hostile faces, at Lou and Albert positioned to guard the exit as Bill left without a backward glance. He shrugged and took himself back to the stool by the fire. Feigning nonchalance, his mind struggled to work its way through this unwelcome turn of events.

He was out on his ear. On his own. Now what was he going to do?

CHAPTER 47

'Couldn't Rab's mother do that?' Hannah's mother declared in exasperation. 'You've got your hands full with wee Bobby on top of your other chores.'

Hannah wiped her arm over her forehead to brush the sweat out of her eyes and applied herself again to the heavy sheet she was feeding through the mangle in the wash-house.

'His mother's got her hands full with his dad,' Hannah reminded her. 'That stroke hit him hard and he needs looked after every minute of the day. She's got no time or energy for more work. And anyway...'

And anyway, Hannah thought, *it's something I can do for him.* But she could not share that thought with her mother and watch the inevitable pity in her eyes. She swallowed down the hopelessness.

As the days and weeks had passed after Belle's death, she had watched the man she loved grow thin and grey, and she knew there was no way she could reach him. He had rejected the infant so Hannah had brought the child home, and now wee Bobby was thriving.

But it was Rab Hannah worried about. He had thrown himself into his work and there never seemed to be a chance to speak to him. Except perhaps on a Sunday when he attended the same church as she and her parents did. So Hannah bided her time, waiting for him to leave church and then accosted him as he turned towards his parents' house.

'I want a word with you,' she said, planting herself squarely in his path.

He had looked at her in surprise. Everyone else had left him to his misery.

'This won't do,' she told him. 'Look at you!'

He looked. His clothes looked like they had been thrown on, the shirt in need of a wash. He ran a hand over his whiskers, momentarily shamefaced. Then memory returned and with it anger.

'None of your business,' he snapped and took a step towards her as if to push past. But Hannah stood her ground.

'It is,' she said. 'Somebody has to tell you and it seems I'm the only one who will do it. I'm looking after your son...' He began to protest but Hannah put her hand up to silence him. 'Yes, I know. You don't want ever to see him. Well, you needn't but you're still his father and legally responsible for him. He's needing clothes and things...'

At this Rab's eyes sharpened into focus on her.

'Baby things,' he growled. 'There's plenty in the house.' He thought a moment. 'No. I won't bring them. I don't want to see him. You can come and get them.'

'Now?' Hannah asked.

'Why not?' Rab said mockingly. 'It's as good a time as any.'

And they walked back in silence to Rab's house. He pushed open the kitchen door and pointed to the stairs. 'Up there,' he said. 'In the back bedroom. You'll find whatever you need. Help yourself.'

Gracelessly he threw himself into a chair by the kitchen table. 'And hurry up. My mother's expecting me for my Sunday lunch.'

One glance at the state of the kitchen told Hannah all she needed to know. Rab had let himself and his home go. The place was filthy as well as untidy. She took a deep breath and headed up the stairs. As she passed the open door to the front bedroom, she saw matching mess. The whole place reeked of neglect.

The back bedroom, however, was tidy. It had been set out for the arrival of the baby and Hannah soon found what she needed in the chest of drawers beside the brand-new, unused cot. Belle as usual had spent lavishly and there were more than enough garments and nappies and powders and creams for wee Bobby now and for a while to come.

Hannah bundled together a selection of things and came slowly downstairs.

'I'll need something to carry this lot in,' she told Rab.

He jerked his head towards the back door. 'There's baskets and stuff through there.'

Hannah cleared a space on the table and set her bundle down, then went across to the cupboard beside the back door and selected a wicker basket. As she packed the things into it, she said conversationally, 'Not doing well, are you?'

'What do you mean?' Rab snapped. 'How do you expect me to...'

'I know, I know,' Hannah said peaceably. She continued folding items into the basket. 'I was just thinking...' He did not react so she continued, 'You could do with a bit of help in the house.'

'I'm not having some nosy stranger poking around in my house,' Rab said.

'Fair enough,' Hannah said matter-of-factly. 'I just thought maybe I could pop in and give it a bit of a once-over from time to time. Keep it from getting too bad.' She waved her hand round at the mess.

'Then I could pick up what the baby needs… I can't carry it all with me today. That cot…'

Rab pulled himself to his feet and went over to the dresser. He opened a drawer and rummaged in it. When he came back to the table, he flung a key down in front of Hannah.

'Do what you like,' he said. 'I don't care. Here's the key. You can let yourself in. Just don't bother me.'

Hannah nodded and calmly finished packing the baby things into the basket, but her heart glowed. She felt she had won a major victory. And so it became her habit to pop in when Rab was at work to give the house a swift clean and tidy. From time to time, she would leave a pot of stew or a homemade pie on the table for him to find when he got back from work. Seeing laundry piling up on the bedroom floor, she took the clothes home and brought them back, washed and pressed. Emboldened, she stripped the bed and made it up with fresh sheets.

Little by little, she became familiar with the house and the ways of the man who lived there, and she made sure that he was comfortable and well looked after.

Her arms ached as she turned the handle on the heavy rollers of the mangle. She had become Rab's invisible helper. They seldom encountered one another, and then the only sign he gave that he was aware of her was a grunt.

But Hannah took a deep pleasure from caring for him – from being allowed to care for him. If it was the only way she was ever to be allowed to express her love – caring for him and his son – then so be it. It gave her joy.

CHAPTER 48

Nancy struggled up to a sitting position in the big bed.

'You're just going to let him go?' she cried. 'But what about me? I won't be safe! Last time…'

Marie Alexander patted her hand. 'Not this time,' she soothed the girl. 'You're perfectly safe. Bill has left two of his men on guard in the bunkhouse and he'll make sure they escort Geordie off the property come first light.'

'But why just let him go?' Nancy protested. 'He killed Hughie, your nephew! And he killed the boy he bought the stake from. Shouldn't he face some kind of justice?'

'Oh, he will,' Marie said quietly. 'Have no doubt about that.'

Nancy's eyes brightened. 'Then he'll hang,' she announced with satisfaction.

'I wasn't thinking of that kind of justice, my dear,' Marie told her. 'Hanging is… just the body. Quite quick, and it's over. Geordie now, if he doesn't mend his ways, will one day have to face a greater Judge and an eternity of torment.'

Nancy gazed wide-eyed at Marie. 'Do you believe that?' she asked.

'Yes, I do,' Marie told her. 'It's what the Bible says. And the Bible says it's not our place to judge Geordie...'

'He's a bad man,' Nancy said bluntly. 'He deserves everything he gets.'

'None of us deserve what we get,' Marie said quietly.

Hungry crying burst from Hugh junior and Marie went over to the makeshift crib. She lifted the red-faced squalling baby from the soft shawls he had been resting in and brought him over to his mother.

Nancy settled the child at her breast, her eyes soft as she watched the infant suckle.

'You're right there,' she whispered, stroking the child's soft cheek with loving tenderness. 'This beautiful little one. I don't deserve him.' She looked up at Marie and now there were tears in her eyes. 'I was a bad girl,' she said. 'I told you. I'm not a fit mother for someone as precious as Hughie's son.'

Marie put her arm round Nancy. 'Never say that, my dear,' she admonished her. 'If the good Lord decided to gift you with this child, then it's your job to take care of him as best you can. And we'll help – as much as you want us to.'

'Why?' Nancy asked. 'Because he's Hughie's?' There was deep sadness in her voice.

Marie squeezed the thin shoulders and dropped a kiss on Nancy's head.

'No, my dear,' she said. 'Because Jesus told us to love one another – and if you'll let me, I'd like to do that – for you and the baby.'

Nancy looked up at her with wondering eyes. 'Love?' she said slowly. 'I've never known love.' Her thoughts drifted as she looked down at the baby in her arms. 'My mother was furious when she realised she was pregnant. She couldn't get away fast enough after

I was born. The other girls looked after me. I was passed from hand to hand, always a nuisance. Till I was old enough to earn my keep.'

Marie was watching her with sympathetic eyes.

Nancy continued, 'And the men... the punters. That was work. Geordie told me to be friendly to Hughie. That was no different from any of the rest. He was a nice boy...' She looked up hesitantly. 'I'm telling you the truth here,' she said. 'You need to know...'

'It makes no difference,' Marie assured her. 'Jesus didn't pick the holy good people for His friends and He doesn't expect us to either. Everyone is welcome. "Love one another," He said. So it makes no difference what you've done. You're here now and you can have a fresh start. You and the baby.'

'Your Jesus sounds nice,' Nancy said wistfully. 'I wish I knew the things you do. It seems to make a big difference.'

'Oh, it does,' Marie said with a smile. 'It makes all the difference in the world.'

'Would you...' Nancy hesitated. 'Would you teach me? I think I've got such a lot to learn. I don't think I know anything very much!'

'Do you want to know my Jesus?' Marie asked. 'Because that's the only way to make a real fresh start. If you want to...'

Nancy's eyes were filled with new determination. 'Oh, I want to,' she said. 'I want that fresh start, and I want... I want to be like you. If that means knowing your Jesus, then that's what I want.'

'Do you know about praying?' Marie asked her.

'Not a lot,' Nancy admitted, adding with a laugh, 'Only when things are really desperate!'

Marie laughed too. 'I understand. Well, when Jesus is your friend, you can talk to Him all the time, get His help all the time, with everything...' She saw Nancy's amazement. 'Yes, everything!'

She laughed again. 'He helps me keep my temper. He helps me sort out the laundry… and the baking… and… oh, everything!'

'Everything? Like helping with the baby? Like what I'm going to do?' Nancy asked.

'Yes,' Marie said. 'Jesus will help you with everything. So shall we talk to Him now?'

CHAPTER 49

Hannah slipped quietly into the house, setting her laden basket on the table, before reaching for the spill to light the lamp. Late afternoon on an overcast day, the room was dark. She knew this place as well as she knew her own home now and needed no light to guide her path to the range with its glowing banked fire in the grate. Quickly lighting the taper, she turned back towards the lamp and stopped with a gasp.

'Rab! What are you doing here?'

Rab Cormack was sitting in a chair by the table.

'It's my house,' he growled.

'Yes, but...' Hannah swallowed hard and concentrated on lighting the lamp and putting the glass cover back on, to give her whirling thoughts and emotions a chance to subside. She blew out the taper and took a good look at the man on the other side of the table.

'I wasn't expecting to find you here,' she said, as steadily as she could, taking in the unshaven face and the dead eyes.

'No?' he answered, uncaring.

'No,' she said. 'And you're going to get under my feet if you stay here. I need to get this floor swept and...'

He waved a dismissive hand. 'I wouldn't bother,' he said. 'It doesn't matter.'

'Yes, it does,' Hannah protested. 'You can't live in a pig sty!'

He shrugged. 'I don't care,' and his voice was filled with defeat and despair that tugged at Hannah's heart. Tears leapt to her eyes but she fought them down. It would do no good to give in to softness now.

'Fine,' she said. 'I'll just put these things away and leave you to wallow in your misery.'

As she hoped, he reacted to her words as if stung.

'You're a hard-hearted piece,' he declared. 'Why shouldn't I be miserable?' His voice rose. 'Belle is gone. My beautiful Belle...'

Hannah picked up the lamp and headed for the stairs with Rab's freshly laundered clothes, quickly suppressing the retort that came so readily to her lips. Just how much good had his beautiful Belle done any of them when she was alive? But he could not see that. Silently Hannah climbed the stairs, her heart torn by the pain of the man sitting alone in the kitchen.

It had been a whole year since Belle died but it seemed Rab's grief was as fresh as the day she had gone. What kind of a hold had she had on this man? Hannah shook her head as she tidied away the things she had brought upstairs.

Rab seemed to have run through the full range of emotions after Belle's death: rage at the unfairness of it, unrelenting unforgiveness towards himself as if he were to blame, overwork to fill every waking hour, and now broken despair as nothing worked. How like Belle that her poison continued to fester a whole year after her death!

Hannah girded her loins for the battle and sallied back downstairs. She placed the lamp in the centre of the table. Rab had not moved. He sat with his head in his hands, the picture of despair.

Ignoring him for the moment, she moved the kettle to the hottest part of the range and gathered together teapot and cups. The whistle of the kettle as it boiled seemed to rouse him and he watched as she poured water into the pot to heat it, rinsed it round and poured it out, then added three spoonfuls of tea from the caddy and filled the pot with boiling water. She set the pot on the side of the range and poured milk into two cups.

'Is there anything to eat with this?' she asked.

He nodded his head in the direction of the larder. 'There'll be some biscuits in there,' he said. 'You should know. It's you that brings them.'

'And it's you that's supposed to eat them,' she replied waspishly.

'True,' he said. 'And I do, sometimes.'

'But there may be some left?'

'May be.' And before she could answer, she was pleased to see him get to his feet and head over to the larder, returning with the biscuit tin. He took the lid off and set it on the table. 'There,' he said and sat down.

Hannah inspected the contents – a few pieces of her home-made shortbread remained.

She poured the tea and handed him a cup, setting her own on the table opposite his. She took a piece of shortbread and sat down. He looked at her, as if waiting, but when she said nothing and only bit into her shortbread, he too reached for a piece from the tin and began to eat.

Hannah picked up her cup and drank. It was a start.

CHAPTER 50

The pale light of dawn and the promise of a fine August day. Geordie's saddlebags had been loaded on to his horse, the gun found and removed. Now he himself was escorted, none too gently, from the bunkhouse and assisted into the saddle.

'Is there anything you want to say before you go?' Bill asked.

Geordie opened his drink-reddened eyes a slit. 'I never wanted your rotten farm!' he sneered. He patted his saddlebags. 'I've still got my gold unless one of you lot have stolen it...'

The ranch-hands stirred angrily but Bill raised a hand to quiet them.

'We haven't taken your gold,' he said.

'I'm going to be a rich man,' Geordie said. 'When you're all still scratching in the dirt!' He spat contemptuously.

'Then it's time you were on your way,' Bill said. His hand came down smartly on the rump of Geordie's horse and it obediently moved off. 'And don't try coming back,' Bill called after him. 'We'll be watching out for you.'

'I wouldn't come back if this was the last place on earth,' Geordie called over his shoulder. 'God damn the lot of you!'

Watching him go, Bill shook his head sadly. 'I think he's the one that's damned,' he said. 'Unless he changes his ways.'

He turned and walked back to the house, letting himself quietly into the bedroom where Marie waited.

'Gone?' she asked.

Bill nodded.

'Good.'

A cry from the room next door told them that young Hugh had woken up hungry again. But the cry was quickly hushed and Bill and Marie could hear Nancy's voice softly singing while she fed the child.

Marie smiled and patted Bill's hand.

'I think all will be well,' she said. 'Now that man has gone.'

CHAPTER 51

The dairy was cold in the morning. All the better, Hannah told herself, for keeping the milk fresh. She turned the handle on the churn. The pretty wooden butterpats carved with thistles were set out ready for use. She had to keep busy.

But her mind kept returning to Rab Cormack and the problem of his son. Young Bobby was growing fast and would soon want answers to questions. As the butter separated from the milk, the churn handle took more effort to turn. As Bobby's questions would be harder to answer if they allowed this ridiculous aversion of Rab's to his son to continue.

But what could she do? Rab still insisted he wanted nothing to do with the boy. Oh, he provided money for the lad's needs so Bobby wanted for nothing. But he refused to see him.

'Come and see your Auntie Hannah,' her mother's voice came from out in the yard. A moment later the door to the dairy was pushed open and a small red-headed child, warmly bundled up, came toddling in. He stopped for a moment then stretched out his arms.

Hannah laughed and stopped churning, to pick up the beguiling youngster. 'And what are you doing out here, may I ask?' she teased him. 'Have you come to help me with my work?'

The lad chuckled, deep dimples showing in his chubby face. Hannah kissed him tenderly and set him down on the floor.

'Would you like a glass of fresh buttermilk?' she asked.

'Hannah, you're spoiling him,' her mother remonstrated gently. 'He's fat enough already!'

Hannah shook her head. 'He's not fat. That's just his warm clothes,' she declared and, taking the toddler's hand, led him across to the table where she poured him a glass of the fresh buttermilk.

Bobby downed it rapidly, leaving a creamy ring round his mouth. Hannah reached down to take the glass from him. As she set it back on the table, her mother said quietly, 'This can't go on.'

'What do you mean?'

Her mother motioned towards Bobby with her head. 'The... situation. I know Rab's still not got over Belle's death but it's time he took more of an interest...'

A wave of fresh resentment against Belle's destructive influence rose suddenly in Hannah's heart. She thought she had dealt with that, she thought despairingly. She had taken it to the Lord so many times...

Her mother was waiting for an answer but Hannah could only shake her head.

'Oh come, Hannah,' her mother said. 'You know this can't go on.'

'I'm happy to look after wee Bobby,' Hannah told her quietly, 'for as long as needs be. I'm happy looking after him.' And it was true. She stooped to pick up the little boy again and dropped a kiss on his tousled curls. Each kiss for the boy full of love for him – and his father.

Her mother's eyes were sad. 'Hannah, you don't have to give up your life...'

Hannah's head came up then and her eyes were bright and fierce. 'I'm happy to do it,' she said again.

Her mother lifted the boy out of Hannah's arms. 'If you're sure... though I worry.' She paused. 'Don't make an idol out of the boy now. You can grow too attached... get to *worship* him.' Her mother watched Hannah's face. 'You understand what I'm saying?'

Hannah nodded before returning to her work. 'I understand.'

She heard her mother leave the dairy, and only then did she look up, the tears shining in her eyes. Her mother's words had struck deep into her heart. Was that what she had done? Made an idol first of Rab Cormack and then when her love was not returned, poured it all into that wee boy, making an idol of him?

Hannah looked down at her work-reddened hands and sighed. There was only one thing to do. She closed her eyes. Deliberately, unwillingly, she folded her hands and prayed.

'Forgive me, Lord...' The tears poured down her face as she relinquished the two she most loved on all the earth into the keeping of God. 'Yours, Lord. And Your will be done in all our lives.'

Drawing a ragged breath into her aching chest, Hannah wiped her eyes and got back to work.

CHAPTER 52

Geordie Sinclair sat in a quiet corner of the saloon bar and watched the young man struggling up from his seat. He was probably in his late teens with money to burn and the girls had already got him sized up. And he, despite the amount of drink he had consumed, still had enough of his wits about him to try fending them off.

With little success. They were like flies on a fresh-killed carcase, Geordie thought. He watched with amusement as the boy became increasingly entangled, redder in the face, louder in voice. Geordie quickly checked round the bar. No one else seemed to be paying any attention to the boy's predicament.

He waited a little longer, then rose and ambled in leisurely fashion towards the hubbub.

'Now, girls,' he said in a softly menacing voice. 'If the gentleman isn't interested, the gentleman isn't interested.'

The girls clustering around the young man fell back.

'Leave him alone, there's good girls,' Geordie said. He reached in his pocket for a handful of notes and threw them towards the young women. 'Go on now!' He smacked the rump of the girl nearest him and she giggled and caught some of the money, tucking it down the front of her dress. The others scrabbled for the notes that had dropped on the floor, then within moments, they had all gone.

Geordie made as if to leave but the young man stopped him. In a strong Spanish accent, he said, 'I owe you thanks, *señor*.'

Geordie waved it away magnanimously. 'No problem,' he said. 'I could see you're new here. The girls don't mean any harm but they can be a bit… persistent!' He laughed and the young man laughed with him, his composure now fully restored.

'Well, I must go now,' Geordie said, turning away.

'No, no!' the young man said. 'I am in your debt. I am Federico Ronaldo de la Vega of Buenos Aires, Argentina.' He bowed in a stately fashion. 'To whom am I indebted?'

Geordie bowed in turn. 'George William Sinclair,' he said solemnly.

'St Clair?' The boy pronounced the name hesitantly.

Geordie smiled. 'Yes, indeed. George William St Clair.' It sounded much better, more impressive. He added, 'Late of the Klondike, and Manitoba, Canada. Before that, Scotland.'

'Scotland?'

'That's right.'

'That is a long way away,' the boy said wonderingly.

'I was left a stake in the Klondike and came to look it over,' Geordie said carelessly. 'I've left folk up there working it…'

'A gold mine?' Federico asked, wide-eyed.

'You could say that,' Geordie laughed. 'That's what the Klondike's famous for.'

'And Manitoba?' The boy stumbled over the unfamiliar word.

'Ranching,' Geordie said carelessly. 'Wheat. It's good business.'

'And now?' Federico enquired. 'What are you doing? Where are you going?'

'I came to San Francisco a while back,' Geordie said. 'I've got some business here.'

'More gold?' Federico asked.

Geordie smiled. 'What about you?' he asked Federico. 'What's your story?'

The boy's open face creased in a sulky scowl. 'My father sent me to school here in America. There was a small problem and I am supposed to go home.' He looked around the saloon with some dissatisfaction. 'I thought I would have some fun before I got on the boat.'

'Yes, of course,' Geordie said. 'A young man like you, of course you should. But this isn't the place.' He waved his arm dismissively at the saloon bar. 'If you like, I can show you some much better places. I've been based here for a while and I know the ropes. Let me show you.'

'Would you, Señor St Clair?' Federico asked eagerly.

'Of course,' Geordie said, clapping him on the shoulder. 'I'll make sure you have a really good time.'

241

CHAPTER 53

'Do I smell rock buns?' Hannah's mother asked as she came into the hot kitchen. She sat down heavily by the table and looked at the tray of freshly baked buns, spicy tantalising steam rising off the crisp golden treats.

'He likes them,' Hannah said defensively.

Her mother looked up at her daughter, tender concern in her eyes.

'Which he?' she asked gently.

Hannah flushed awkwardly. 'Both of them,' she said, turning her back on her mother and busying herself at the sink with the washing up.

Her mother sat in silence as Hannah washed the utensils and the baking bowl in the suds and placed them on the draining board. She made to rise to help but Hannah forestalled her.

'No, no. Just you sit and rest. I'll finish this.' She reached for the tea towel. The passing years and her mother's increasing frailty had placed the responsibility for the household tasks on Hannah's shoulders. When she had finished and turned back to the table, her mother opened her mouth but Hannah forestalled her.

'I was baking anyway, so I just thought...' she said softly. She came to sit across from her mother. 'I made plenty. We could have some with our tea,' she offered.

'You know your father prefers scones,' her mother demurred.

Hannah waved her hand at the tea-towel covered cooling rack further down the table. 'I've made some,' she said.

'Yes, of course, my dear,' her mother said. 'You're a good girl.'

'Not so much a girl,' Hannah said ruefully.

Her mother reached out and patted her hand. 'Is it not maybe time you thought more about yourself, my dear? Time is passing and...'

'Grandma!' a cheerful voice greeted her as Bobby erupted into the kitchen, swinging his school satchel on to a chair. He planted a cheeky kiss on his grandmother's cheek while one hand snaffled a rock bun. 'Oh! Still hot!' he declared.

'Fresh out of the oven,' his grandmother said.

'Can I have a glass of buttermilk?' he asked Hannah.

'Yes of course, my love,' Hannah said. She stood up and went past him out to the dairy.

'You're spoilt,' Bobby's grandmother said.

A cheeky grin split his face. 'I know,' he mumbled, his mouth full of rock bun. 'I'm lucky.' He looked up as Hannah re-entered the kitchen bearing a glass of the creamy liquid. 'Thanks, Auntie Hannah. You're an angel.'

'And you're a scamp!' she told him affectionately.

'I know,' he said blithely, beaming at both women.

They watched him swallow down the buttermilk, then he grabbed another rock bun. 'That was good,' he declared. 'I'm going out to play now.' And he was gone like a mini whirlwind.

Hannah and her mother laughed.

'He's a good boy,' Hannah said.

'Thanks to you,' her mother said. 'You're the one bringing him up. That Rab Cormack…' She caught the look in Hannah's eyes and bit back her words. 'I know. I know, my dear.' She sighed, then ploughed on. 'But isn't it time Rab took on his responsibility for the boy? And let you get on with your life?'

The bleakness of that prospect – a life without either Bobby or Rab in it – threatened to overwhelm Hannah.

'Hannah?' her mother prodded gently.

But Hannah simply shook her head. She could not talk about it. Resolutely she reminded herself that she had entrusted the whole situation to her Lord and she was waiting on Him to sort it out. In the meantime…

'I know you're right, Mother,' she said. 'But it's not in our hands.' She took off her apron and set it down, walking unhurriedly towards the stairs. 'Let's talk about it later.'

Her mother shook her head fondly. Hannah was as steadfast as always.

But once in the sanctuary of her bedroom, Hannah sank on to her bed and covered her face with her hands. Her mother was right. She had to admit it. It was way past time for Rab Cormack to take over the upbringing of the boy. A house with one elderly man and two women in it was no home for a lively boy like Bobby. And it was past time for him to get to know his father – and for his father to get to know him.

But it would be a wrench. And once Bobby moved out to live with his father, her life would change for ever. Her only reason to see Rab, to talk with him, would be gone. And there was no sign that he had any inclination to do any of that of his own accord. Once Bobby had gone, she would have to step aside from the pair of them. Losing

Bobby meant losing Rab – what little she had of him, and any hope of any more.

Hannah flung herself on her pillows and wept – quietly so no one would hear. Then she forced herself to sit up and wipe her eyes dry.

She would not regret what she had done with her life. She loved Rab and she loved Bobby. So that was all there was to it. She had chosen to do this out of love. Knowing that there might be nothing at the end of it, no response from the man she loved more than life itself.

She reached for her Bible, her only comfort. It opened at a well-thumbed page in the Gospel of St John: chapter 14 verse 1: '*Let not your heart be troubled: ye believe in God, believe also in me.*'

'I do, Lord Jesus,' Hannah whispered. 'I will trust You. Help me keep trusting.'

CHAPTER 54

Geordie Sinclair reckoned he could cut a swathe through downtown San Francisco but young Federico de la Vega appeared to have stamina as limitless as the wad of cash that he had stashed in his fancy jacket pocket. By the early hours of the morning, Geordie decided enough was enough. He had relieved Federico of a generous amount of his money and was trying to offload the lad on to some willing girls at one of the bars. But Federico was having none of it.

'No, no,' he cried. 'You are my amigo, Señor St Clair. Where you go, I go.'

The only problem with that, as far as Geordie could see, was that he had no plans for going anywhere. After the debacle at the Alexanders' ranch, he had ridden cursing back to Brandon and got a train to Vancouver, thinking maybe he would return to the Klondike and Hughie's claim. But when he reached Vancouver, the word was that the Klondike was finished and there was a new gold rush at Nome in Alaska. Watching all the hopefuls stampeding to get there, Geordie decided he would go in the other direction and found himself in San Francisco, a city where he quickly found his feet in the saloons and gambling dens. But as to the future…

'A man like you, Señor St Clair,' Federico was saying. 'There will be room in your fine residence for me, I am sure. Plenty of room. Come,' he declared. 'Let us return to your residence and get a little sleep. Then you can show me more of this fine town.' And swaying gently, he placed his arm round Geordie's shoulders and leaned heavily on him.

'Which way do we go?' he enquired and hiccoughed drunkenly.

Geordie looked down at the foolish face of the rich young man and a sudden idea came to him. Surely he could turn this situation to his advantage? But first he had to think fast. The cheap doss-house he had been staying in would not do for Federico to share, not if Geordie wanted to maintain his image as a rich successful man – and that would be necessary for the plan that was beginning to take shape in his mind.

One by one he discarded the places that would welcome him and the lad at this time in the morning, till there was only one possibility left. Jessie ran one of the most upmarket bordellos in San Francisco. True, she had thrown him out when he had not had enough cash to pay his dues, but once she saw the colour of the lad's money, she would surely be glad to take them both in. And show her appreciation.

Geordie brightened. 'This way.'

By the time the two of them reached Jessie's elegant parlour house on one of the better streets of San Francisco, Geordie had concocted what he thought was a convincing tale.

'My housekeeper can be a bit difficult,' he apologised to Federico. 'I'm not here often enough to keep her in check!'

'Ah yes,' the lad agreed sleepily as Geordie led him into the mansion. By the time Jessie arrived, Geordie was prepared and the lad more than half asleep.

'So you're back!' The large woman in the dark red dress stood arms akimbo, every inch the irate person in charge. 'What do you think...?'

'A little late, I accept...' Geordie cut across in a loud determined voice and a gesture that at once alerted Jessie. Her eyes narrowed. She came closer.

'Who's that?' she asked. 'And is he alive?'

Federico had slumped, one arm still round Geordie's shoulders, with Geordie doing most of the work of holding him up. The lad had fallen fast asleep.

'I'll explain in a minute,' Geordie hissed. 'Don't worry. He's got plenty of money. Help me get him to bed. On his own,' he admonished. 'And he needs to think this is my place, okay?'

'You've got a nerve...' Jessie began.

'Trust me,' Geordie told her. 'It will be worth it. He's got enough money on him to buy this place twice over...'

'So why don't we just take it off him now?' Jessie demanded.

For a moment Geordie was tempted, then he remembered what the boy had said: 'Where you go, I go.' Where this boy was going was sure to be a rich family back home in Buenos Aires who would reward the man who looked after their wayward son and returned him safe and sound – and only a little poorer.

'I have a much better idea,' Geordie said.

As he had expected, Jessie's greed overcame her natural suspicion and she allowed him to put Federico in one of the large front rooms of the house. Helping to undress the boy and put him to bed, she was reassured by the large wad of money Geordie removed from Federico's jacket pocket.

'No!' Geordie told her sharply as she reached for the money. 'All in good time.' He gave her a squeeze. 'Trust me.'

249

'Ha!'

They left Federico to sleep. When he roused, late next morning, Geordie sauntered into his room.

'Good morning,' he greeted Federico. 'And how are you today?'

Federico opened a bleary eye. 'Morning already, *señor*?'

'It is, and I have business to conduct in this town,' Geordie replied briskly. 'If you care to rise and accompany me…'

But Federico's response was a groan. Geordie hid a satisfied smile. It was as he had expected.

'Headache?' he enquired.

Another groan and the covers were pulled up over the lad's head.

'I'll send someone up with a remedy for that,' Geordie said cheerfully. 'Well, no matter. I shall go alone. You'll be feeling much better by the time I return.'

No response this time so Geordie left the room and went in search of Jessie.

'Get someone who looks like a servant to take him a glass of seltzer,' he instructed. 'Keep the girls and everyone else away from his room – but keep an eye on him. Don't let him wander around and don't let him out. I'll be back around three.'

Jessie started to protest but Geordie pulled a handful of notes out of his pocket. 'Take these to be going on with,' he said. 'He'll never miss them.'

He strode out of the house and down to the business district where he located the offices of an import/export agency.

'Mr George William St Clair,' he announced himself to the clerk. 'Late of the Klondike.'

It was amazing how that name opened doors, Geordie thought, as yet again it worked its magic and he was ushered into the principal's office. Here he encountered a disconcertingly sharp gaze.

'And how may I be of help to you, Mr St Clair?' the man behind the big desk enquired.

'I need some information,' Geordie told him. 'But I need to come by it discreetly, not using my usual channels.'

The man steepled his fingers together and looked at Geordie with interest.

'Indeed?'

Encouraged, Geordie continued. 'I'm on the point of making a sizeable investment but I should like to have corroboration of some background information about the people involved.'

'I see.'

'They're based in Argentina,' Geordie said. 'Would this present a problem?'

'Not at all,' the man said. 'Our sources are both widespread and reliable.'

'In that case,' Geordie continued, 'the name is de la Vega…'

CHAPTER 55

'Auntie Hannah?'

Hannah looked up from the shirt she was ironing. She set the heavy iron down for a moment and turned to look at the boy doing his homework on the kitchen table.

'Yes, my love,' she responded. 'What is it? An arithmetic question you can't get right?'

She made to move over to help but Bobby shrugged away her query.

'No, no, I can manage those fine. No. That's not it.'

He paused and then, searching her eyes, he finally ground out, 'Why doesn't my dad like me?'

The boy took a deep breath and, his face red with emotion, added, 'Is it true that I killed my mother?' The words then came in a rush. 'Is that true? And is that why he doesn't have any time for me? Auntie Hannah, it wasn't my fault! But the boys at school… They all say… They all say it's not surprising. Why should he have any time for me when I killed my mother?'

Hannah was by his side instantly and enfolded him in her arms, pressing his head to her bosom as she stroked his hair and tried to comfort his sobs.

'There, there, my dearie,' she soothed. 'It certainly was not your fault.'

She raised her eyes to Heaven as a fresh flare of anger towards Belle surged through her. The woman had a lot to answer for.

'Women do die in childbirth,' she explained gently. 'It's a risk for every woman, and things just sometimes go wrong.' She gave Bobby a tight squeeze then stepped back so she could look in his face. 'I'm very glad that the midwife was able to save you. We could have lost you too.' She smiled at him and ruffled his hair affectionately. 'And where would I be without you?'

'But my dad,' Bobby persisted, refusing to be sidetracked. 'He doesn't want me. He wishes… He wishes it was *me* that died and my mother that was saved.'

Lost for words to refute the lad's only too accurate perception, Hannah gathered him in her arms again.

'You won't hear anybody in this house say that,' she muttered fiercely.

Bobby pulled away and stared at her.

'Why?' he asked with the clear-eyed curiosity of a child. 'Was she not nice? One of the boys at school…'

'Don't you pay any attention to what the boys at school say,' Hannah told him. 'Shall we just say she was nice to the people she wanted to be nice to.'

'People like you?' Bobby persisted.

Hannah sighed. She did not want to tarnish Belle's memory in the child's mind but how could she tell him the truth?

'Enough questions,' she said gently. 'I must get on with my work.'

'Ironing Dad's shirt.' It was a flat statement, but then Bobby enquired, 'Why? Why do you do his washing and his cleaning and bake nice things for him when he never comes here or does anything for you?'

Hannah swallowed hard. How do you explain love to a seven-year-old, especially unrequited love?

Her mother's footsteps coming downstairs saved her from answering.

'Grandma!' Bobby rose to give the old lady a hug. When she had sat down, Bobby announced, 'We were just talking, me and Auntie Hannah.'

'Oh, were you?' her mother responded, casting a sharp glance at Hannah.

'We were,' Hannah said and bent to her ironing, wondering what the lad would say now.

'Am I going to stay here with you for ever and ever?' Bobby asked.

Hannah kept her head down and waited for her mother's reply.

'Well, Bobby, that depends on your father...'

'He doesn't want me! He's never wanted me!' the boy burst out.

His grandmother raised her hand to quiet him. 'Never say that, my boy. We don't ever know what another person is thinking or feeling.' She smoothed the front of her skirt thoughtfully. 'We were happy to look after you when your mother died. Your father couldn't look after a baby on his own.' She watched as Bobby nodded reluctantly.

'But I'm a big boy now,' he said. 'The boys at school say...' He stopped suddenly, biting his lip.

Hannah and her mother exchanged glances.

'What did the boys say?' his grandmother probed gently.

'It wasn't nice,' he muttered.

'No, I can imagine that,' she said. 'Out with it!'

'They said I'll grow up to be a great big sissie living in a house with just old women.' He got the words out with difficulty.

'Oh dear.' It was true that since the death of Hannah's father, there were just the two of them living with young Bobby. A twinkle lit her mother's eye for a moment. 'In that case we'd better get Auntie

Hannah married off so you'll have a man around the house.' She was greatly amused to see the matched horror on Hannah's and Bobby's faces.

The lad was up on his feet and hurling his arms around Hannah's waist, crying out 'No! Don't do that!'

He turned back to his grandmother. 'I'm happy living here with you both. I don't want anyone else here.' His intrinsic honesty forced him to add, 'Except my dad. The only man I'd want to live with is my dad… if he'd have me.'

Hannah bit her lip. Those were her sentiments exactly!

CHAPTER 56

It was easy enough to get the lad to talk about his family.

'My sister is the most beautiful girl in Buenos Aires,' Federico boasted proudly. 'And we are one of the richest families. So she is always chaperoned to protect her from fortune hunters!'

Geordie exchanged interested glances with Jessie.

'I'm sure your mother is missing you, though, Master Federico,' Jessie said, playing her part as the faithful housekeeper as she lifted the breakfast tray from the table.

The lad looked up at her and shrugged. 'Yes, of course. I am Mama's favourite.'

'How proud she'll be when you go home all grown up,' Jessie prompted and the young man preened, but then his face fell.

'Thank you, Jessie,' Geordie said in the voice of the master of the house. 'That will be all. We will be out for dinner this evening.'

Jessie hid a grin and gave a dutiful nod before removing the tray and herself from the room, carefully closing the door behind her. So far the plan had worked. She had been able to keep the girls away from the rich young man and left him to Geordie's ministrations. Federico seemed to have accepted that Geordie was master of this impressive, elegantly furnished house and rich in his own right – completely unaware that it was his own money that was funding their expenses.

'Tonight,' Geordie said, leaning back comfortably in his chair, 'I thought I'd take you to one of my favourite places. It is a discreet establishment where gentlemen gather and can play cards, that sort of thing.'

Federico looked worried. 'I don't seem to be very lucky at cards, *señor*,' he stammered.

'Then perhaps it is time for your luck to change,' Geordie said cheerfully, slapping the young man on the back.

But as the evening progressed and Federico continued to lose heavily, it was clear that the youth was no longer enjoying his experience as a man about town.

Finally, he threw down his hand. 'This is useless,' he declared. 'I'm never going to win!'

And despite the protestations of the seasoned card-sharps that Geordie had carefully placed around him before wandering off to find his own amusements, Federico continued to insist that he wanted to go home.

Geordie took his time returning to his side.

'There you are, Señor St Clair!' Federico exclaimed. 'I wish to go home now. I am not winning and I have had enough of cards!'

Geordie smiled at his collaborators and, taking Federico's arm, led him away from the table.

'But another drink?' he suggested.

Federico shook off his arm. 'I have had enough to drink and it made the cards worse,' the lad said sulkily. 'I want to go home.'

'We could try another gambling house…'

But Federico had clearly had enough. 'I want to go home,' he said petulantly, sounding very young indeed.

'Then that's what we'll do,' Geordie agreed. He escorted Federico back to Jessie's and wished him goodnight, ignoring the lad's emotional state.

In the morning, he was prepared for Federico's outburst when he finally went down to join him at the breakfast table.

'Good morning, Federico,' he began.

'I want to go home!' the lad burst out. 'To Buenos Aires! But what am I to do? I haven't got enough money left! I lost it all in those card games...'

'Ah, is that what is worrying you?' Geordie said smoothly. 'I'm sure we can sort that out.'

'I am not going to another gambling house,' Federico said fiercely. 'I will lose what I have left!'

'No, no,' Geordie said, helping himself to eggs and steak and hash browns. 'No, I have a better idea.'

Federico threw himself back into his chair, his face a picture of despair. 'I can't imagine what it is! My father will be furious...'

'Do you need to tell him?' Geordie enquired.

'Well, of course! How else am I to get home? I will have to wire him and plead with him. Tell him everything and beg for the money to get me home!' The young man threw his head in his hands.

Geordie tapped his arm to get his attention. 'No. You don't have to do that. Do not worry. There is a better way. Listen to me.'

He set his plate of food on the table and sat down. 'You have told me such interesting things about your country and about your city that I have a mind to see it for myself. I think there may be some good business opportunities for me there.' Geordie suppressed a smile. His words spoke only the truth – but the business opportunities he had in mind were far from what the boy might think.

Geordie continued, 'Since I shall be booking myself a passage on a boat to Buenos Aires, why don't I book for two and you can accompany me? I would enjoy your company. And when we get to Buenos Aires and you have been reunited with your people, you can show me around.'

Federico looked up, hope dawning in his eyes.

'What do you say?' Geordie said in an unconcerned voice as he applied himself to his food.

'Say?' Federico said in a voice of great joy. 'Why, thank you, Señor St Clair! I am forever in your debt. How can I ever thank you!'

Geordie hid a grin and continued eating.

CHAPTER 57

Bobby's words had nagged at Hannah. She did not think he would grow into 'a great big sissie' as the taunts of the boys at school had said. There were plenty of men about the place. When her father died, her eldest brother had become head of the family, taking over the running of the carting business that continued to operate from the yard at the back of the house. There were stablemen working there who welcomed Bobby and talked to him. He knew the drivers who came and went every day.

There *were* men in his life, she protested to herself. Decent men who offered him good examples of honest working lives.

Yes, but not the love and guidance of a father, her heart told her. She raised her eyes from her Bible and reminded the Lord, 'There's You. You're our Father!'

She could almost see the loving, reproving smile and she had to accept the truth. The boy needed his earthly father. But what was to be done?

Hannah sighed and firmly pulled her mind back to her morning devotions. This time was precious. She woke early to be with the Lord in the quiet and calm of the morning, to sit in His presence and absorb His peace before the busyness of the day got underway. It provided a reservoir of strength that she could draw on throughout the day – and often plain and simple words of guidance that she so needed.

She opened her Bible now and prayed. 'You know I want the best for Bobby. But I'm afraid. I'm afraid Rab will reject him outright, to his face, and hurt him beyond mending. And I'm afraid of alienating Rab completely by pressing him. I'm afraid of his anger with *me*. Help me, Lord. Let me see what's right to do – and give me the strength to do it, for the boy's sake. Oh, You know I'd hang on to Bobby happily! He's so welcome here – and he… well, I see Rab so much in him. I've come to love Bobby for his own sake, but at the start it was for Rab's sake, a way of expressing my love for Rab. Serving him… But maybe I'm being selfish, keeping Bobby here. As the crucial link in a chain that exists only in my imagination – that links Rab and me.'

As she prayed, Hannah's heart calmed. Yes, she thought, it was time there was reconciliation between Bobby and his father. Time for Rab to accept his responsibilities and his son. For a moment, Hannah remembered Belle's defiant declaration that she did not know whose child the coming baby was, then she pictured Bobby in her mind's eye. Though the red hair clearly came from Belle, in her mind there was no doubt. Bobby was Rab's son in looks and in character. There was no impediment there to reconciliation.

But how was it to be done? 'We're Yours and You'll need to sort this out,' she whispered. 'But I'm willing to do whatever You tell me to.'

She gathered her concentration and began to read. That morning's portion of scripture was 1 Samuel chapter 25. It was a lovely story of King David. Still on the run from King Saul, David and his men were in need of food and had sent to ask politely for supplies from a man named Nabal. The response was churlish and angered David who determined to get even with Nabal.

But Nabal had a wise and beautiful wife, and his workers came and told her the problem. At once she organised generous supplies of food and set off to prevent any bloodshed. When she met David, she bowed before him in humility but then she spoke. It is a long speech for a woman in the Bible. Wise and careful, but really a reproof. She is a straight-talking woman and David heard her out. *'Blessed be the LORD God of Israel who sent thee this day to meet me: and blessed be thy advice, and blessed be thou, which hast kept me this day from coming to shed blood, and from avenging myself with my own hand'* (1 Samuel 25:32–33).

And King David heeded Abigail.

As Hannah read, her eyes widened. 'There's no need to ask, is there, Lord?' she whispered. 'It's time for some straight talking and I've got to do it. The outcome is in Your hands.'

She set her Bible back on her bedside table and rose. Reaching for her coat and hat, she hurried downstairs.

Her mother looked up in surprise as Hannah appeared at the breakfast-room door dressed to go out.

'I'm going over to Rab's,' she said. 'If I go now I'll catch him before he goes to work. We need to talk about the boy.' She paused, hand on the door jamb. 'Pray he'll take it right,' she said. Her mother nodded and began praying.

Her prayers were echoed by Hannah as she paced nervously along the road to Rab's house. As always she slipped round the side and entered the kitchen by the back door. Rab, on the point of pulling on his overcoat, turned at the sound of the door opening.

'What's the matter?' he asked, sudden concern on his face.

'Bobby,' Hannah stated, coming into the kitchen and standing in front of him.

Rab halted, then more slowly pushed his arm into the sleeve of the coat and drew the coat closed. His eyes searched her face.

'What's the matter with him? Is he ill?'

Feeling her knees weaken, Hannah pulled out a chair from the table and sat down.

'Hannah!' Rab insisted. 'What's the matter? Tell me!'

'Why should you care now?' she asked him. 'Do you care?'

'Of course I care!' Rab declared angrily. 'He's my own flesh and blood! He's all I've got...'

'No,' Hannah said.

That pulled him up short. 'What do you mean, "No"? The boy's mine...'

'Since when?' Hannah asked him. 'He's been more mine than yours. I've looked after him, seen to anything he needed...'

Rab began to protest but Hannah waved his words away. 'Yes, yes, I know. You paid for what he needed – but only when I came and told you what was wanting. You never came to see him. You never acknowledged him as your son. You rejected him. And the boy knows that. And he feels it. He knows you never wanted him.'

'That's not true!' Rab protested. 'I was so happy when Belle told me she was pregnant! But then when she died...'

'Yes, we know what that did to you,' Hannah said crisply. 'But it did just as much to Bobby. He's a poor motherless boy – but did he have to be a fatherless one too? Belle's death was a horrible tragedy, yes. But what you've done to Bobby is your own deliberate choice – and he knows it and just can't understand.'

Hannah sailed on. 'Despite everything, the boy loves and admires you. He'd give anything for a kind word from you. And to live with you, to really be your son, is his most precious dream.' She ground to a halt, suddenly afraid she had gone too far.

Rab stared at her. 'He said that?'

Hannah nodded. 'Yes. He said that.'

Rab squared his shoulders and took a deep breath. 'Then maybe it's time I did something about it.' He turned to the door. 'But for now, I must go to work. I'll come over later.'

And with that Hannah had to be content.

CHAPTER 58

Geordie stood, deep in thought, on the deck of the ship that was bringing him to Buenos Aires. It had been a long journey, over five weeks from San Francisco and round the Horn of South America, but compared with his initial voyage from Liverpool to Canada, it had been a luxurious delight. Thanks to Federico's money, he had been able to arrange first-class accommodation for them both.

Everything had gone exactly as he had hoped but now he had to deal with Federico's family. The lad was an innocent. If he was lucky, Federico's family would be equally as unworldly. He had encouraged Federico to wire his parents from San Francisco telling them that he was on his way home, signing himself their obedient son. Geordie said there was no need to mention him, just to say he was travelling with a friend. They had left San Francisco with Federico in high spirits and eager to see his home and family again.

As the ship nudged its way into one of the berths at Puerto Madero, the lad's excitement had sunk to nervous apprehensiveness as he waited to face his father. He scanned the busy port area, the quaysides thronged with people. Finally Federico spotted his father amongst the crowd and waved to attract his attention.

'There, Señor St Clair,' he told Geordie, relief and anxiety in his voice. 'My father has come to meet me.'

Disembarkation was a lengthy process but at last they were walking down the gangway on to the quayside and making their way towards the well-dressed, silver-haired gentleman who awaited them, his face stern and unsmiling.

'Papa!' Federico cried and flung his arms around his father. The embrace was returned, Geordie noted, though more coolly.

'And who is this?' his father asked, indicating Geordie at Federico's side.

'Permit me to introduce my friend – and saviour!' Federico declared, bringing Geordie forward.

Geordie could see Federico's father's eyes narrow as he considered this information.

'Indeed?' he enquired, unmoving.

Geordie bowed. 'George St Clair at your service, *señor*.'

'Señor St Clair is come lately from the gold fields of the Klondike. We met in San Francisco where he has some business, and a beautiful home,' Federico said. 'He has been of great help to me.'

Now it was the turn of Señor de la Vega senior to bow. 'I am grateful to you,' he said formally. 'I shall hear more of this later. Meanwhile…' He took Federico's arm. 'Your mother and sister are waiting.' He nodded to Geordie. It was a dismissal.

Geordie bowed again, a pleasant relaxed smile carefully in place.

'Then I will bid you farewell,' Geordie told Federico and moved away to locate his luggage. As he walked away, his ears were pricked for Federico's voice calling him back, but the call did not come. Geordie shrugged. He had plenty of time.

Once the necessary customs formalities had been carried out, Geordie secured a carriage to take him and his luggage to a fine hotel in the centre of Buenos Aires. The hours listening to Federico prattling on proudly about his home city had been very useful. Geordie had detailed plans for his first few days in the city, sightseeing and being seen.

He was descending the grand staircase late in the afternoon when a voice hailed him.

'Señor St Clair!'

It was Federico, who came hurrying up. He seized Geordie's arm.

'You must not stay here!' he declared.

'Why?' Geordie looked bemused. 'It appears a perfectly respectable place to me.' He had chosen the establishment with care.

'Yes, yes,' Federico said. 'Of course, that is true… But my father insists… You must come and stay with us while you are in Buenos Aires. The family is in your debt.' He dropped his voice and confided, 'I told my papa everything. How I lost so much money gambling.' He shrugged and smiled. 'It is something we understand in this city! Papa was not pleased but when I told him how you helped me and enabled me to get back home… He says it is the least we can do. So, *señor*, will you please accept our hospitality while you are in Buenos Aires? The carriage is outside. We can have your bags brought later.'

Geordie hid a satisfied smile. 'There is no need…' he began.

'My father sent me,' Federico began to protest. 'He insists!'

Geordie laughed. 'I understand! It is most kind of your family. I shall be delighted to accept.'

CHAPTER 59

Rab wasted little time, appearing in their house at tea time, just as he used to when he was courting Belle.

'Rab?' her mother had greeted him, casting a quizzical eye at Hannah. She had simply taken his coat and offered him tea and fresh-baked scones.

The three of them had then sat in uncomfortable silence, the awareness of the two people missing from their midst – Belle and Hannah's father – heavy in the air.

At last Hannah had risen to offer Rab a second cup of tea but he had waved it away.

'I've come about Bobby,' he announced.

Again her mother's eyes flew to Hannah but she simply said 'Yes?' peaceably.

'The boy should be living with me,' Rab said.

Hannah's mother raised her eyebrows. 'Are you not satisfied with how Hannah has been looking after him?'

Rab waved that away. 'That's not the point. You've done a fine job when he was little and I couldn't look after him, but now he's growing up, his place is with me.'

'But do you want him?' Hannah's mother queried.

Hearing a faint noise at the door, Hannah realised that Bobby was out there, listening. She held her breath as she waited for Rab's answer. And she prayed fiercely, fervently: *Dear Lord, please let him say the right thing – for Bobby's sake! Don't let him say anything that will hurt the boy or damage the possibility of a relationship between them. Please, Lord, please!*

The seconds ticked by as Rab gazed into his now-empty teacup.

'When Belle died, I felt I had died too. My whole future – I'd bound up with her, in her.' He looked up at Hannah's mother as if willing her to understand. 'What I did was wrong – turning my back on the baby. But I was hurting so much, I didn't think. So now is my chance to make it up to Bobby, to start again.' He added hesitantly, 'If you think he'd let me?'

The sincerity rang clearly in Rab's words and before Hannah's mother could make any reply, Bobby had rushed into the room and placed himself squarely in front of his father.

Hannah watched as Rab gazed at the boy, taking in Belle's red-gold hair and the determined face that was so like his own. She watched, holding her breath and keeping her prayer going. *Please, Lord! For Bobby... and for Rab.*

Rab set his teacup down on the table by his side and stretched out his hand. He placed it gently on Bobby's shoulder and looked deeply into the boy's eyes.

'I think it's time you came home and lived with me,' he said. 'What do you say? I'm not such a good cook as your Aunt Hannah or...'

But Bobby's eyes had lit with joy.

'Oh yes!' he said. And to Hannah's delight, Rab opened his arms and his son went into them for a first – if awkward – hug.

Thank you, Lord, Hannah prayed. *I think it's all going to be all right.*

It fell to her to pack Bobby's things, and in no time she and her mother were waving the lad goodbye.

'But I'll come and see you,' he assured them.

'Yes of course,' her mother agreed, but as Hannah discovered, occasional visits were not at all the same as having Bobby living with them. The house seemed to echo hollowly without his cheerful presence and Hannah felt his absence like another death. She missed him with an almost-constant ache that she tried to relieve with hard work. She insisted that it was no bother to continue doing his and his father's laundry, but her mother, coming upon her in tears one day over the ironing, chided her.

'This will not do, Hannah. You need a man of your own, a family of your own. Don't waste your life in hopelessness!'

And Hannah remembered Belle's spiteful words: 'I'll make him promise never to marry again. You'll never have him!'

And as the years went by, it seemed that Belle's words were true.

CHAPTER 60

Geordie Sinclair felt he needed to pinch himself. Surely he was in Heaven itself! Buenos Aires was all and more than he had ever dreamed of and the welcome from the de la Vega family had exceeded his wildest hopes.

With Federico chattering nineteen to the dozen, he had been driven in a smart liveried carriage through Buenos Aires to the Palermo district where the de la Vega family had their town villa. Fine wrought-iron gates were flung open by servants and the carriage swept through and up a broad driveway to the porticoed front entrance.

Geordie was glad that he had used some of Federico's gambling losses to buy suitable apparel for himself. He would need to play his part carefully if his plan was to work.

Climbing down from the carriage, his hand was wrung by Federico's father who came out to meet him and bring him into the house. A servant took his hat and cane, and Federico's father ushered him through cool marbled corridors to an elegant drawing room where three women were seated in comfort. Oscar de la Vega led him first to a ripely beautiful, dark-haired matron who had clearly been a beauty in her youth.

275

'My wife, Dona Ana Emilia.'

Geordie smiled a greeting and bowed. Dona Ana Emilia inclined her head graciously in response.

'And my daughter, Sofia Maria.'

The girl was as lovely as Federico had boasted and still very young. Geordie bowed. She smiled directly at him, and the older woman at her side scowled and muttered something in Spanish.

'And this is Sofia Maria's duenna, Dona Consuela,' Oscar de la Vega explained. 'It is our custom that young women are chaperoned.'

Sofia Maria laughed, a delicate silvery sound, but her attention all the while was fixed boldly on Geordie. A duenna, Geordie thought. But by the look of the girl, that was not likely to be a problem. He engaged the girl's eyes for a moment, acknowledging her interest, then turned back to her father.

'You have a fine family,' Geordie complimented him.

At a signal, a servant silently stepped forward with a tray of gold-rimmed crystal glasses filled with wine and Geordie's health was drunk with great ceremony.

'I hope my boy has not been too much trouble?' Oscar de la Vega said, eliciting appreciative laughter from his wife and daughter.

'He is a fine lad,' Geordie told them. 'But boys away from home, alone...' Geordie shrugged. 'It is not to be remarked on that little problems arise.'

'Indeed?'

Geordie waved away the question. 'He reminds me of my younger brother,' he said. 'I was happy to be of assistance.'

Federico's mother smiled. 'Ah, you have family, Señor St Clair?'

'I have left my mother and brothers and sisters back home in Scotland,' Geordie replied. He smiled sadly. 'But it was necessary. I had business matters to see to that could not be left to others.'

'Successfully, I hope?' Oscar de la Vega asked.

'Indeed.' Geordie allowed himself a satisfied smile. 'And I hope my trip will continue to be successful.' He allowed his eyes to rest on Sofia Maria de la Vega for a moment. A faint blush stole across her pretty cheeks but her smile told him all he needed to know. Innocent the girl might be, like her brother, but like her brother she would be an easy little chicken to pluck.

'We hope you will think on us as your family while you are in Buenos Aires,' Federico's mother said.

'You are most kind,' Geordie responded politely.

'And if there is anything I can do to assist you with your business,' Oscar de la Vega said. 'Some of my connections might be useful...'

'Thank you,' Geordie said. 'I should be most grateful for any introductions you felt able to offer.'

'Oh, there is plenty of time for business tomorrow,' Federico's mother put in a trifle pettishly. 'This evening we are going to the zarzuela and we hope you will come with us.'

'Zarzuela?' Geordie queried.

'Theatre,' Federico explained. 'A kind of play with music, dancing...'

'Everybody goes,' Sofia Maria said.

'Everybody?' he queried.

Oscar de la Vega slapped his shoulder. 'Everybody. We go as a family so as our guest you will come with us, yes?'

The girl's eyes were fixed on him, waiting. Geordie paused only for a moment.

'I should be delighted,' he said. 'That is most kind of you.' He set his empty glass on the hovering servant's waiting tray.

'Manuel,' called Oscar de la Vega. Another silent-footed servant appeared. 'Manuel will show you to your rooms,' he told Geordie. 'If there is anything you need, please do not hesitate to ask.'

'We dine at six,' Dona Ana Emilia said.

Geordie bowed. 'Thank you,' he said and followed the servant out of the drawing room, his mind racing.

Led through the house to a generously proportioned suite of rooms in one wing, Geordie discovered that his luggage had arrived and been unpacked.

'I shall be looking after you while you stay here, Señor St Clair,' Manuel said. 'If there is anything you require...'

Geordie threw himself on to the large comfortable bed, his hands behind his head. He studied Manuel. How useful could he be?

'Anything?' he queried casually.

A conspiratorial smile broke out on Manuel's face. 'Almost anything, Señor St Clair,' he declared. 'Though the more difficult comes at a price.'

'Good,' Geordie said. 'We understand one another. Now,' he said, 'tell me about this zarzuela...'

CHAPTER 61

'Lord, I commit all my ways to You,' Hannah prayed, but then the anguish in her heart overtook her calm and she cried out, 'You *know* I do! I always have! But Lord, it's been so long and still I go on waiting and trying to trust...'

'Hannah!' Her mother's thready voice came from the next-door bedroom.

'Coming, Mother,' Hannah replied. She set aside her Bible and went through to see what her mother needed.

'I'm sorry...' her mother began, her once-strong voice a whisper of what it used to be.

'No, no,' Hannah said. 'No need for that. I'm here. What was it you wanted?'

Her mother gestured to the bedside table. 'Could I have my Bible and my glasses, please? I can't reach them and I'd like to read for a little while.'

Hannah leaned over and plumped up the pillows behind her mother's thin shoulders, then she helped her into a more comfortable position for reading. She reached for the Bible and the spectacles and handed them to her mother, watching the shaky hands lift the glasses into place.

Her mother smiled weakly. Even that had been an effort. Each day brought more visible weakness, Hannah thought sadly, as she went downstairs. Each day she could see her mother slipping away from her.

Tears came to her eyes. When her mother died, she would be on her own. So far her older brothers and sisters had been happy for the two of them to remain in the house, but when her mother died it would belong to her oldest brother. He already ran the business that operated from the yard behind the house so it would make sense for him to move into the house. His wife Joanie had been eyeing the place assessingly on her last visit, Hannah recalled. Would they let her stay, she wondered? She would be able to contribute to her keep by continuing to look after the dairy.

The thought struck a terrible chill into her heart. Was this the future for her? The ageing spinster sister endlessly making herself useful to her family so they would not throw her out on to the streets?

Hannah shook herself. *Talk sense*, she admonished herself sternly. *They're not like that. And anyway, the Lord is in charge. He knows what He's doing. He's got it all in hand.*

But as she filled the kettle and put it on to boil for tea, the worrying thoughts continued to claw their way up into her mind.

CHAPTER 62

How his friends back home would laugh, Geordie Sinclair thought, and how envious they would be. The months of keeping his nose clean were at last about to pay off. Very soon he would be able to relax and enjoy the fruits of his labours.

He had courted young Sofia Maria de la Vega according to the strict code of her family and her society, because of the one stumbling block he had not foreseen. A duenna. He had heard of such people but had always thought them a joke, women who could be relied on to assist rather than hinder the determined suitor. But Dona Consuela had proved to be the one duenna who could not be suborned or subverted.

Geordie had tried simple persuasion at first and received a firm refusal. No, she would not leave the room and allow him to sit unchaperoned with Sofia Maria, not even for a few moments.

He had attempted bribery. Here Manuel had been very useful in discovering her penchant for bonbons. But the gift was accepted and the favour refused. No, she would not permit Sofia Maria to walk alone with him.

He tried offering money. It vanished into her reticule. But again she refused to allow them any time alone together.

'Find out about her,' he instructed Manuel. 'If there's any dirt, dig it up.'

But there was none. Dona Consuela was a respectable widow from a respectable, traditional Argentinian family. There was nothing in her background that Geordie could use against her.

Inwardly he railed. He had planned for a swift seduction of the innocent Sofia Maria and an easy entrance into the de la Vega family to assuage their shame, but clearly it was not to be. He had hardly had a moment alone with the girl since Sofia Maria was accompanied by Dona Consuela at all times, both at home and outside, and nothing would prise her from Sofia Maria's side.

The only opportunities for a few words or a smile came during the interval at the opera or the zarzuela, but even there strict protocol operated with the gentlemen required to sit behind the ladies. Geordie had found himself accompanying the family to church where it was possible to seize a few moments with Sofia Maria while her parents greeted friends and acquaintances.

But always Dona Consuela was there, frowning and watchful, so there was nothing for it but to play by the rules. For the first time in his life. The gambler in him calculated the odds and decided that the pay-off would be worth it. He would make sure it did.

And so Geordie minded his 'p's and 'q's and gradually won her father's acceptance as a worthy suitor for his daughter's hand. The rich traditional families of Buenos Aires tended to marry within their own circle, but rules could be bent for a newcomer with high enough social status – and plenty of money.

Geordie smiled to himself. The time and effort lavished on impressing Federico in America and on the journey to Argentina had been well worth it. The lad's innocent pronunciation of his name had helped. St Clair had much more cachet that Sinclair and then all it took was a casual flick of the hand, a shrug, mention of the family name, and the assumption of family land. A few details let slip – a castle (so easy to point to Sinclair and Girnigoe Castles on a map), a mention of grouse shooting and salmon fishing, royal connections (for everyone knew how Her Majesty loved Scotland!) – and let the de la Vegas fill in the gaps from their own imaginations.

As for money, it was just as well that the *porteños*, as the residents of Buenos Aires called themselves, shared his enthusiasm for gambling. Every Sunday, men, women and children of all classes went to the races. Oscar de la Vega was a member of the Jockey Club, the most celebrated in South America and with the finest race track where such notables as the President and the top brass of the army and navy could be seen. And every single person indulged in betting on the horses. The huge grandstand, big enough for ten thousand people or more, was filled week on week, and the stream of men going to place bets seemed never-ending. To Geordie's delight, his luck seemed to be holding and he had won enough at the Sunday afternoon races to bolster his funds for the time being.

Checking his appearance in the cheval mirror in his room, Geordie allowed Manuel to brush a speck of lint from the shoulders of his elegant jacket. Manuel had become his right-hand man, tried and true. He produced a flower and tucked it into Geordie's buttonhole with a cheeky conspiratorial wink.

'Thank you,' Geordie said gravely, then permitted himself a wintry smile.

His bride awaited him downstairs, with her family and a priest ready to officiate at the private marriage service. Afterwards there would be a huge party with all the grand people of Buenos Aires invited. He had carefully perused the invitation list and saw no reason for concern. There was no one here who could know anything of the true antecedents of the man passing himself off as Señor George William St Clair.

Geordie shot his cuffs and pulled down the points of his lavishly embroidered waistcoat. All his plans were coming to fruition. Once he was married to Sofia Maria, he would be part of the de la Vega family and all the doors open to them would be open to him. Not to mention the young heiress's dowry.

He smiled at his reflection in the mirror. The thing was as good as done.

CHAPTER 63

It was hard to say goodbye to her mother. Somehow it felt like desertion to stay behind in the kitchen while the menfolk went to the cemetery, but that was how it was done. There was no place for a woman at the graveside. Only in the grave itself, Hannah thought with sudden bitterness.

But there her mother would rest – in the grave with the man she had loved all through her long life. And they would be reunited in Heaven. Hannah was sure of that. It was a small comfort.

She sighed and fussed with a plate of sandwiches. Anything to keep busy. Her sister-in-law Joanie had scolded her, telling her that her place was with the other women of the family in the front room, awaiting the men's return from the cemetery, but Hannah knew she could not bear that. She could not bear their small-talk, their prideful chitter-chatter about their children and husbands while she sat, unable to contribute anything to the conversation, excluded by her spinsterhood.

Bobby had come to the funeral to say goodbye to his grandma and now he had gone off to the cemetery with his father. They were doing fine, that pair. The move from the nearby house where Rab had lived with Belle had been a wise one. They had made a new start together, Bobby excited and happy, Rab determined. He still worked too hard.

A noise at the door told Hannah the men were returning. Young Nell came through to the kitchen.

'Auntie Hannah, Mum says you must come through now.'

It was peremptory, Nell echoing her mother's sharp tones. Hannah wondered in anguish how she was to live in this house with them now her mother was gone.

'Auntie Hannah!'

'Yes, my dear,' Hannah responded softly. With a smile to the helper ladies in the kitchen she turned and followed Nell through to where ranks of plump and well-satisfied women sat in her mother's chairs, sipping tea from her mother's best china, all centred on her sister-in-law Joanie in pride of place in her mother's favourite chair.

Hannah paused in the doorway and the low murmur of conversation stopped abruptly as they caught sight of her. A few faces turned a little rosy. A few pairs of eyes were averted. But Joanie's were as sharp as ever.

'Come in, Hannah,' she instructed her. 'Your place is here with us, not in the kitchen.'

'Thank you, Joanie,' Hannah replied, trying very hard for calm and composure. *Help me, Lord*, she prayed desperately. She would only get through this ordeal under the shelter of His wings. She quickly looked round the room. The only vacant seat was one of the hard chairs lined up against the back wall.

Determinedly straightening her back as she seated herself against the wall, she observed Joanie raise her hand to the queue of mourners who now filed into the room to offer her their condolences. Few glanced Hannah's way or noticed her.

'Hannah?' Rab seemed to have materialised at her side. 'What are you doing there? You should be...' He waved to where Joanie was holding court.

'It doesn't matter,' Hannah said, forcing back the sudden tears that sprang to her eyes. Rab had seen and had taken pity on her and that erased all the pain. She smiled then and looked into those beloved brown eyes. 'Truly. It doesn't matter.'

'Auntie Hannah?' Bobby slipped his hand into hers and leaned confidingly against her.

'Yes, my love?' she asked.

'It was cold in the cemetery, but Dad said to wear my warm coat so I was all right.'

'Oh, that's good,' Hannah said approvingly. He was looking after the boy.

Rab shrugged it off, then moved away as a man on the other side of the room called to him.

'I'm sad about Grandma,' Bobby said. 'But she *was* very old.'

Hannah smothered the slightly hysterical grin that threatened. 'True, my love.'

Bobby's face was serious now. 'My dad is quite old, and so are you. You won't die, will you?'

A light tenor chuckle startled her. 'Good heavens, young man,' the owner of the voice said with a warm smile for Hannah. 'Your auntie is much too young for you to be even thinking such a thing!' His smile widened and he held out his hand confidently. 'I'm Alec Gunn. I've been away for a while – working down south – but I'm home now. My parents needed me on the farm.'

Hannah accepted the hand. It was nice to be smiled at. He was a good-looking man of around her own age, smartly dressed in a dark suit. She was glad she had gone to a bit of trouble with her appearance, knowing that Rab would surely attend the funeral and the tea afterwards.

'Mr Gunn,' Hannah said.

'Ah no!' he protested. 'Alec. Don't you remember me? I was one of those annoying boys that set the turkeys on your sister when you came out to visit your uncle's croft.'

The memory came clear and bright. How she had enjoyed seeing Belle being chased by a trio of noisy turkeys almost as tall as she was! She smiled at Alec then.

'I remember.'

He winked at her. 'I thought you might.'

'So you're home now?'

'Yes. For good. Maybe you didn't know?'

Hannah shook her head. The last few months caring for her mother up till her death had excluded almost everything else.

'My older brother was lost in an accident six months back,' Alec explained. 'So my parents needed me to come home and take over the running of the farm.'

Hannah nodded her understanding. Brothers taking over family businesses – and the homes that went with them – was something she knew about, she thought, with a glance to where Joanie was holding court.

Alec Gunn was continuing to speak. 'Would you like to come out and visit us some time?' he asked. 'My parents would be glad to see you.' He paused, then added, 'And so would I.'

CHAPTER 64

Geordie lounged in a comfortable armchair as he watched Sofia Maria place a heavy gold necklace set with emeralds round her lightly tanned neck. She sat in front of the elaborate dressing-table mirror in their bedroom in the villa her parents had given them as a wedding present, her reflection quite clear in the candlelight.

He held out his hand. 'Give it to me,' he said softly.

Sofia Maria's eyes flew in horror to his. 'But they were a gift from my parents,' she stammered. 'I cannot…'

'Cannot?' he challenged. He rose slowly from the chair and began to move toward her, his eyes hard on her face. It paled and fear came into her eyes.

'George,' she pleaded, the tears starting in her eyes. 'Please don't make me… My parents…'

He stood behind her so she could see him in the mirror, his face fixed and implacable, his hand held out.

'Give it to me,' he repeated.

She whimpered and clutched at the necklace.

'You're mine, remember?' he taunted her. 'That means everything you have is mine now…'

He watched her watching him, the face he had once thought so pretty revealed in its childish weakness, the once-seductive lips trembling, tears brimming her eyes. The starting bruise from yesterday slipping out from the shoulder of her dress.

'Don't make me have to take it from you,' he threatened.

She shuddered and her hands began to move slowly to lift the necklace and place it in his hands. He closed his hands around it, stuffing it in his pocket, then he smiled in triumph.

'Good girl,' he said. 'You're learning. I'm going out now.'

She opened her mouth, then seeing the look in his eyes, quickly closed it.

He nodded in satisfaction. 'I'll be back when I'm back. No questions, right?'

He bent to press a kiss on the back of her neck and felt the instant recoil as his lips touched her flesh. He straightened and caught her eyes in the mirror.

'Or shall I stay home tonight and see how my lovely young wife can entertain me instead?'

His lip curled as he saw the panic flare in her face. He gripped her shoulder hard where the bruise was and squeezed. Tears sprang from her eyes.

'George!' she pleaded but he ignored her, his grip tightening. He waited till she crumbled, then he threw her from him.

'I can find much better entertainment almost anywhere else!' he taunted her and without a backward glance strode from the room.

'Manuel!' he called.

'Yes, *señor*!' His faithful servant came running.

'Alessandro's tonight, I think' – Geordie mentioned a famous gambling saloon in Palermo – 'and then I think a visit to Madame Caleche's. I won't be back till morning.'

CHAPTER 65

'Auntie Hannah! Auntie Hannah!'

Young Nell came rushing into the dairy where Hannah was hard at work churning butter.

'What is it, Nell?' Hannah looked round to ask, her hand still methodically turning the handle.

'You've got a visitor. Mother's entertaining him in the parlour but he says he's come to see you.' Nell cast a disparaging glance at Hannah's working clothes. 'You'd better go up to your room and change before you see him. He says you're going out!'

She laughed incredulously and danced away, leaving Hannah open-mouthed in surprise. Who would want to see her? It couldn't be Rab because Nell knew him well and would have said so.

Slowly Hannah let go of the churn handle. She did not know of anyone who would come to see her. Since her oldest brother and sister-in-law Joanie had moved in to her home with their family, Hannah had felt her position in the household reduced from one of family-member to poor relation. Close to servant status. And servants were not encouraged to have visitors, let alone visitors who had come to take them out. Joanie would not be pleased.

Strangely that thought lit a moment's pleasure for Hannah. She was sure there was some mistake. Nobody would come to take her out, but while the misunderstanding lasted, there might be some quiet amusement in the situation.

Knowing that Joanie would be even more displeased if she were kept waiting, Hannah shook herself out of her thoughts and walked briskly across the yard to the house. Since this was a misunderstanding, what she was wearing would make no difference. She would be back in the dairy shortly.

She pushed open the parlour door and peeked in curiously. Alec Gunn sat on the sofa being entertained by her sister-in-law. At the sound of the door opening, Joanie looked up sharply and, seeing Hannah in her old work dress, frowned. She waved her into the room.

'Hannah dearest!' She spoke in honeyed tones. 'What are you doing in that old dress? I've told you that you don't need to help in the dairy.' She turned to Alec Gunn and said, as if speaking indulgently about a child, 'She will insist on making herself useful, as she calls it! And there's really no need. We've got plenty of paid help. And this is still your home, isn't it, Hannah?' She waited, gimlet-eyed, for Hannah's response.

Alec Gunn rose from the sofa and came over to take Hannah's hand.

'Hannah,' he said. 'How are you?'

'I'm well, thank you,' Hannah said, waiting to find out what this was all about.

'Mr Gunn…' Joanie began but Alec Gunn cut in.

'I was in town on business and I wondered if you'd like to come back with me to visit my mother and father? They've been asking after you since we met at your mother's funeral.'

'What a lovely idea!' Joanie gushed. 'Yes, of course Hannah would be delighted, wouldn't you, Hannah? It will be nice for her to get out among friends.' Again the gimlet stare. 'Go up and change, Hannah dear,' Joanie instructed her. 'She'll only be a few minutes, Mr Gunn.' She gave a dismissive wave to Hannah, but Hannah was not so easily dismissed.

'That's very kind of your parents, Alec,' she said. 'But are they indeed expecting me today?'

He had the grace to demur. 'They've said you should come to see them many times so I thought that since I was in town today…'

'What is the matter with you, Hannah?' Joanie said, the irritation showing in her voice. 'It's a kind invitation.' 'And you're in no position to be choosy' was the message in her eyes.

It would indeed be a pleasant change to get out of the suffocating atmosphere of Joanie's constant patronising supervision. And what she could remember of Alec Gunn's parents she had liked well enough. Of the man himself she was not so sure. There was something just a little too smooth and confident about him… And she had no idea why he was showing an interest in her.

'Hannah?' Joanie's voice was peremptory. Hannah bowed to the inevitable, taking herself upstairs to change into her better costume, hat and coat.

As Alec Gunn helped her into the seat of the pony trap that was waiting outside the house door, Rab Cormack rounded the corner of the street. His quick eyes spotted her and he slowed to a stop.

'Hannah?' His voice held a question.

'This is Alec Gunn,' she introduced them. 'Perhaps you remember him. He's taking me to visit his parents at the farm.'

'Is he indeed?' Rab said. 'Then I hope you enjoy your visit. Gunn.' He acknowledged Alec in a frosty voice and strode away.

'Your brother-in-law keeps a friendly eye on you, does he?' Alec enquired as he clicked the reins to start the horse moving down the street.

'No, not really,' Hannah responded. Rab did not usually notice her at all these days. Then a sudden thought occurred to her. Perhaps having Alec Gunn to squire her around a little could make Rab pay attention? She looked up at the confident young man perched beside her, waiting for an answer. 'I suppose it's just that the families were connected.'

'That'll be it,' Alec agreed cheerfully. 'It would be greedy of him to be looking at a second of the Reid girls, now wouldn't it?'

He smiled winningly and Hannah realised with surprise that he was flirting with her. She took a deep breath. If it would get Rab to pay attention to her, maybe it would be worthwhile playing this game.

She smiled and settled back to enjoy the journey out to the Gunn farm.

CHAPTER 66

The priest rattled through the words in a heavy Italian accent.

'Mumbo-jumbo nonsense,' Geordie sneered to himself.

All he had to do was remain upright a little longer, then he could have a drink. That would be another drink, his memory taunted him. There had been quite a lot of wetting the baby's head over the past few days, including that very morning. The de la Vegas were delighted at the new addition to their family and Papa de la Vega certainly seemed to be looking on him with renewed favour.

For a short while Geordie had wondered if his gambling and other activities had come to Oscar de la Vega's notice. He recalled the evening his loving wife had thrown his choice of evening entertainment at him. Only once. His face twisted in satisfaction. He had taught her that he was master in his house and not to be criticised or checked. She showed him proper deference now. Geordie glanced up and caught her anxious gaze on him. He gave her a brief sardonic nod and she quickly averted her eyes.

Yes, he had had a moment's concern that perhaps his father-in-law was cooling towards him but the arrival of a son had brought the de la Vega smiles back in full force. There had been champagne and man-to-man satisfaction. Geordie smiled at the memory. As always, his luck was good and he seemed able to do no wrong.

All he had to do was stay upright and carry off this ridiculous charade. He realised someone was speaking to him. Papa de la Vega. His father-in-law.

'The name, George. What are you naming the child?'

Ah yes. The priest needed to know the name of the child. He had given that a lot of thought. With one stroke he could cement the bond with the de la Vegas.

'Jorge de la Vega St Clair,' he said.

It had a fine-sounding ring to it. And as Geordie watched the pleasure on the faces of the de la Vega family and the impressed smiles and glances of the attendant throng of friends and relations, he knew he had got it right. Just like everything else in his life.

Geordie preened. He had done well, he thought, as he watched the priest sprinkle the water and name the child. Everything was going well.

CHAPTER 67

'Are you going to marry that man, Auntie Hannah?' Bobby asked.

They were sitting in what Joanie liked to call the parlour. Rab had brought Bobby on one of his infrequent visits and Joanie had insisted on serving afternoon tea and being present.

Now she tut-tutted. Joanie firmly believed that children should be seen and not heard.

'I don't think you should be asking your Auntie Hannah that kind of question.' And as Bobby opened his mouth to respond, Joanie sailed on, 'Though I must say *I* would like to know the answer!' She glanced sideways at Hannah.

Sleekit like a cat playing with a mouse, Hannah thought. She ignored her sister-in-law, carefully taking a bite of scone so her mouth was full and she could not be expected to answer. But Joanie was not to be deterred.

'You've been walking out with Alec Gunn for a good six months now,' she said. 'You visit with his parents regularly. Should we not be expecting an announcement shortly?' Her smile was coyly expectant.

Hannah chewed stoically on her scone. She tried not to look at Rab. Her ploy of allowing the very personable Alec Gunn to squire her around had been purely in an attempt to make Rab notice her – to see her differently, as a woman who was attractive to men, maybe even to make Rab a little jealous. But it simply had not worked. Rab was as indifferent to her as he had always been. Belle retained her poisonous grip on his heart.

And Hannah had got herself into a terrible tangle with Alec Gunn.

Not that she had really *encouraged* him. It was more that he was difficult – even impossible – to *discourage*! She tried not to sigh but it was hard to keep her feelings from showing.

It had all come to a head the day before when he had thoroughly embarrassed her by going down on bended knee and proposing marriage to her.

'Say yes, Hannah,' he had said, smiling and confident that she would.

When she protested that it was too soon, that she needed more time to get to know him, time to think, he had become... almost sulky. Like a spoiled child refused a treat.

Hannah had managed to put him off but he was pressing for an answer.

'I won't give up,' he told her. 'I'll come back tomorrow. That should give you time to think it over. We're not getting any younger, you know. Think about it, Hannah.'

Without pausing for breath, he had continued, 'My parents like you. You'll fit in perfectly on the farm. We've a fine dairy for you to take charge of... Mum and Dad will move down to the cottage and we can have the farmhouse. I can have it refurbished exactly as you want before the wedding – whatever you want! We can go and look at furniture...'

As if she was interested in such things, Hannah thought. On and on he went, enumerating all the advantages there would be for her in their marriage. He had not, she noticed, said a word about loving her. It seemed to be a comfortable business arrangement he was looking for. And that, sadly, was why it would be so easy to say yes to Alec.

It would get her out of the increasingly uncomfortable situation as poor relation, ageing spinster aunt in Joanie's household. Not that Joanie or her brother or their children were deliberately unkind. Just that they were not exactly … kind – and it was obvious to them all that Hannah simply was in the way. It was awkward for everyone.

Marriage to Alec Gunn would be a most respectable way out for them all. Joanie would be delighted.

And he was offering her a comfortable life. The farm was prosperous, the dairy modern with experienced staff. She got on well with his parents. She liked him fine.

But for one thing. And that one thing was that she was still in love with Rab Cormack. Rab who showed not the slightest interest in her.

She looked at the expectant faces of Bobby on one side of the fire and Joanie on the other.

'I don't know,' Hannah told them honestly. 'I haven't made my mind up.'

CHAPTER 68

Geordie Sinclair threw back another brandy and slammed the empty glass on to the spindly table by his side. He snapped his fingers and a servant came running with the decanter to refill the glass.

'That will be all,' he said and watched, brooding, as the servant obeyed his instructions. He lifted the glass and stared through the dark golden liquid into the fire. The evenings were cool and he felt the cold. Strange when he considered the freezing days and nights he had endured in his home country, not to mention in the deep snows of the Klondike.

But there were more kinds of cold than plain physical chill and here, in sultry Buenos Aires, he was aware of a definite frost in his relations with the de la Vega family. More pressing than that, however, was the problem of Manuel – loyal, faithful Manuel who had obeyed every instruction with alacrity and imagination.

Even the removal of young Federico, erstwhile heir to the de la Vega fortune. Geordie smiled. That had been accomplished in a most effective way. Yellow fever. Most probably caught on one of his forays into the seedier parts of the city, as some of the mourners who had come to pay their respects whispered behind their hands. Dona Ana Emilia de la Vega had applied her delicate lace-edged handkerchief to red-rimmed eyes and clung to Sofia Maria, apparently unaware of the gossip about her only son's tragic death.

But Oscar de la Vega had been outraged, and shamed, turning some of his fury on Geordie.

'Could you not keep the boy out of trouble?' he demanded.

Geordie had spread his hands wide in innocent appeal. 'He had his own friends,' he protested. 'I could not watch over him every hour of the day.'

And then Sofia had miscarried their second child. The de la Vegas were plunged once more into mourning, and finally Oscar de la Vega had come to him and offered him what he had wanted, what he had planned for, so long ago, back in San Francisco: the family business – the ranches out on the pampas, the warehouses and offices on the quaysides, the ships that carried the meat to Europe.

'There is no one else,' Oscar said. 'And you need to be able to take care of Sofia Maria when we are gone.'

Geordie had demurred, graciously. 'Surely there is someone closer in the family? And I – I have family and land in Scotland...'

But Oscar would not have it. 'For Sofia Maria's sake, I ask you to stay here in Argentina and learn the business. I will stand at your shoulder for as long as I am able.'

'But I know nothing about ranching as you do it here,' Geordie had said.

'Then it is time for you to learn,' Oscar told him. 'I have excellent managers on the ranches but you need to get out there and show yourself so that they will know you and respect you.' Oscar had clapped him on the back. 'Say your farewells to Sofia Maria. We will ride out on Monday. Expect to be away for a week.'

A week on the pampas had not been part of Geordie's plans. The city was much more to his taste, not the cattle and the gauchos. Saddle-sore and resentful, he watched as Oscar de la Vega received deference and respect and *he* was eyed up as if he were the sweepings from the saloon floor!

But he would show them, Geordie fumed. Once it was all in his hands, he would not waste his time out there. The managers would deal with it all while he enjoyed the proceeds. Yes, that was how it was going to be.

But then the erstwhile faithful, loyal Manuel showed his true colours. He had accompanied them to the pampas, his eyes watchful and greedy, and on the night of their return home, as he unpacked and brushed Geordie's clothes, he raised the stakes.

'You will be very rich,' Manuel said thoughtfully. 'This is a well set-up enterprise. It runs like clockwork.'

Geordie had agreed, sitting in front of the fire, brandy glass in hand. He had preened. Everything was working out exactly as he had planned.

'You would not want it to go wrong,' Manuel said. 'Not now, when everything is so nearly in your grasp.'

Geordie had shrugged. 'Nothing will go wrong. Trust me. I've got it all worked out.'

'I would not be so sure,' Manuel said softly.

Geordie had raised his eyes and caught Manuel's crafty look.

'And what could go wrong?' Geordie enquired.

Manuel had lifted an expressive eyebrow. 'Who knows? Someone might say a word to Papa de la Vega – about his lovely daughter's unhappiness. How it was that she lost the baby…' He paused as Geordie considered. Only Manuel knew of the state of his relationship with Sofia Maria. Only Manuel knew of the beating he had given Sofia Maria…

Manuel continued. 'And it would be sad if someone were to tell Papa de la Vega what really happened to his beloved son.' He folded the clothes carefully.

Geordie sipped his brandy. 'So it would,' he said, holding on to his temper with both hands. 'But it is unlikely that Papa de la Vega would take the word of a servant against that of his son-in-law.'

Manuel had smiled. 'Ah, yes,' he said. 'Señor George St Clair, the rich gentleman from Scotland with the family lands and the castle. Such a prize for the hand of his lovely daughter.'

'Indeed,' Geordie said.

Manuel continued with his work. 'I was down in the port the other day. Having a drink in one of the bars.' He hung a jacket up carefully in the armoire. 'There are quite a few men from your country coming to find work amongst the sheep-farmers of Patagonia.' He cast a quick glance at Geordie. 'They are a friendly people. Interested in everything. Quite talkative.'

'And?' Geordie ground out.

'And it would appear that none of them know of a gentleman named St Clair' – he pronounced it carefully – 'with a St Clair castle in that part of their county.' He shrugged. 'What they told me was very interesting. And I think Papa de la Vega might also be very interested.'

Geordie Sinclair stilled. Now was not the time for Papa de la Vega to find out the truth about his background – the truth about him. Too much hung in the balance.

'Especially when it could be prevented,' Manuel said.

'Prevented?' So that was what this was about, Geordie thought with sudden relief. A little bit of blackmail. He could handle that. In fact he would have been disappointed in his henchman if he had not been unscrupulous enough to try it.

Manuel had mentioned a manageable sum and Geordie had nodded as if it were nothing.

'I do not see that there needs to be any problem over this,' Manuel had said as he bade Geordie goodnight.

And Geordie had thought so too. But as the weeks and months passed, he had come to realise that he was wrong. He had miscalculated both Manuel's greed and Oscar de la Vega's tight control of the family purse-strings.

And now de la Vega had decided it was time for Geordie to return to the pampas – for a month! He had been only too aware of Geordie's aversion to the countryside and the work of the ranches. Geordie snorted. He had not come all this way to make his fortune, successfully avoiding farm work in his own country, just to labour under a relentless sun in another country, working with smelly cattle and contemptuous gauchos.

He had used ploy after ploy to put off Oscar de la Vega's requests for him to return to the ranches. Sofia Maria was sick. Young Jorge was unwell. Each time, the relationship between himself and his father-in-law chilled a little more till the frost was obvious to all.

Geordie threw back the brandy. Tomorrow, if he wanted to maintain the lifestyle he had become used to, and that of the leech Manuel who clung to his pockets, he would have to overcome his reluctance and head out west.

But not tonight. Tonight he would go into the city and visit some of his favourite places. And perhaps he would find a poker game with worthy opponents and a prize worth playing for.

CHAPTER 69

Walking down the street together, Bobby was clearly in a fidget.

'What's the matter with you?' his father asked the boy.

'Aunt Hannah!' Bobby said, his face gloomy.

'What about your Aunt Hannah?'

'We've got to stop her!'

'What do you mean?'

'Marrying that man Gunn,' Bobby burst out. 'I don't like him.'

'I don't like him either,' Rab Cormack said with a smile. 'But that's not our problem. Only your Auntie Hannah has to, if she's going to marry him.'

'Yes, but I don't think he's a nice man and I don't think she's going to be happy with him. I don't think she really likes him,' Bobby exploded.

'Oh aye?' Rab queried.

'Aye,' Bobby told him. 'She's only thinking about it because it's horrid for her now that Auntie Joanie lives in her house and bosses her about and it's not her house any more and...' He trailed to a stop, his face brightening as an idea occurred to him.

'And?' his father queried.

'Well, I was going to say "and there's nothing else she can do, to get away from Auntie Joanie." But there is.' Bobby's eyes sparkled.

'Oh yes?'

'Yes!' Bobby said gleefully. 'If we can stop her marrying that man Gunn, then you can marry her instead!'

Rab glowered at his son. 'I don't want to marry anyone. When I lost your mother...'

But Bobby burst in, 'My mother? How long was she my mother? A few minutes! Auntie Hannah has been more of a mother to me all these years and still is. She looks after me like a mother. She always has. She washes our clothes and presses them, she bakes for us and makes sure we eat properly. What would happen to us if she decides to marry that Alec Gunn?'

Rab paused and looked at his son's impatient face. 'That's just a wee bit selfish, isn't it, son? Thinking only of yourself?'

Quick as a flash Bobby responded, 'And isn't that what you've been doing all these years? Thinking only of yourself and letting Auntie Hannah be a mother to me, and doing all the housework and stuff like a mother would, and never getting married so she could have her own home and her own children and...'

Rab stared at Bobby as his words struck their target.

'Well, put like that...' he said slowly. 'I just hadn't thought.' He shook his head. 'It never occurred to me.'

'It's true though,' Bobby persisted.

'You're right, son. Out of the mouth of babes!' Rab teased ruefully. He clapped Bobby on the shoulder.

'I'm eleven,' Bobby shot back.

'I know. Eleven years your Auntie Hannah has looked after the pair of us and barely got any thanks for it.' Rab sighed. 'Are you sure she really isn't interested in that man Gunn?'

CHAPTER 70

Geordie Sinclair threw the cards down in disgust. Lady Luck was still not smiling upon him. He looked up into the greedy face of Manuel who was watching the play closely, then round the faces at the table. His losses tonight were worse than ever and he knew he could not pay them.

Papa de la Vega, though willing enough to use him as a worker in his vineyard, had not been at all trusting when it came to opening the coffers and letting him help himself. Geordie smiled to himself. That had not stopped him though. He had simply allowed his creditors to assume that he was entitled to the de la Vega fortune. Well, he was, wasn't he, as the last male in the family after Papa de la Vega? They accepted his notes of hand happily. The estates were large enough and they were in no hurry to kill the golden goose while he was still playing – and losing.

But tonight, tonight something was different. He was tired. Tired of the sneering, supercilious faces of the *porteños*. He would never be one of them. Never accepted in this society. And now always looking over his shoulder lest someone who knew who – and what – he really was should cross his path from the boatloads of men coming from

Caithness into Buenos Aires en route for Patagonia. Someone whose knowledge would put an end to his comfortable existence. So far he had managed to hold Manuel off but it would only take one stray traveller to encounter Papa de la Vega...

Geordie rubbed his bleary eyes. It was early morning and he had been drinking heavily since he had left the house – and his lovely wife. What a disappointment she had turned out to be. Instead of being the key to open the de la Vega coffers, she was a whining nuisance, a burden. He would have been better off with one of the welcoming whores that skirted polite Buenos Aires society.

But they cost money.

Always it came down to money. And his was long gone. He was living on credit, backed by the assumption that Oscar de la Vega was his banker. Geordie's fist clenched in his pocket, his finger catching the ring that lay at the bottom. The engagement ring he had bought for Sofia Maria those years ago when he had thought her worth the investment. He had torn it from her finger before he left the villa tonight. The last of her jewels.

He took it out and looked at it, turning it in his hand. It was worth money, serious money – though not enough to cover tonight's losses. However, perhaps one last throw? To cover them all? He caught Manuel's eye and winked confidently. His luck was due to change.

'Double or quits?' he cried.

He slammed the ring down on the table as his stake. The men at the table muttered. One or two set their cards down and picked up their winnings, pushing back their chairs to leave. Then there were only five men left. Geordie, three other players, and Manuel, watching.

Geordie dealt the cards carefully. This time he had to win. The men bent over their cards. Geordie tried to clear his fuddled weary mind and concentrate.

'Send your man away!' one of the players demanded. 'He is standing too close.'

Geordie waved Manuel away but not before Manuel had time to frown a warning at him. Geordie ignored it and stared down at his hand. It was not as good as he had hoped. But that was not a problem. Guile and deceit would win out as they always had before.

First one man then another slapped his cards down on the table and left, muttering darkly. At last there was only the pair of them, Geordie and a small dark man with hard eyes.

He looked up. '*Señor?*' the man enquired. 'You wish to end our game now, like them?' He waved derisively at the departing backs.

'No, no,' Geordie declared airily. 'I'm happy to continue... If you are?' It was a challenge and the man raised a black eyebrow, glanced down at his cards with a satisfied smile and replied, 'Indeed, *señor*, I am happy to continue.'

As play began again, a small crowd gathered and Geordie began to sweat. The cards were not running in his favour and his opponent seemed to delight in the torture, looking up from time to time as if to satisfy himself that Geordie knew he was being steadily beaten.

His mind working furiously, struggling against the fog of the drink that he had consumed, Geordie looked up to see Manuel trying to signal to him. He was looking very worried and pointing at the other player, then jerking his thumb to show Geordie that he thought he should give up and leave. But how could he? The hand he held could in no way be a winning hand. He had nothing left to put in the pot except worthless credit notes that had now risen so high, Oscar de la Vega would surely kick him out when the creditors came calling for settlement.

What was there left to do? From the distant past came a memory of a trick he had learned aboard the ship that had taken him from his home in Scotland to the gold fields of the Klondike. He had used it a few times in the saloons of Dawson City and it had never failed.

Geordie brightened. He waved Manuel away, looked down at his cards and began his bluff, not noticing his opponent's quick flickering gaze take in the change in his demeanour.

Card followed card. Geordie began to feel more confident. It was working. It always had in the past. Lady Luck would not let him down now! Any moment now, his opponent would concede and he could gather up the pieces of paper, take the ring home to his loving wife, and everything would be all right.

As a satisfied smile curved his lips, he looked up to see his opponent standing up from the table. Yes! All was well. How could he ever have doubted himself? He was the clever one! He had triumphed once again!

But the man did not concede. He pushed his chair back and stood facing Geordie squarely.

'I think perhaps there is some mistake,' he said gravely, looking round the little crowd that remained around the table. He laid out the cards in his hand – then with his other hand, he flipped over the deck that Geordie had been dealing from. There, neatly and unnaturally stacked at the bottom of the deck were three aces. The men around him murmured angrily.

He fanned the aces.

'Your explanation, *señor*?'

Geordie thought furiously. The only way out was double bluff. He staggered to his feet and blustered angrily, 'What do you mean, *my* explanation? You shuffled the cards before I began to deal. You could as easily have...'

The man's face sharpened into fury. 'Are you calling *me* a cheat?' he hissed. His words echoed in the suddenly silent room.

The faces blurred. The word rang in Geordie's ears.

'Cheat? Cheat?'

Yes, that was what he had done.

He opened his mouth and said what was in his head.

'Yes.'

In the next moment he heard only two things. Manuel crying 'No!'

And the sound of the shot.

The last thing he ever heard.

CHAPTER 71

Hannah stood beside Rab in front of the minister, the words floating across her consciousness.

'Do you, Robert Cormack, take this woman, Hannah Reid…?'

No, it was not how she had imagined it would be. They were both a lot older. And maybe wiser too.

Out of the corner of her eye, she could see Bobby bouncing up and down in excitement. He really felt he had brought them together and now they could be a real family.

Joanie looked smug and satisfied. With the last loose end tidied away, she could enjoy being mistress of the Wellington Street house.

Yes, for all their sakes, Hannah was sure she was doing the right thing, though what Rab thought he was doing was another matter entirely.

He had come banging on the house door, barely half an hour after he had left, urgently demanding to see Hannah. Joanie had sent young Nell up to fetch her. Hannah had been sitting on her bed, tears drying as she searched her Bible yet again for words of comfort. Little had she imagined what awaited her.

Nell said breathlessly, 'Mum says you've got to come downstairs. Now!' So Hannah had splashed some water from the ewer on to her face, mopped it dry, patted her hair and descended the stairs behind Nell. She expected a scolding. She knew Joanie wanted her to marry Alec Gunn – according to Joanie 'an excellent prospect' whose linkage to their family could only do them good socially.

So Hannah squared her shoulders, sent up a swift prayer for forbearance, and entered the parlour. To find not a cross-faced Joanie awaiting her, but Rab, standing with his back to her, gazing into the fire.

He turned, his eyes searching her face. He held his hat in his hands and he was turning it round and round, a sure sign that something was bothering him.

'What is it?' Hannah moved swiftly across the room to him. 'What's the matter?'

There was something in the way he stood four-square in front of her that stopped her instinctive rush. She slowed, stopped a few paces away, and waited.

Eyes on the carpet, Rab began slowly. 'Hannah, I owe you an apology.' The words were clearly hard for such a proud man to say.

Hannah began to protest but he simply waved the hat at her to silence her and went on. 'All these years since…' he stumbled, swallowed hard, then determinedly ploughed on. 'Since Belle died, you've been there for us – the boy and me. You took him in when he was a baby.' Rab raised his eyes to hers and she glimpsed a depth of pain in them that caught her breath. 'You brought him up, single-handed, when I wasn't there for him.'

'Rab!' Hannah protested, shocked to see this man expose his feelings to her.

'It's true, Hannah,' he said. 'I let him down and you stepped in. I went to pieces when Belle died and you were there to help the both of us. And eleven years later, you're still at it!' He gestured to the clean, ironed shirt he was wearing – one she had delivered to the house just the other day.

Hannah froze, dismay and hurt welling up in her. He was going to tell her it had to stop. He was going to sever this last flimsy connection between them. He was going to break her heart. She closed her eyes, willing the prickling tears back.

'Hannah, it can't go on like this.'

The death knell sounded and Hannah was surprised she managed to hold back the sob that choked her, the tears that threatened to deluge down her face. She was surprised she remained standing and had not simply crumpled on to the ground.

'You've given up everything for us. It's not right. You've years left. You could marry...'

She began to protest but he interrupted, 'You haven't said yes to Alec Gunn?'

She could not lie to him. She could never lie to him.

'No,' she whispered.

'And you won't?' he persisted.

'No. I won't.'

'Good,' Rab said dismissively. 'I know things about him. You've made the right decision there.'

He stopped. Hannah could not bear to look at his face; all she could see was the hat turning and turning in his hands. He cleared his throat awkwardly.

'Hannah, the only way I can see to make it up to you, if you would consider it...' Again he hesitated, then asked, 'What if *we* got married?'

Her gasp was shock and her eyes flew to his, but he was looking at his hat, turning and turning it in his hands.

'I've built the business up, the new house is bigger and more comfortable. The boy would love to have you there.'

He waited, turning the hat round and round.

Hannah watched it. Round and round, like her thoughts. Rab was asking her, in his roundabout way, to marry him. The one thing she had longed for, prayed for, dreamed of, it seemed, all her life.

And now it had come. But what could she say? He spoke never a word of love for her, or even affection. What he was offering was compensation for eleven years of hard work, of mothering his son, and taking care of him.

Marriage to Rab. Her fondest and lately her most hopeless dream. She looked at him, exasperated tenderness in her eyes. She still loved him, this clumsy man who could not see love when it stared him in the face.

Could she marry him? Enter into this loveless marriage he was offering?

Hannah squared her shoulders. It would not be loveless. She – and God – surely had love enough for both of them.

'Yes,' she told Rab. 'Yes, I will.'

And 'I do' she said to the minister's prompting. 'I do.'

Lightning Source UK Ltd.
Milton Keynes UK
UKOW04f1917091215

264451UK00005B/357/P